OFF
THE
GRID

Also by Robert McCaw
Death of a Messenger

OFF THE GRID

A KOA KĀNE HAWAIIAN MYSTERY

ROBERT McCAW

OCEANVIEW PUBLISHING

SARASOTA, FLORIDA

ISBN: 978-1-60809-361-8

Cover design by Christian Fuenfhausen

Published in the United States of America by Oceanview Publishing

Sarasota, Florida

www.oceanviewpub.com

10 9 8 7 6 5 4 3 2 1

PRINTED IN THE UNITED STATES OF AMERICA

To Calli, my devoted wife, without whose
patience and encouragement
this story would never have been told.

CHAPTER ONE

THE PLUME OF smoky steam rising like a sulfur cloud from a volcanic vent told Hilo Chief Detective Koa Kāne he'd been called to a nasty scene. He eased his Ford Explorer past the patrol car partially blocking the remote country road just outside tiny Volcano Village on the Big Island of Hawai'i. Ahead, an ambulance and a fire truck barred the way. The air was thick with sauna-like humidity. Ditches and giant *hāpu'u* fern trees crowded the edges of the narrow lane, leaving no room to pull off, so Koa parked his police SUV behind the ambulance.

He skirted the fire truck, stepping over a thick hose snaking up the road. Oily smoke billowed from the flaming hulk of a brown Honda Civic about thirty yards ahead. The badly crunched and partly obscured car lay upside down in a ditch under the front end of a dump truck. The yellow color and Hawai'i County seal on the door marked the truck as property of the county highway department.

The pump on Engine 19 from the Volcano fire station screamed at full power, feeding pressurized water to two firefighters battling the blaze, trying to slow the flames enough so other firefighters, kept back by the heat, could douse the flames with chemical foam and carbon dioxide. Through the acrid fog of water, steam, and smoke, Koa recognized Deputy Fire Chief Darryl Opatta commanding the effort. Darryl's round face and coarse black hair made him look younger than his forty-some years. They'd worked other bad fire scenes together and taught safety and fire prevention to schoolkids. Opatta was a good man. Koa waved and the deputy fire chief acknowledged the gesture.

Koa reconstructed the accident in his mind. The Honda must have been traveling toward him on the one-lane asphalt road when it was blindsided by the dump truck coming from a crossing dirt lane. The truck must have been barreling along to have rolled and crushed the smaller vehicle, rupturing its gas tank and igniting the contents.

As chief detective, Koa rarely attended the scene of even the worst traffic accidents. The dispatcher had alerted him to this crash only because he lived close by and the first responding patrolmen hadn't been able to locate the truck driver. The empty truck left Koa puzzled—county employees were never supposed to leave the scene of an accident. A hit-and-run by a county employee involving a fatal accident could saddle Hawai'i County with damages in the millions.

The firefighters, shooting water onto the burning hulks, inched closer to the fire. The flames receded and the smoke lessened. As Opatta yelled instructions, the firemen gradually closed in on the crushed vehicle. Suddenly, a scream rent the air, prickling the hairs on the back of Koa's neck. Someone—it sounded like a woman—had survived the accident only to be trapped in the flames.

Acting on instinct, Koa sprinted toward the vehicles. It was a stupid move. Opatta yelled at him, but he barreled ahead. He was twenty feet from the smoldering wrecks when they exploded in a fireball. The front end of the dump truck rocketed upward, absorbing most of the force of the explosion. Still, the shock wave spread like a tornado, slamming him to the ground. An explosive thunderclap deafened him, so he barely heard the whine of flying metal, but something hammered his left shoulder and pain spiked down his arm. For an instant, he was back with the Fifth Special Forces Group in Mogadishu, Somalia, caught in a toxic hailstorm of rocket-propelled grenades and automatic weapons fire. Odd how an explosion could transport you ten thousand miles in an instant.

The buzzing in Koa's ears subsided. He rose to his knees, testing himself for injuries. His shoulder hurt like blazes, but he wasn't bleeding. He'd been near vehicle explosions before, but not like this—not like a five-hundred-pound bomb exploding in his face. Vehicle explosions happened in war zones . . . or in terrorist attacks. What the hell was inside that Civic?

He faced a new terror. The two firefighters knocked down by the blast had lost control of the fire hose, which thrashed back and forth like a mad python, threatening to decapitate anything in its path. The hose swung away, smashed into the ground, and whipped back toward Koa with deadly force. Only his combat training saved him. He dove to the ground and heard a whistling noise as the nozzle slashed through the air just inches over his head.

The runaway hose collapsed. Opatta, closest to the pumper truck, had killed the power. As Koa climbed off the ground for the second time, he flexed his arm and checked his shoulder, testing his upper bicep where he'd been struck. He'd have the mother of all bruises, but he'd been lucky. One of the two firefighters previously manning the hose got up, but the other man was unconscious. EMTs ran forward to attend to him.

"Get on that hose, now!" Opatta roared. Firemen scrambled to retrieve the hose and were soon again fogging water on the burning wrecks. The explosion had sucked the energy out of the fire, and the flames died rapidly. The blast had torn apart the Civic, leaving little more than the engine block and twisted frame. The screaming woman inside was no more, vaporized in the explosion.

"Damn," Koa swore, joining Opatta. "What the hell was that? More like a bomb than a gas tank explosion."

"Christ almighty, you got that right." Opatta's eyes were wide, and he seemed disoriented. "Christ almighty," he repeated. Opatta appeared to be suffering a post-traumatic effect. Koa had commanded troops who'd been stunned after a nasty fight.

He put a hand on Opatta's shoulder. "You okay, brah?"

Opatta let out a long sigh. "Yeah," he said slowly, "I'm okay." He shook his head and seemed to regain control. "I need to get my arson guys out here."

"And an expert forensics guy. Get one of those explosive consultants from Oʻahu," Koa suggested.

"Good idea. I'll call 'em."

"I've never seen a fire hose break away like that. It damn near took my head off."

"Damned strange," Opatta agreed. "Never had one of those safety nozzles stick open like that. Something must have jammed it, maybe from the explosion."

"What do you make of all this?" Koa waved his arm, taking in the destroyed vehicles.

"Quirky. The whole scene is quirky as hell." Opatta jabbed a meaty finger at the yellow truck. "That county truck . . . what the hell is it doing here? These roads are private. There ain't no county maintenance in here. Where's the truck driver? He's done a goddamn runner. And speed. That truck was movin' fast, fifty miles an hour, maybe more, on that shit-ant dirt road. Plus, no skid marks." Opatta turned, pointing toward the intersection where the dirt lane dead-ended into the narrow macadam road. "Where's the skid marks? Something's fishy. Like the crash was deliberate."

Koa was thinking the same thing. A staged accident killing whoever had been driving the brown Honda would add up to murder.

"Engine 19, this is Volcano station, do you copy?" the radio on Engine 19 blared.

The fire chief grabbed the handset. "This is Fire Two, I copy."

"Fire Two, is Chief Detective Kāne with you?"

"Roger that," Opatta responded.

"Have him call Sergeant Basa. He's got a possible 701."

Koa's head snapped around. 701—police-speak for first-degree murder. First, a vehicular homicide and now a murder? Koa felt a surge of adrenalin and a flicker of fear at what he might find.

CHAPTER TWO

THE WOMAN'S SCREAM echoed in Koa's ears, and he continued to see afterimages of the exploding wrecks. They, like other searing memories, had become a part of him, adding layers to the burden he, other soldiers, and first responders carried. But Koa's memories were personal. Like the twisted face of Anthony Hazzard, the sugar mill manager he'd killed. Or the awful firestorm in Mogadishu, Somalia, where he should have died.

Such experiences haunted some, hollowing them out inside. It happened to a lot of cops, but Koa had learned to tame his demons. Instead of being consumed by thoughts of the men he'd killed, Koa channeled his guilt and revulsion into a passion to exact justice. A grizzly crime scene only made him more determined to nail the perp. It might not work for other cops, but it was his way. He turned his outrage at the senseless violence in his world into something he could live with.

Koa first confronted death when his father, a simple sugar worker, had fallen, or been pushed, into the giant steel rollers of a cane-crushing machine. Eighteen at the time, Koa had seen the brutality of the sugar fields suck the life out of his dad. In just a few years, the vibrant, fun-loving man of his early youth had become stooped and withered long before his time. Along with other workers,

his dad had tried to unionize, only to be brutalized by the mill manager, one Anthony Hazzard, and his overseers before the giant steel
rollers of the cane-crushing machine had finished the job.

Already angry about the abuse his father had suffered under the
ruthless regime of the sugar barons, Koa was devastated by his father's
death. Then he heard rumors from other sugar workers that the
death had been no accident, but rather a warning to other laborers
against unionizing. Koa's despair turned to outrage, and he set out
to make the bastards pay for their treachery. His fury focused on
Hazzard, the mill manager, and Koa exacted his revenge.

Almost a year later, Koa signed up for the Army and left Hawai'i.
Pushing himself hard, he earned a place in officer candidate school
and then the Special Forces. In nightmares, he died on godforsaken
battlefields in faraway places. God's retribution for what he'd done
to Hazzard. On his tour of duty in Somalia, the awful dreams nearly
became reality in a maelstrom of violence, like nothing he'd ever
imagined. Things had been hard growing up poor in Hawai'i, but
life had been precious. Not in Somalia, where crazed fanatics
seeking martyrdom lurked around every corner. Koa pumped himself up with a dozen kills, but his brothers-in-arms, like Jerry, his
buddy and dearest friend, were not so lucky.

He and Jerry had been together since the first days of their training,
supporting each other and watching the other's back. They'd lived in
swamps and mountains, eaten snake meat side by side, and picked
lice from each other's hair. Jerry pulled him out of quicksand during
a swamp march and covered for him when he faltered. Jerry often
spoke of his future, back in his home town of Seattle, where he
planned to become a policeman, like his father. He talked about it so
much the guys nicknamed him the "damn cop."

In Mogadishu, they'd been tasked to capture Mohamed Farrah
Aidid, a Somali warlord, and his followers in the Habr Gidr clan.

Although operational commanders requested tanks and armored vehicles, penny-pinching civilian politicians refused. As a result, Koa's team went in ill-equipped in the face of unexpectedly strong Somali opposition.

During the operation, he, Jerry, and six other members of the team came under heavy fire and were forced to hole up on the second floor of a burned-out building waiting for reinforcements. Koa had been on lookout at a window with Jerry behind him. Koa had seen something out of the corner of his eye and ducked reflexively an instant before a sniper fired. The bullet marked for him hit the "damn cop." Jerry died less than fifteen minutes later. Koa knew that he, not Jerry, should have been going home in a body bag.

Jerry's death hit Koa like an epiphany. He owed Jerry. He owed Anthony Hazzard. Getting killed in the Special Forces wouldn't pay those debts, but there was a way to honor Jerry's dream and atone for his own recklessness. He returned to Hawai'i, and as Jerry had intended, became a cop. He recognized a certain irony in his decision—killer becomes policeman—but maybe having disguised his own crime, he'd be one step ahead of the next killer. A commitment to the police became his penance for Jerry's death and atonement for his own sins. His commitment gave his life a sense of balance and purpose he'd lost in killing Hazzard. At the same time, his secret made him intensely suspicious of others.

Forcing thoughts of his past away, Koa called Sergeant Basa on his cell. Basa was Koa's go-to man. Although he lacked Koa's military background, the bearlike police sergeant had worked his way through a half dozen jobs in the department. He'd started off walking a beat in Hilo, then he'd worked out of a patrol car, served as a dispatcher, and graduated to shift supervisor. He now supported the detective bureau.

Basa, like Koa, had gotten ahead through hard work and personal sacrifice—the old-fashioned way. That reinforced the bond between them. They'd worked dozens of cases together. Basa was tough, attuned to happenings on the street, and had a keen sense for what had to get done at a crime scene. Koa hoped one day he'd decide to become a detective. Professional buddies, they were fierce competitors when it came to *keihei wa'a*, outrigger canoe racing.

The sergeant, expecting Koa's call, answered on the first ring. "Koa?"

"I'm listening. Tell me about the 701."

"We just had a call from the rangers at HVNP."

Koa felt a shiver run down his spine. After three serious, but failed, relationships, he'd finally met *the one*. Nālani had been a technician at the Alice Observatories when they'd first met, but had long dreamed of becoming a ranger at Hawai'i Volcanoes National Park. She had previously served as a park ranger and passed all the exams but had to wait for an opening. Then, several months ago, a spot at HVNP had finally opened, and she'd been sworn in as a park ranger. They'd celebrated with a bottle of Moet & Chandon champagne.

Koa had been smitten from the first time he'd seen her smile, but could hardly believe such a babe could fall for a forty-three-year-old, hard-boiled cop. An image of her smooth, round Hawaiian face, bright black eyes, and flowing black hair popped into his mind. He'd been surprised when she'd accepted his invitation to dinner. Once they began dating, neither his job nor the eight-year gap in their ages had seemed important. Still, Koa often wondered if she'd stay with him if she knew he killed a man and gotten away with it. The dirty truth in his own past made him suspicious that others also harbored vile secrets, and Nālani was no exception. He'd checked out her background.

She was an island girl. Like too many Hawaiian children, she'd come from an illicit affair. An older Hawaiian man had impregnated her teenage mother. Nālani had barely known her father before he disappeared into prison when she was four. Five years later, after giving birth to her second illegitimate daughter, Nālani's mother overdosed on meth. Even before her mother's death, Nālani had been raised mostly by her grandmother—her *tūtū*—in the tiny town of Hōlualoa, south of Kona.

She'd been a lucky orphan. Her *tūtū*, who'd nurtured a dozen grandchildren and other relatives, had been quick to spot the spark that set Nālani apart and demanded excellence in everything she did from schoolwork to sports. She'd escaped the poverty that trapped so many Hawaiian children, including her half sister, and won scholarships, opening the door to a first-class education in college and graduate school in California. She'd become a biologist, worked for a pharmaceutical company, and been a park ranger before returning to Hawai'i. Like many other natives, the islands were in her blood and drew her home.

After they'd dated for three months, she'd moved into Koa's cottage near Volcano. She'd changed his life. They hiked for miles through the forests and craters of the national park, where she taught him to recognize Hawai'i's unique bird and plant life. She'd studied *kapa*—bark cloth making—and showed him the many plants, like *'akala*, *kōlae*, and *milo*, used to create the dyes that made Hawaiian bark cloth special. He invited her to join him in teaching young teens in the art of *keihei wa'a*, outrigger canoe racing. She'd had a natural way with the kids and soon attracted several young women to their Saturday afternoon canoeing classes. Koa smiled as he remembered the first time they'd made love—after dinner around a fire under a star-speckled sky high up the slopes of Mauna Loa, they retired to their tent for a night of unrestrained bliss.

Koa asked Basa, "It's not about Nālani, is it?"

"No, no, she's not involved," Basa reassured his friend, and Koa felt relief. He didn't need more personal troubles. Ikaika, his youngest brother, on parole following a felony conviction, had managed to find trouble again. Eight years Koa's junior, Ikaika had flunked out of high school and been a delinquent since his preteen years. Big, rough, and wild as a cornered boar, he'd served two stints in juvie lockups and two more at Kūlani, the Big Island's isolated prison facility. Although he and his brother shared a criminal past, Koa's crimes were secret, and Ikaika's legal troubles created an uncomfortable conflict for Koa as a cop.

"They've got a body," the sergeant continued, "a partially burned body."

At the words "burned body," Koa flashed back to Somalia.

"You still there?" Basa asked.

"Yeah. I was just thinking. Where in the park?"

"*Ma kai*, downhill from Pu'u 'Ō'ō, near the old Royal Gardens subdivision."

"Royal Gardens?" Koa pictured the lava-encrusted remnants of the destroyed community below the Pu'u 'Ō'ō vent on the eastern slope of Kīlauea volcano. "Lava burned through that place years ago. How'd anybody find a body out there?"

"Three rangers hiking in to check on the Pu'u 'Ō'ō lava flows stumbled on it about an hour ago. Called it in on their radio. They're still out there, asking what they should do."

"What makes them think it's a homicide?"

"Not sure. Something about his being dead before the lava got to him."

"Damn!" Koa swore. The Big Island typically had fewer than ten murders a year, and now he had two unrelated killings on the same day. The gods must be angry. He weighed his priorities. He had a bizarre fatal automobile accident and now a partially burned body in a possible homicide. His chief would want him to investigate this accident. The hit-and-run could bust the budget and maybe even cost Mayor Tenaka his job. Chief Lannua was tight with Tenaka. Koa had no doubt about the chief's priorities, but all Koa's instincts told him to get to the HVNP murder scene. The chief might be unhappy, but it wouldn't be the first time.

"I'm at the scene of a bizarre accident involving a county maintenance truck—"

"You been demoted to the traffic division?" Basa interrupted.

"Very funny. No, it looks like a hit-and-run with a county truck driver doing a runner."

"County? That's going to cost big bucks."

"Exactly. That's why I'm here. But I'm going to bail on this scene and go out to HVNP. Get Piki out here. Tell him to talk to Chief Opatta."

Pika Piki, at twenty-six the youngest detective in the department, radiated energy. In his first months, he'd been ribbed about his alliterative name, but he'd taken it well. Now everyone just called him Piki. He had great drive as well as superb Internet research skills, but his exuberance often led him to superficial judgments. Koa guessed he'd been a hyperactive child. Piki was, in Koa's view, a work in progress. Some days there was a lot of progress . . . other days, not so much.

"I'm on it."

"Can you join me out at HVNP?"

"Sure."

"Good. We're going to need transport." From long experience on the mostly rural Big Island, Koa thought through the logistics. "Come out in the police chopper and meet me at the USGS observatory on the Kīlauea crater rim. I'll tell Opatta what's going on, so he can work with Piki."

"Be there as soon as I can," Basa responded. "You want support, photographer, medical, and crime-scene techs?"

Basa was a self-starter, which made a huge difference to Koa. "Photographer and crime-scene techs." He paused. "I guess we'd better have medical, too. Although Shizuo won't do us much good." Koa referred to the seventy-six-year-old Japanese obstetrician who functioned—or, more accurately, failed to function—as the county's coroner. Koa had a quarrelsome relationship with the incompetent physician after repeatedly, but unsuccessfully, trying to get him replaced.

Forty-five minutes later, Koa, Sergeant Basa, police photographer Ronnie Woo, and two crime-scene specialists, along with Dr. Shizuo Hori, hovered over a natural war zone on the northern edge of Hawai'i Volcanoes National Park. Just to their west along the east-rift fault line, sulfur-laden plumes of smoke rose from the volcanic cone of Pu'u 'Ō'ō. Two miles north along the fault, *Pele* had vented her wrath again at Kupaianaha. The volcanic vents—the most destructive in Kīlauea's recent history—looked like pumice pimples on a blackened landscape, hardly large enough to have poured out millions of cubic yards of lava, destroying buildings, roads, a church, and many historic sites.

Below the chopper, tangled rivers of black lava filled the landscape for more than five miles, stretching from the Pu'u 'Ō'ō and Kupaianaha vents down to the ocean on the east and far off to the north toward the town of Pāhoa. Smoke rose from breakouts where fresh lava ignited the forests at the fringes of the flow. The lava was mostly *pāhoehoe*, the smooth, sooty charcoal-colored brand of Mother Nature's excreta.

Only an occasional *kīpuka*, an oasis of old vegetation, left untouched but surrounded by new lava, broke the barrenness of the landscape. Here and there a clump of wizened trees clung to life, somehow having survived the searing heat.

The eastern slope of the Kīlauea volcano hosted even more bizarre *kīpuka* areas—remnants of human civilization. Royal Gardens was one. In the speculative land boom of the 1960s, developers carved up 1,800 acres of volcanic wasteland into one-acre homesites, lacking water, electricity, telephone, and sewage, and sold them to the unsuspecting public for $1,000 per lot. Advertised as directly adjacent to the "spectacular attractions" of Hawai'i Volcanoes National Park, most buyers had no idea their lots were within an earthquake zone, judged by the USGS to be at extreme risk of volcanic activity. By the early 1980s, the community harbored sixty-some homes awaiting the wrath of *Pele*, the Hawaiian goddess of volcanic fury.

In January 1983, the ground ruptured and lava fountained along the fault line at Pu'u 'Ō'ō, and in July 1986, the eruption moved to Kupaianaha—places not far upslope from Royal Gardens. The buyers got their promised spectacular attractions, but the volcanic fireworks produced streams of molten rock pushing through the streets of Royal Gardens, consuming homes, cars, and everything else in their path. *Pele*, capricious as always, left remnants of scattered buildings, stop signs sticking out of solid rock, and occasional stretches of unimproved road going from nowhere to nowhere. In other places, she buried the community in over one hundred feet of new lava.

The helicopter rocked dangerously in the gusting winds. After three tries, the pilot finally planted the skids on the barren rock. Two hikers, wearing wide-brimmed hats to shield them from the sun and thick-soled boots to guard their feet, approached the helicopter as the police team disembarked.

"I'm Makani Mano," a ruggedly handsome Hawaiian, nearly as tall as Koa, greeted them, screaming to make himself heard over the roar of the helicopter. "From the USGS volcano observatory. This is USGS volcanologist Randy Pape." Pape, a shorter, heavyset man, nodded his head in acknowledgment.

"Chief Detective Koa Kāne," Koa yelled back. "Didn't catch the first name . . ."

"Makani, the name's Makani Mano."

"Got it." *Shark Wind*, Koa thought, translating the man's name from Hawaiian, when recognition dawned. Nālani had mentioned Mano's name more than once, and Koa wondered if he was a competitor for her attention. It wouldn't be surprising that her male colleagues in and around the national park would pursue her. He'd have to keep an eye on Mano and run his name through the computer.

"Sergeant Basa, police photographer Ronnie Woo, Chip Baxter, and Georgina Pau." Koa pointed to each in turn. "Chip and Georgina are crime-scene technicians. And this"—Koa turned to the medic—"is Dr. Shizuo Hori."

Mano waved a greeting as they all moved away from the whirlybird.

Koa came straight to the point, yelling to make himself heard. "You found a body out here?"

"Yes, sir. He's over there." Mano pointed toward a lone figure in a Smokey the Bear hat, standing a couple of hundred yards away. "Near Aouli. Aouli Kim, she's a park ranger."

Although he'd never met Aouli, Koa also recognized her name from something Nālani had said. "Let's have a look." Koa started toward the park ranger.

"Hold up. Hold up," Mano protested. Koa stopped and turned back.

"Sir . . ."

"You can drop the sir. Just call me Koa."

"Okay, Koa. There's new lava out here, and it's dangerous. Maybe you and your people could follow me?"

Koa instinctively looked down at his shoes but didn't see anything cooking. "Sure."

"And watch your footing. It's easy to bust an ankle," Mano warned. Koa, well aware of that risk, said nothing.

Mano led them in a wide arc downhill before angling back toward the lone figure of Aouli. It was rough going, especially for Woo with his camera bag and the techs with their equipment cases. Deep crevices, many large enough to swallow a man, separated lobes of ebony rock. Porous charcoal-like stubble coated the recently cooled lava, and brittle bubbles of rock left by air pockets crunched beneath their feet. The smell of sulfur gas came and went with the wind gusts. The sooty surface absorbed the fierce heat of the sun until it scorched the soles of their shoes. The distance, maybe three hundred yards even with their circuitous route, seemed like a mile. Despite the trade winds blowing puffy clouds from the east, sweat drenched the team long before they reached their destination.

When Koa approached Aouli, he pegged her as a Hawaiian in her late twenties—younger than his girlfriend, but lacking Nālani's grace. Up close, he registered the distressed look on her face.

She offered no *aloha* or other greeting. "There." She pointed at a dark rain poncho, anchored to the ground with rocks along the sides. "It's over there."

Koa took a deep breath and mentally prepared himself for a gruesome sight.

"Be careful," Aouli warned with an edge in her voice, making him stop. "See that toe?"

"Toe?"

"It's a small finger of the lava flow." She pointed at a long snake of dull black stone that appeared to end under the poncho. "That's a new flow within the last thirty-six hours. It'll support your weight, but it's still hot inside."

Avoiding the new lava, but nevertheless feeling the heat it radiated, Koa knelt next to the plastic and removed the rocks anchoring one side. Before he could lift the sheet, a gust of wind caught the edge, whipping it away. The ugly odor of decomposing flesh assaulted him. "Jesus Christ . . ." The words were out before he could control himself.

He'd seen scorched bodies—way too many of them. Men caught by mortar fire or too close to an exploding RPG. For years after Somalia, reddened, blistered faces shorn of hair had joined Hazzard's face in his nightmares. Now he faced another scorched corpse. For a moment, the sight triggered horrible memories, but with great effort, he forced them away. He had to concentrate, to focus on the present, on his job. Get the job done for Jerry . . . for his own redemption. That's how he'd become chief detective.

He forced himself to study the corpse, taking in every detail. He'd taught himself to go slowly, to absorb every facet of a crime scene, to look not only for what was there but also for what was missing. And false clues. His experience with Hazzard made him paranoid.

The shriveled, naked, partially burned corpse lay in an irregular gap between two lobes of lava rock. The new toe of lava had extended into the hole, covering most of the corpse's left arm. The heat in the confined space must have been horrendous.

He turned his attention to the remains, starting with the man's face. Birds had pecked out the man's eyes, leaving gory sockets. Heat had seared the man's flesh, but Koa noted the high, wide forehead and pointed jawline. The man's nose had been broken earlier and healed with a distinctive twist to the left. His lips had shriveled and his mouth hung open in a grin. The man's teeth were stained a brownish yellow, like the teeth of a smoker or a coffee addict, and he had a double gap in his upper front teeth.

Koa turned his attention to the rest of the man's body. The hot rock must have ignited the deceased's clothes, leaving burnt scraps of blue denim. The man had been wearing jeans. Strangely, a thick leather belt, although blackened, had resisted the heat, and lay unbuckled atop the body. That puzzled Koa. The lava couldn't have unhooked the belt or stripped it from around the man's waist. Heat had roasted the man's skin, but a series of deep circular burns disfigured the man's chest, groin, and thighs. At first Koa assumed flecks of burning lava made the marks, but as he examined the scars, he suspected a more vicious cause.

The loose belt suggested the man had been dumped with the belt discarded on top of the body. The appearance of burn marks pointed to torture, probably with cigarettes. There were lots of burn marks. It was a bad scene. The man had suffered unimaginable pain before he'd passed. What kind of animal tortured another human being like this, and why? Had this man sought to hide some secret?

Lifting his head, Koa examined the surrounding area. It was desolate, with nothing but ebony lava for a half mile in every direction. He doubted the man had been tortured out here in the open, not with active lava so close. More likely, the poor devil had been tortured elsewhere, and his killers had dumped the body so the advancing lava would hide their crime. But where? And how had the killer or killers transported the body to this wasteland?

Sergeant Basa knelt beside Koa and peered into the small pit. "Poor guy. Looks like he fell and got trapped in the lava. Hell of a way to die."

"I'm not so sure." Koa added up the factors in his head. "Look at those burn marks and the belt. How'd his belt come loose and land on top of him? And I'm wondering whether the heat burned the clothes off his body, or he was naked and his clothes were thrown in on top."

Basa leaned down to get a better look at the burns. "You're right. And there's a pattern to those circular burns. They're all the same, like cigarette burns. You're thinking torture?"

"Yeah, it looks that way," Koa said. "And like the killers discarded the body."

"Killed elsewhere and dumped so *Pele* would bury the evidence," Basa suggested.

"Yeah, only *Pele* didn't cooperate." Koa pointed to the toe of lava covering only a small portion of the body. "Another couple of yards of lava flow, and no one would ever have found this poor bastard."

The two policemen exchanged a hard look. "Jesus, you think Shizuo can sort this out?" Basa asked.

Koa let out a short, dispirited laugh. "He couldn't tell the time of death if he witnessed the killing. But that's no matter. We need to protect this site until we can get the body out of here. We'd better get some fire and rescue folks to cut this poor slob out of the lava."

Koa stood and signaled Ronnie Woo forward. The diminutive Japanese photographer was a genius with his Nikon. Koa never worried about the quality or thoroughness of Woo's crime-scene shots. "Looks like a homicide. Shoot a full set of photos. Get a picture of the belt on top of the body and close-ups of the burn marks on the torso and groin." He thought about warning Woo about the hideous sight but didn't. The photographer never showed the slightest emotion no matter how horrible the crime scene. For a second, Koa wondered how Woo dealt with violent death, then let the thought go.

Koa joined Mano and his colleagues standing a short distance away. "How'd y'all stumble on the body?"

"This," Mano responded, holding up a piece of charred blue denim. "We found this hooked on an outcropping of lava, and then saw the swarm of flies. Aouli went to check and found the body."

"Any of you move anything or touch the body?"

"Touch that corpse? No, sir. We just put a rain poncho over the hole to keep the flies away." Koa checked the others for their replies and was rewarded with a "no" from Aouli and a headshake from Pape.

"Any idea about his identity?"

"You kidding? I wouldn't recognize anyone from . . . what is left." Mano's face, like Aouli's, had taken on an ashen color.

Koa understood. A human corpse discarded in a lava moonscape—let alone one savagely burned—would turn anyone's stomach. "How does one get in or out of this area?"

"Drive, hike, or fly—"

"Drive?" Koa interrupted. "I thought *Pele* destroyed the roads into Royal Gardens."

"Lava flows cut all the roads and destroyed most all the buildings, but residents still get in and out on ATVs and motorcycles. They're mostly crazy, but they do it."

"People still live here?" Koa looked around at the desolate expanse of black rock.

"The sensible ones left when the eruptions first threatened Royal Gardens. Some had to be forcibly evacuated just before their homes went up in flames. But there are diehards, and *Pele*'s nothing if not fickle. A few buildings, including a couple of partial homes, survived in islands surrounded by lava. And there's folks who live in tents or shacks."

"And they ride motorcycles in and out?" Koa was incredulous despite the explanation.

"Yeah. Motorcycles and ATVs, right past county emergency personnel, who'll have to evacuate them next time *Pele* throws a tantrum."

"Just *pupule* . . . nutty," Koa remarked, although his thoughts were already trending in a different direction.

He signaled to Basa, who joined them, and asked the sergeant to have patrolmen canvass the surrounding area for anyone who might have seen anything out of the ordinary. As Basa set out with his new task, Ronnie Woo shouted that he'd completed the crime-scene photos. Koa walked over to where Shizuo Hori waited.

"Your turn, Doc." He deliberately shortened the honorific, knowing it would irritate the presumptuous baby doctor. Shizuo was a self-important little prick, and to Koa, a royal pain in the ass.

Koa pointed at the body. "There's something odd about the burn marks. Be good to know if they're premortem or postmortem and whether there are any other signs of possible torture."

The little medical man bristled. "You telling me how to do my job?"

Koa responded mildly, "No, Shizuo, just letting you know what questions the chief and Mayor Tenaka will likely have." That got Shizuo's attention. He pandered to the mayor, who steadfastly supported the incompetent quack, probably because Shizuo—famous for staying in high-stakes games when even a poker rookie would fold—lost a ton of money in their Thursday night poker matches. But, Koa reflected, the obstetrician had an ulterior motive— gambling losses were his ticket into Mayor Tenaka's inner circle. It was just the sort of corruption that drove the Hilo establishment.

The Japanese medic strutted toward the corpse only to falter on the rough terrain. He nearly fell down before picking his way forward and spreading a white cloth on the ground. The prissy little doctor, Koa thought, didn't want to dirty his pants. Shizuo knelt next to the body, but immediately got up, only to fold the cloth in quarters before again kneeling on it. Koa almost burst out laughing. The lava wasn't that hot. Shizuo's inability to turn the lava-locked corpse forced him to truncate his examination. When he finished, he stumbled back across the lava. "I can't do my job in these conditions," he whined.

"I'll ask the next killer to take that into consideration," Koa responded. "What can you tell me?"

"He's dead maybe thirty-six hours, but I don't know. It's difficult. The heat, you know, distorts conditions."

"Cause of death?"

"The body's strangely emaciated. Could be the roasting, but . . ."

"But what?"

Shizuo shook his head. "Blood loss, maybe. Hard to tell with the heat."

The evasions had started. "Roasted premortem or postmortem?" Koa asked.

"Can't tell."

"What about the burns?" Koa asked.

"Odd, like cigarette burn marks. And the spacing looks man-made. Perhaps I can tell you more once they get the body back to the hospital."

Koa doubted it.

The helicopter, previously dispatched by Basa to collect fire and rescue personnel, returned and disgorged more people. Rescue workers erected a small tent over the site and firefighters began the laborious process of cutting the shriveled body out of the surrounding lava. Who, Koa wondered, had died in this godforsaken place?

CHAPTER THREE

ON THE WAY back to police headquarters, Koa spotted four teenage vandals with cans of black spray paint, running from one political poster to the next, defacing the advertisements with large black letters: "NO." Nāinoa Nihoa, currently a Hawai'i state representative, was running for governor. His campaign had turned normally placid Hilo into an urban combat zone. Adolescents and adults alike defaced political posters. Vandalism reports, drunken brawls, and even domestic disturbances had multiplied in the three weeks since the campaign started.

Deterring street crime wasn't Koa's role, but he still stopped and got out of his Explorer. The teenagers scrambled in different directions. He started after one of them, then gave up, shaking his head in disgust.

Koa avoided discussions of Nihoa's policies. He didn't have much truck with politicians, and people were either for or against Nihoa. Staunch Republican, former military officer, and deputy undersecretary of the Army, State Representative Nihoa campaigned on an unusual alchemy of native Hawaiian sovereignty, states' rights, and Tea Party financial conservatism. He preached tribal sovereignty for native Hawaiians, home or charter school learning for Hawaiian children, drastic cuts in the state budget, and a return to traditional Hawaiian environmental practices.

Koa harbored mixed feelings about the man. He and Nālani supported Nihoa's environmental and educational policies. Nālani, an avid environmentalist, had taught Koa about the fragility of Hawai'i's environment. Pigs and cows, introduced into an island chain where the bat was once the only mammal, had caused irreparable damage, cows destroying the native *koa* trees and pigs tearing up the forests. Together with bad land-use planning, negligent water management, overfishing, and invasive species, they did great harm to the islands Koa and Nālani cherished. Just a mention of the thousands of feral cats roaming the island, destroying the native *manu*, native birds, was enough to prompt Nālani to condemn the "advocats" groups, whom she regarded as hopelessly misguided.

Then there were education and public services. Hawai'i's public school system ranked near the bottom in national surveys and was plainly deficient in preparing children for college. Native children performed poorly, with high teen pregnancy rates. Cronyism and featherbedding caused havoc with the efficiency of governmental functions. People stood in line for hours just to renew their drivers' licenses.

Yet Nihoa's platform held a dark underside. In his teenage years, Koa, like many poor Hawaiian kids, had been an ardent supporter of the sovereignty movement, but his military service had changed his perspective. He now thought of himself as an American first and a Hawaiian second. He rejected the sovereignty movement's efforts to create special rights and privileges for people just because their remote relatives had lived in the islands before the United States had overthrown Queen Lili'uokalani in 1893.

He also worried that the sovereignty message harmed tourism and curtailed business, costing the islands precious jobs. But most of all, Koa opposed Nihoa's use of sovereignty to curtail government services. He feared budget cuts would cripple the already over-worked and underresourced police department. He knew from personal experience that many crimes went undetected, and having witnessed chaos in Somalia, worked as a cop for a dozen years, and served as chief detective for six years, he understood acutely that the police guarded a fragile line between civilization and anarchy. Anarchy was never far away.

Nihoa's message had potent popular appeal among native Hawaiians, taxpayers, and parents with school-age children, but generated fierce opposition from Hawai'i's traditional political con-stituencies, public employees, the business community, and tradi-tional elected officials. These divisions produced the most vitriolic, and sometimes violent, political campaign in Koa's memory. The news that Nāinoa Nihoa planned to hold a political rally the fol-lowing week in Hilo had sent apprehension soaring within police ranks.

When Koa entered the police headquarters conference room, Chief Lannua, Deputy Chief Foster, the head of the patrol divi-sion, the head of technology, and a half-dozen other leaders pounced on him about the murders. He shocked them by de-scribing first the vehicular explosion and then the torture victim. Two brutal murders on the same day had the group buzzing for several minutes.

The chief called the meeting to order. A tall, strapping, prema-turely balding man, S. H. Lannua exuded an air of authority. For as long as Koa had known him, no one aspect of the chief explained his influence. At times the chief's sway seemed to emanate from a certain patrician manner. Something intangible in his posture and demeanor made those around him defer, waiting for the chief to speak.

Unfortunately, he possessed only one of the two qualities Koa considered essential for management of the island's police department; he had political clout. Chief Lannua's family had lived on the island for generations, had large land holdings, and commanded the respect of nearly everyone with political influence. Politicians thought twice before double-crossing Chief Lannua.

But his strength was also his weakness. He was a politician. All too frequently, he shared details of police investigations with the mayor and the mayor's cronies, and sometimes thwarted investigations that cast the mayor in an unfavorable light. In Koa's view, he yielded too easily to supposed political realities. Too close to the mayor and the council, he failed to fight for the funds the police department desperately needed to maintain adequate levels of staffing and competence. And he was too old school to embrace the technological changes needed to modernize the force.

They had a turbulent relationship. The chief, Koa knew, depended upon him to tackle the department's toughest cases. They had repeatedly battled over Koa's unrelenting push for a bigger budget, more detectives, and especially resources for police technology routinely used by mainland police. But the real fireworks exploded when the chief tried to steer an investigation away from the island's power brokers. In Koa's experience, the rich and powerful surrendered to criminal impulses just as often as the common folk.

The group got down to the business of preparing for the rally. A giant map depicted the route of Nihoa's motorcade from Hilo airport to Wailoa Park outside the county government offices, where the candidate was expected to address the largest political rally in Hilo history. Lieutenant Orsini, the head of the Intelligence Division, presented an update on the plans for the rally. "I'm predicting a crowd of thirty to thirty-five thousand," he said, stunning everyone. "That's roughly one-fifth of the island's total population." Koa had never seen that many Big Islanders gathered in one place.

Deputy Chief Foster announced the state police would send officers, the FBI would lend undercover agents, and the TSA, DEA, and the county sheriff would also send personnel. Police on Oʻahu and Maui would each send officers. Seventy-five percent of the cops in West Hawaiʻi would be shifted to Hilo for rally day. All departmental leaves would be cancelled and all officers would be expected to pull twelve-hour shifts. Foster outlined the patrol division assignments along the motorcade route and around the rally area. He asked Koa to have all his detectives in civilian clothes, mingling with the crowd, alert for suspicious activity.

The mayor's head of emergency management outlined street closures, first aid stations, and a temporary holding area for anyone arrested during the rally. Selected county employees with green armbands would assist in crowd control. Two fire companies would cover rally-related fire and rescue, and another fire company equipped with water cannons would be ready in case the crowd got out of control. Collectively, they were about to mount the largest police operation in Hawaiʻi County history.

* * *

Koa thought of his own history as he headed back to where a woman had almost certainly been murdered in the explosion of the Honda. He, too, had murdered although it hadn't been premeditated. Having blamed Hazzard for driving his father beyond the breaking point and suspecting Hazzard had been behind his father's fatal accident, Koa had set out to teach the son of a bitch a lesson. He'd tracked the manager to his hunting cabin high in the Kohala Mountains, and hidden in the forest, biding his time. By sunset, Hazzard, a big, heavy man, had downed a half-dozen shots of bourbon and stood unsteady on his feet. While they were both over six feet, Koa figured his training on the wrestling mats and his quickness would more than compensate for Hazzard's weight advantage. He'd seized the moment and attacked, jumping Hazzard and choking him with bare hands until the man went limp. Wanting to punish, but not kill Hazzard, Koa had relaxed his grip. In an instant Hazzard shot up and broke free. As the two men faced off and circled each other, Koa sensed he was outmatched and grabbed a fire iron. Like a wild horse, the enraged mill manager charged Koa, kicking and swinging his arms. Koa struck with the iron. Hazzard went down. Appalled at his own violence, Koa tried to revive the man, but the poker had done its deadly work.

* * *

When Koa got back to the scene of the wrecked Honda, the fire truck and ambulance were gone. A heavy-duty wrecker had moved the dump truck far enough to clear a working space around the charred skeleton of the Honda. A few dozen red and yellow pennants sprouted within the hundred-foot square cordoned off with crime-scene tape. Inside the tape, Sam Ikeda, the fire department's arson investigator, perched on his haunches, combing through a pile of twisted metal parts. Known in the fire department as "serious Sam," Ikeda was a short, dour, balding man of Japanese ancestry, known for hard work and his utter lack of humor. Koa wondered if he ever laughed.

"Permission to enter," Koa said. He never sought permission to enter a crime scene except when Ikeda worked an arson case. Precise, skilled, and compulsively thorough, Ikeda exercised absolute dominion over his work areas.

"Sure, but come in that way." Ikeda pointed. "And don't step on any of my markers."

Koa picked his way through the maze of flags to where Ikeda squatted. "The medics get the body?"

"You mean the pieces of flesh charred beyond recognition?" Ikeda grimaced. "DNA's gonna be the only way to get an identity. Not much left here either."

Koa looked around the blackened area.

Ikeda frowned. "I can't figure it out."

"Talk to me," Koa said.

"Heat. This damned fire burned way too hot." Ikeda held up a metal bracket, the end of which drooped like melted chocolate. "I've never seen this kind of damage in a gasoline fire."

"I thought gasoline was a pretty good accelerant."

"It is for wooden buildings. But with a maximum temperature around 1,250 degrees Celsius, there's no way an open-air gasoline fire melts steel like this. No fuckin' way." Ikeda picked up another piece of melted metal.

"Propane?" Koa suggested, thinking that the locals used and frequently transported propane tanks.

"Where's the tank? I've sorted through all the wreckage." Ikeda spread his arms to take in the whole area. "No sign of a tank, not a single scrap. And besides, even a propane fire wouldn't be hot enough to melt steel."

"What, then?"

"It's driving me crazy." Yet in another moment Ikeda's voice became determined again. "I might have an answer after I get some of this debris to the lab."

"What about vehicle identification? You find a license plate?"

"No way. When steel melts, tin evaporates. We'd be lucky to find droplets of the license plate someplace in this mess."

"A Vehicle Identification Number?" Koa asked hopefully.

Ikeda shook his head. "Not even on what's left of the engine block." He stood up and led Koa across the cordoned area to the front of the dump truck. "Let me show you something."

"Damn!" Koa exclaimed. Some phenomenal force had destroyed the front of the truck, blasted the engine block backward through the dashboard, and shredded the front of the massive steel frame. The front axle hung in three separate parts. The front wheel rims were burned clean of any semblance of tires. Some of the metal parts appeared partially melted. "That looks like bomb damage."

"Exactly, except I haven't found any explosive residue. Hell of a mess, this is."

"Koa!" a voice called from up the road. Seeing Piki approaching, Koa carefully picked his way outside the crime-scene tape to meet his young detective colleague.

"There's something fishy about this accident!" Piki said. He was constantly in motion, making gestures with his hands and shifting from foot to foot.

Whenever Piki got excited, Koa tried to calm him down. "What do you have besides the explosive fire?"

"The truck went missing from the highway maintenance yard at Kurtistown."

Koa felt the spark of excitement that came with a clue. "When?"

"The highway department reported it stolen yesterday morning, but they're not sure when it went missing."

"Any word on the driver?"

"No. And the crime-scene boys found the cab wiped clean."

"Weird," Koa remarked. "You've canvassed the neighborhood?"

"That's where it gets even weirder. A woman, Mrs. Furgeson, in a house down there"—Piki pointed down the cross lane from which the truck had come—"says the truck was sitting there for about an hour, like it was waiting for something."

"Lying in wait for the brown car?" Koa asked.

"Sounds that way. Looks like a deliberate accident, like a murder." Piki's eyes glowed with the revelation.

Koa had already reached the same conclusion. "That's the way we're gonna treat it," he responded. "Did this Mrs. Furgeson see the accident?"

"No. You can't see this far up the road from her place."

"Any word on the driver of the brown car?"

"Not yet. Since the road dead-ends about five miles up the hill"— Piki waved an arm toward Mauna Loa in the distance—"I figure the car most likely came from one of the houses up there." His hand fluttered as though taking in the houses. "Two of Sergeant Basa's boys are going door to door."

A dirty brown Chevy with a blue police bubble bumped down the country lane. Officer Johnnie Maru stopped next to the two detectives. Maru, one of Basa's recruits, was always in trouble, usually for something stupid, like a dirty uniform or showing up late. Basa defended and protected him, repeatedly telling Koa that Maru could be trained. Koa believed in rigorous training, but it was no substitute for brains. Maru came up more than a little short in that realm.

"What do you have, Maru?" Piki asked.

"I ain't too sure. A half mile or so up the hill, a witness told us some woman named Mrs. Campbell drives a small brown car—an old Honda. Says she saw Mrs. Campbell drivin' this way just before the accident."

"What's this witness's name?" Koa asked.

Maru consulted a dog-eared notebook. "Alice . . . Alice Montog. After talkin' to her, I went by the Campbell place, a banged-up squat set way, way back up a rutted dirt track. The windows and doors are open, but nobody's home. And I didn't see no vehicle no-where's around."

That, Koa thought, should be enough to get an ID. He called Basa. Five minutes later, Koa had confirmation that Gwendolyn Campbell, with a post office box in nearby Volcano Village, had registered a brown 1994 Honda Civic.

"Let's go talk to this Alice Montog and have a look at the Campbell place," Koa said.

Maru led them up the lane until the asphalt gave way to gravel. He pulled up in front of an attractive yellow house with a riot of red and pink ginger flowers in a meticulously kept front yard. A kneeling, middle-aged woman in dirty shorts and a stained blouse tended the flowers.

"Mrs. Montog?" Koa asked.

"That's me." She smiled brightly.

"I'm Chief Detective Kāne. I understand you saw a brown car."

Her smile faded. "Is Gwendolyn all right?"

"Why don't you tell me what you saw?"

"Like I told that other officer over there"—she dipped her head toward Maru—"Gwendolyn Campbell drove by this morning just before I heard that awful noise down the street."

"You're sure it was Campbell, and she was driving a brown Honda?" Koa persisted.

Alice Montog didn't suffer fools gladly. "She was driving fast, too damn fast, but I know that car, I know Gwendolyn Campbell, and I got eyes. What are you getting at?"

"I'm just trying to get the facts straight."

"Well, I got my facts straight."

Koa smiled inwardly at her response. "Where does this Campbell lady live?" he asked.

Mrs. Montog pointed up the road toward Mauna Loa. "She's got a place in the forest up the hill."

That made sense given the location of the crash site. "She live alone?"

A cloud of disapproval passed over Alice Montog's face. "She lives with some guy, but I've only seen him a couple of times. He must be up there somewhere." She again waved her hand toward the mountain.

Her attitude alerted Koa to pursue the issue. "Is there something peculiar about Mr. Campbell?"

"He's very"—she appeared to hunt for the right word—"fleeting, almost like he's not here. I rarely, if ever, see him."

That's odd, Koa thought. The explosion had given him a bad feeling, and it was only getting stronger. The policemen continued up the road until the gravel petered out, and their vehicles stuttered over the washboard of a rough dirt lane. A mile later, Maru turned into a barely discernible track that wound over rock outcroppings and tree branches deep into the rain forest.

They bounced up the rutted trail for almost a mile before reaching a tiny clearing, harboring a dilapidated carport, a weather-beaten house on stilts, and a shed. The forest encroached so close that tree branches touched the house's moldy sides and rusty roof. A tree had fallen, damaging a corner of the roof, and lay in a tangle of branches beside the foundation. Blistered gray paint peeled from the walls. Four propane tanks were lined up along the left front wall, and irregular electric wires ran haphazardly from the shed to the house. Clearly, the occupants lived off the grid. Mosquito netting covered the open windows, and the front door stood ajar behind a battered screen. A pervasive dampness, coupled with the hum of insects, gave the place a clammy, foreboding feel.

A black cat scampered under the house when Koa climbed the rickety steps. He knocked loudly on the screen doorframe. "Anybody home?" Silence. He peered through the screen. Despite the dark interior, Koa got the impression of objects cluttered everywhere, filling the space and covering the walls. He shouted, "Police. Is anyone home?" Silence.

Koa had no legal basis to enter the house, yet he felt an urgent need to identify the victim, especially given the suspicious nature of the accident. And if Gwendolyn Campbell had died in the brown car, he needed to find her next of kin, presumably her husband. Returning to his SUV, Koa retrieved a flashlight. "I'm going to have a look around inside," he said. "Piki, you and Maru check out the shed. We're looking for anything that might tell us more about Gwendolyn Campbell or her husband." Always vigilant against Piki's zealousness, he added, "But don't go crazy, all right? We don't have a warrant."

"You got it, boss," Piki responded.

The screen door creaked on rusty hinges as Koa stepped into the dimly lit interior of the house. Starting to his left, he swept the beam of the flashlight slowly around a great room that combined the kitchen with a work area and made up at least two-thirds of the ground floor. He might as well have wandered into a garage sale. All manner of odd and mismatched objects—a gilded birdcage, a row of Chinese urns, European figurines, miscellaneous chairs—filled every corner and most of the floor. Piles of books and other assorted belongings left only narrow aisles for passage toward the kitchen. Shelves overflowed with bric-a-brac. Asian tapestries and cheap oil paintings covered most of the wall space. The dim, overstuffed room felt overwhelmingly claustrophobic.

Koa looked through the clutter, seeking some unifying theme. He focused on canvases, drawings, and art books covering the counter along the front wall under the windows. Sketches, paints, and brushes lay scattered on two long worktables. An easel, supporting a partially finished drawing, screened the living space from the 1950s kitchen. He'd entered an artist's studio.

He moved cautiously down one of the narrow pathways toward the kitchen until the smell of burned coffee assaulted him. He directed his light toward an ancient propane range where a melting percolator sat atop a barely simmering gas burner. He turned off the gas, at first thinking the over-warmed coffee meant that someone was around, but then the pieces snapped into place. If the misshapen coffeepot had been full that morning when the Campbell woman raced away down the street, the stove might have been on for hours. The coffee might have slowly boiled away.

But who, he asked himself, leaves a coffeepot simmering on the stove? People living off the grid became paranoid about fire hazards, especially in wooden houses buried deep in the forest. Could Gwendolyn have been planning a quick return? He thought about distances. It seemed unlikely Gwendolyn would have left the coffee heating while she went to the store. The Montog woman had seen her driving fast. Had she, he wondered, been called to an emergency? Or maybe run from something.

He stood in the middle of the studio, looking for anything that might tell him more about the inhabitants of this remote dwelling. He saw no mail, no newspapers, no computer, and no desk, nothing to help him identify the person or persons who lived there. He guided the light around the walls, checking for photographs, plaques, or certificates. Nothing.

He examined the half-finished painting on the easel. A forest scene with birds, butterflies, and other creatures. A large, mostly bare canvas rested on the front counter between the windows. An overhead projector, like the ones used in the police department when he'd first joined the force, stood on a small movable table. A sketch on transparent paper rested atop the projector's light box. The artist, he thought, must have used the projector to transfer sketches to canvas.

He needed to find Mr. Campbell or whatever male lived here. Alice Montog had mentioned "some guy," but the guy wasn't here.

He phoned Sergeant Basa. "Double-check for any vehicle registered to a Campbell in the Volcano area."

"Already done. The one I gave you, registered to Gwendolyn Campbell, that's it."

Koa returned to the door, found Maru, and instructed the patrolman to start re-canvassing the neighbors, asking about Mr. Campbell—where he worked, where he might be found.

Piki swept around the corner. "There's not much out back. Just the generator in the shed and one sweet Boss Hog motorcycle, top of the line." Piki's eyes glittered with admiration.

"You get the plate number?" Koa asked.

"No plates on it, but it came from Pete's Hog Shop, and I got the VIN."

"No plates? That's odd." Koa wondered what kind of motorcycle enthusiast owned an expensive machine without license plates. A Boss Hog—a big, heavy machine—suggested a male rider. Likely Mr. Campbell's wheels. If the Campbells had registered only one vehicle, and they'd found the man's motorcycle, Mr. Campbell should be around. The whole scene began to feel increasingly strange . . . disorienting.

Koa returned to the house. Two doors opened off the great room. He opened the first door and stepped into a small bedroom. Piles of drawings and fabrics three and four feet tall covered the small bed. A closet without doors bulged with more stuff. The place, he thought, must be inhabited by hoarders. Nothing adorned the walls, except a large, and now terribly familiar, Nāinoa Nihoa political poster.

He'd turned to leave when an odd detail stopped him. The wall-sized advertisement read: "Nāinoa for State Representative." The poster dated from an earlier campaign, not Nihoa's current run for governor. As Koa took in the candidate's handsome face—his bushy eyebrows over penetrating, ice-blue eyes—he saw three short, feathered darts piercing Nihoa's left eye. And numerous tiny black holes evidencing repeated target practice. Another of Nāinoa Nihoa's many detractors, Koa thought as he returned to the great room.

After finding nothing of interest in a small bathroom, Koa climbed the stairs to the second floor. Three doors opened off a short hall. The first led to another small bedroom filled to overflowing with stacks of canvases, art books, and assorted other paraphernalia.

The second door gave access to a bathroom. An assortment of women's underwear hanging from the rod over the combination bath-shower, along with men's shaving gear next to the sink, confirmed that a couple shared the residence. He noted water puddled in the bottom of the tub. One of the towels felt damp. Someone had bathed that morning. He checked the medicine cabinet. No prescription medicines to identify the occupants. Nothing else of interest.

The only door off the right side of the hallway opened into the master bedroom, filling the rear of the second floor. This spacious room with windows and a decrepit balcony overlooking the rain forest offered a respite from the clutter of the rest of the house. An unmade bed with two sets of pillows, both bearing marks of recent use, provided further confirmation of joint residency, as did the pair of matching dressers.

Orchid plants lined the windowsill, and more orchids, all in bloom, sat on the broken-down balcony. The colored blossoms and the light coming through the cheap glass balcony doors gave the room a cheerful quality the rest of the house lacked. So, he thought, Gwendolyn Campbell loved orchids, lots of different varieties of orchids, many of which he couldn't name.

Nothing adorned the walls except a large portrait of a man dressed in U.S. military camouflage fatigues and combat boots with the double silver bars of an Army captain sewn onto his lapel. The officer stood with his right hand on the handlebar of a Boss Hog LS445 motorcycle. Piki hadn't exaggerated. The powerful machine seemed to imbue the man with energetic authority. His left arm hung by his side and held a pistol. Koa examined the gun. It appeared to be a Heckler & Koch HK45—a semiautomatic pistol typically carried by Navy Special Forces, not Army, personnel.

Koa opened the nearest dresser drawer. Women's underwear. He closed the drawer and switched to the other dresser. He found the gun in the top left-hand drawer. Using a cloth to avoid smearing fingerprints, he checked the gun—ten rounds in the clip and one already chambered. He removed the clip and ejected the round from the chamber.

The powerful weapon felt familiar and brought back memories of his years in Somalia and his pre-9/11 days in Afghanistan. He checked the safety and slid the weapon into a plastic evidence bag. He doubted the gun was registered in compliance with Hawai'i law, but a trace on the serial number might help identify the owner.

The drawer also contained a commando knife, like the one Koa had carried in the military. Grooved thumb grips on either side of the long, thin blade made it easier to extract the weapon after sliding it between an adversary's ribs. A conical steel point on the back of the handle could deliver a crippling backhand blow. Special Forces operatives carried such knives.

This man intrigued Koa. An officer, an Army uniform, a Navy Special Warfare weapon, a commando knife. Koa returned to the portrait. As he looked into the man's face, he experienced a prickle of excitement, then recognition. He took in the high forehead, crooked nose, pointed jaw, and double gap in the upper front teeth. The man had been younger when he posed for the portrait, but Koa had no doubt he was staring at the face of the corpse from the lava field.

Twin bolts of realization hit him. Gwendolyn Campbell had died in the Honda Civic, and it hadn't been an accident. Her husband had been tortured, murdered, and dumped in a lava field.

Koa confronted a nasty double homicide. He shivered. Instinct told him he'd stumbled into a black hole. Most murders erupted from drunken brawls or domestic quarrels. This was something different, something *weliweli*—dreadful and ferocious.

CHAPTER FOUR

THE FOLLOWING MORNING Basa stuck his head in Koa's office door. "Got a minute?"

"Sure." When Basa closed the door, Koa sensed something out of the ordinary. "What's up?"

"Haven't you heard? The chief is laying off six patrolmen and some of the support staff. They'll be gone by the end of the month."

The news jolted Koa. "You can't be serious! We're already way understaffed."

"It's true. Maru's already got his notice. And Smithy's on the list, too."

"Smithy?" Koa gasped in astonishment. Smithy had been with the police force longer than Koa. As a patrolman, he'd lost both legs when an illegal crystal meth lab had exploded like a Roman candle during a police raid gone sour. Every chief during Koa's twelve-year tenure with the department had found a place for Smithy, who now worked in the dispatch center. Koa couldn't count the number of times he'd heard Smithy's cheerful voice over the police scanner. The man knew more jokes than a stand-up comic and told them with irrepressible enthusiasm.

Basa, who'd befriended Smithy years ago, was especially protective of the disabled policeman. "Yeah." Basa shook his head in disgust. "Smithy got his walking papers yesterday, no fuckin' pun intended. I don't know what he's going to do."

"That's unconscionable," Koa exploded. "Has that word spread?" The police rumor mill put teenage sororities to shame when it came to gossip.

"Yeah. Well, as you can imagine, the chief's stock with the troops is in the toilet—right down the stink hole. I don't know what the hell he's thinking."

Koa had noticed a change in the chief's recent behavior. He'd become overly cost conscious—even downright chintzy—but layoffs took the pattern to a new level. Canning Smithy was nothing short of stupid. Getting hurt on the job was every cop's fear, and an officer expected the department to look out for him or her and their family if the worst happened. That's what being in the police fraternity meant. Besides, there'd been no slump in the island's economy, and Koa had heard nothing about falling tax receipts. Something he didn't understand—something ugly—was afoot.

"Let me check it out," Koa said, struggling to suppress his anger in front of Basa. "But let me know if you hear anything more. Okay?"

"Sure." Basa paused before changing the subject. "I've got a couple reports for you."

Koa leaned forward. "Shoot."

"First, patrolmen checked out the neighbors around the Campbell house. They didn't get much, except for one woman—a Ryan Chang—who seemed to know Gwendolyn Campbell. You ought to talk to her."

"Okay. You want to give me a preview?"

"I don't have much. She apparently hung out with Gwendolyn. Says the husband, named Arthur, was pretty much a recluse. Not much besides that. Johnnie Maru made the contact and, you know him, he's got a room temperature IQ."

Koa knew all too well. "I never understood why you hired that fuck-up."

"It doesn't matter now," Basa shot back with a frown. "The chief just made sure of that." Koa again saw anger in Basa's eyes. They could share gripes about Maru's screw-ups, but Basa had the protective instinct for his people that made for a good leader.

Koa waited, and the storm slowly passed before Basa continued.

"Patrolmen canvassing the squatters in the wasteland around Royal Gardens turned up a possible witness to the lava killing, a dude named Mo."

"What did Mo say?"

"A bunch of crazy shit. Most of those folks out there are serious mental cases, but it sounds like Mo saw something about thirty-six hours before the rangers found the body. You're going to want to interview him. He lives in a discarded shipping container—one of the old Matson line boxes—and won't leave voluntarily. Says people will steal his shit, not that he's got much. I figured he'd clam up if the boys brought him in."

"Okay. I'll talk to Ryan Chang first."

Koa drove out to Chang's place in Volcano. A sign at her driveway advertised specialty mushrooms: "*Ali'i*, shiitake, and oyster mushrooms for the discriminating chef" in English underneath Chinese lettering. When he parked in front of the house, a slight Chinese woman in a large coolie hat left a bucket in the field where she had been working over long, low mushroom-growing boxes and started toward Koa's Explorer. An older woman, she was dressed in baggy pants and a long-sleeve shirt to protect against the sun. Ultraviolet rays and age wrinkles had marred her face, but her small black eyes shone with curiosity.

"Ryan Chang?" Koa asked.

"*Nihao.*"

Koa didn't know much Chinese but recognized the greeting. "Koa Kāne with the Hawai'i County Police. I'd like to talk to you about Gwendolyn Campbell."

The woman's lips trembled, giving Koa his first hint that Chang had been close to the dead woman. "Gwendolyn . . . I hear she have accident. Very bad."

She led him to a large shaded *lānai* and offered him a seat on a mat. While Koa, unused to sitting on the floor, lowered himself awkwardly, Ryan Chang disappeared into the house. While she was gone, Koa thought about taking notes, but as usual, rejected the notion. Note taking discouraged stray comments and slips of the tongue that gave revealing nuance to testimony. Besides, Koa had a near-photographic memory. If he made notes at all, he did so only after interviews or for personal data like names, addresses, and telephone numbers. People expected you to write those things down.

The hat no longer covering her thick black hair, Chang soon returned, knelt opposite him, and placed a clay Chinese teapot and two small Chinese cups without handles on the mat between them. She poured tea into one of the cups and, picking it up with both hands, presented it to him. "Very good for health," she promised.

Her hands were brown and leathery from years in the sun. Crinkles around her eyes gave her a grandmotherly look, although he guessed she looked older than her actual years. She smiled as he took the tea, and he sensed her warmth as well as the heat of the drink in his hands.

"*Mahalo.*" He bowed his head slightly. He waited until she'd poured her own tea and lifted the cup to her lips before he took a sip. It had a delicious smell and a subtle lavender taste, and he thanked her again. "You knew Gwendolyn Campbell?"

"*Shi*, we discover other." She spoke with a thick Chinese accent.

"Discover?" He inclined his head.

"World is big and world is small when two girls from Yulong River, Guangxi Province, become friend in Hawai'i."

"You knew each other in Guangxi, China?"

"*Bú*, we not know other in China, but discover bond in Hawai'i."

"You were related?"

"Not family, but people in Yulong River village share together-ness, like family, like clan."

Koa knew how that worked among Hawaiian families. "How did you meet here in Hawai'i?"

"*Gōng bū*, shiitake, made us one."

"Gwendolyn came here to buy mushrooms, and your common heritage led to a friendship."

"Just so." She nodded. "Gwendolyn born Chaolong Village on Yulong River, upriver from Aishanmen, where I born. Much rural, much poor. Mountains very, very beautiful. Family farm river valley. Hard life, very hard for girl child. We share much. Poor Gwendolyn."

"How did she come to Hawai'i?" Koa asked.

Ryan Chang sighed. "I hear only little her story. Her family much poor, girl children not value in China. But Gwendolyn great beauty. Her father sell Gwendolyn to rich man." As Ryan talked, her hands made tiny birdlike movements.

"Damn," Koa swore softly. "That's awful." He thought of the destitute families he'd seen in Afghan refugee camps. Life's cruel circumstances drove people to extremes, even selling their own children.

"Could be, but he maybe save Gwendolyn. Farm girl child in rural Guangxi Province work dawn to dark in rice paddy. Very hard. Many die very young." Ryan's hands made plucking and planting gestures as though she were back in a Chinese rice paddy. She suddenly stopped and gave him a rueful smile. "Once learn, never forget."

"And after she left her family?"

"Gwendolyn very beautiful. Man, much like, many man."

"She became a prostitute?"

Ryan clasped her hands together. "*Bù*, not prostitute, but many man like." She stopped and sipped her tea.

Koa waited until she replaced the teacup on the mat. "What happened after she escaped China?"

"This I not know. Gwendolyn much secrets, places we not go. I no risk good friendship."

Now they were getting to what Koa wanted to know. "Did she have enemies, people she feared?"

Ryan straightened. "*Shì*, she take great care."

"In what way?"

"Strangers she fear. She want me watch and tell her any not belong and—" Ryan paused.

"And?" Koa prompted.

"*Shì*, she have gun. She always have gun in bag."

This Gwendolyn sounded mysterious and dangerous. He didn't expect this woman to know, but he was curious. He was always curious about guns. Guns, he believed, like jewelry and fashion accessories, were expressions of personality. "What kind of gun?"

"I not know."

"When did you last see Gwendolyn?"

"Two . . . three days before accident. Poor Gwendolyn."

Ryan Chang was proving to be a valuable source of information. Maybe she could explain Gwendolyn's flight in the brown Honda. "Was anything wrong? Was she upset?"

"*Shì*, something happen. She much upset. I see in body, in eyes. Much trouble in eyes. She very nervous." Once again Ryan's hands took flight.

"What about her husband?"

"She no ring but live with Arthur. Maybe married. I not know."

"Arthur Campbell?"

"*Shi.*"

Now they were on to the subject of a man with Special Forces weapons. "Tell me about him."

Ryan became visibly uncomfortable. "Never meet Arthur. Much secret man. Gwendolyn tell me little. I think myself, he much time in forest with orchid. Very, very strange."

"Orchids?"

"Gwendolyn bring orchid, many times. Very beautiful. *Shi*, very beautiful."

The man with the Boss Hog? "Arthur grew these orchids?"

"*Shi*. She tell me."

He remembered the orchids in the bedroom of the Campbell house. He'd assumed they were Gwendolyn's but maybe they'd been Arthur's province. But he hadn't seen any other orchids around the grounds. Strange. He turned the conversation in a different direction. "Did Gwendolyn have other friends?"

"Not much."

Always alert for the nuance as well as the words, Koa followed up. "But some other friend?"

"*Shi*, teacher sell much old Hawai'i things. Him name Howard, maybe more than teacher," she added slyly.

"More than teacher. I don't understand." He thought he did understand, but assumptions could be misleading. He wanted confirmation.

"Gwendolyn very, very beautiful, you understand."

Again, Koa nodded. "Yes. Where can I find this Howard?"

"Green house, near highway." She pointed back down the lane toward the belt road.

That would go on his to-do list. "Can you think of anything else about either of them, either Gwendolyn or Arthur?"

"*Bū*, nothing. You punish truck driver kill my poor Gwendolyn?"

"Yes. We will find him and charge him with her death."

He started to rise, but she held out her hand. "You wait, please." He eased himself back down as she disappeared into the house, and returned with a basket, brimming with shiitake mushrooms. "For you wife. They good eat and good medicine for health. You come back when basket empty."

Koa didn't bother to tell her he wasn't married. Nor that he did most of the cooking. He just accepted the basket and thanked her. On his way back to his Explorer, he reflected that he'd stepped into a nest of secrets. Two brutal murders of two suspicious loners—and he had no idea who they really were or who'd go to such elaborate lengths to make sure they died.

CHAPTER FIVE

"I HEAR YOU guys did great last Saturday," Koa remarked as he and Basa drove southeast along Highway 130 toward Kalapana on their way to see Mo, the half-crazed witness with information about the lava killing. Highway 130 had once run along the southeastern coast, providing access to Royal Gardens before linking up with Chain of Craters Road in Hawai'i Volcanoes National Park. But when *Pele*, in a volcanic tantrum, had destroyed Royal Gardens, she'd covered Highway 130 with lava before sending her rivers of boiling rock into the sea, raising thick clouds of poisonous gases. Now Highway 130 ended as close to the wreckage of Royal Gardens as one could get in a car.

"You heard. We stuffed your best time by more than a half a minute," Basa said. Both of them were fanatic open-ocean outrigger canoe racers, each with a different six-man team.

"You must've had a good caller," Koa shot back. The caller, shouting commands from the second seat, kept the canoe racing forward without wallowing or capsizing in rough water.

"Yeah, right, like all that singing makes the hull move faster," Basa retorted. "Your team gonna be out for the regatta next weekend?"

"Damn straight. We gotta qualify before we can clean your clock," Koa replied.

"You're gonna have to get some powerful paddlers to do that, maybe some born after the age of dinosaurs."

Koa winced. Basa had touched a nerve. The sergeant's bearlike strength, coupled with a ten-year age advantage, made him a formidable competitor. Koa's team had won championships, but he and his teammates had aged and lost a stroke or two. Besides, he'd had spinal surgery and found the grueling open-ocean races took a lot out of him. "Brains will outperform brawn," he said with more conviction than he felt.

They rode in silence for several minutes. When Basa spoke again, he was serious. "Smithy wants to know if he can talk to you about his situation. He's hoping you can put in a good word with the chief, maybe get the chief to pull his pink slip and give him another year or two."

Koa's mind shifted to this latest office intrigue. He'd talked to one of the patrol captains who'd also noticed the chief's new tight-fisted budget priorities. Koa had gotten an earful. Neither of them could get a fix on the chief's motivations. "Sure. I'd be happy to sit down with Smithy, but I don't know if I can help."

"Whatever you can do. I'll let him know."

When they reached Kalapana, Basa maneuvered Koa's Explorer past the first "Road Closed" barrier and over one patch of lava before hitting another stretch of highway *Pele* had spared.

Off to the ocean side, *ma kai* way, a brand-new two-story house with a "For Sale" sign stood surrounded by waves of ebony lava, like a boxy ship on a black sea. Uphill, various habitations—tents, shacks, converted shipping containers—sprouted from a barren lava field. What kind of person, Koa wondered, lived on ground *Pele* might reclaim at her whim? Some of these folks, he knew, had already been burned out of places in Royal Gardens. Maybe seeing their homes go up in fire had driven them mad.

To Koa's surprise, they pulled up next to two of Basa's patrolmen on ATVs. Koa recognized officers Shane and Humana. "Only way to get around on this damn lava," Basa explained.

"Where's this fellow Mo live?" Koa asked.

"Up in the Gardens," Humana responded. "You're in for quite a ride."

Sergeant Basa mounted one ATV behind Shane, while Koa rode behind Humana. Officer Humana hadn't exaggerated. While the charcoal-black *pāhoehoe* lava appeared smooth from a distance, up close deep crevices lay hidden between dips and mounds, outcroppings, and irregularities. For almost thirty minutes, the ATVs rocked and jounced their way up the slope, like tiny boats on a choppy black ocean.

As they reached the former subdivision, evidence of man's inability to withstand *Pele*'s wrath abounded: foundations of burned-out buildings, half-buried cars, a refrigerator bound shut by lava, an isolated road sign sticking out of solid rock. *Kīpuka* areas, islands of older vegetation and trees *Pele* capriciously spared, gave the barrenness only scant relief. Koa could hardly imagine sixty homes had once existed in these blackened badlands.

A few intrepid, or stupid, souls had reoccupied the disaster zone. The policemen passed a couple of shacks before traversing a hundred yards of gravel road, running from one bank of lava to another, and stopped before a battered and rusted Matson shipping container—the forty-footer had long outlived its original purpose. A rough doorway had been hacked through the side, and a blue tarpaulin on tent poles served as an awning. Two cheap folding beach chairs sat ready for visitors, but layers of black dust on the seats told Koa no one had been around for ages.

Officer Shane banged on the side of the steel box. "Mo, you home?"

An emaciated man with a long, dirty gray beard, glassy gray eyes, and a nervous twitch emerged from the container, mumbling, "You better be watching out. You better be watching out . . . the 'itch will toast your ass . . . toast your ass." He wore stained and ripped coveralls without a shirt, and smelled of unwashed flesh, reminding Koa that Mo lived without running water, electricity, or sewage disposal. Koa's experienced eye told him Mo was high on something, probably meth. This was going to be a difficult, and most likely useless, interview.

Koa introduced himself. "You live alone up here, Mo?"

"Live with the 'itch . . . with the 'itch," the man responded. Koa wasn't sure whether he'd said "bitch" or "witch" and couldn't tell whether the man referred to a woman or *Pele*, often pictured as a wizened female with glassy white hair.

"Is she here now?" Koa asked.

Mo replied earnestly, "She comes and she goes . . . a nightmare . . . an awful nightmare."

Koa was thinking of the nightmare of the partially burned body they'd found not too far away. "I understand you saw something up here a few nights ago."

"Nightmares in the night . . . nightmares," Mo muttered.

"Tell me what you saw?"

"Nightmare screams . . . nightmare screams in the night." Mo bobbed up and down and shifted erratically from side to side. His eyes sparkled with an unnaturally bright, shiny look, confirming Koa's suspicion of drug use.

"Mo." Koa spoke slowly, as if addressing a child. "You told Officer Shane over there"—Koa pointed at the officer—"you saw something up here a few nights ago, do you remember?"

"Nightmare screams . . . nightmare screams in the night." More head bobbing.

"You heard nightmare screams a few nights ago?" Koa began to regret the long, bumpy trip over the lava field.

The man nodded. "Like a wounded animal."

Koa stared at the strange, unkempt man, trying to make sense of his ramblings. Mo kept talking about sounds, but he'd told Officer Shane he'd seen something. Koa tried a different tact. "Where?"

"Chinese house . . . Chinese." Mo pointed up the hill toward a ridgeline, but Koa saw no house.

Koa was getting nowhere. "You saw nightmare screams like a wounded animal in the Chinese house?" he asked skeptically.

"I see," Mo responded.

Koa had wasted enough time on this fool's errand. He turned away, motioning to the others to follow, and headed back toward the ATVs.

"I see . . . I see Chinese house," Mo said, his voice louder.

Koa turned back toward Mo, sure the man was hallucinating. He studied Mo, who still pointed excitedly up the hill. Koa decided to give it one more shot. "Where, Mo? Show me where."

Mo grabbed a gnarled walking stick leaning against the container and limped around the end of his makeshift abode. The four officers followed Mo who hobbled slowly up the hill toward a slight ridgeline crowned with scraggly shrubs and partially burned trees. After ten minutes and 150 yards, they reached the scorched vegetation. Mo led them along a path for maybe another twenty yards, then stopped and pointed. "Nightmare screams."

Koa waited for Mo to continue, but the man stood frozen, like a stone monolith on the lava. Something had frightened Mo, and he wasn't going any farther.

The four policemen left Mo and continued along the trail to the edge of the ridge. Koa felt a prick of excitement when he stared down at the remnants of a building, nestled in a hollow below the crest. Crazy Mo might indeed have heard something. Red-hot lava had set one end of the structure ablaze, but rain must have extinguished the fire because a third of the dwelling remained standing, grim evidence of *Pele's* perversity.

They picked their way down the slope and entered what had once been the ground floor of a medium-sized house. Burned timbers littered the ground, but Koa saw that someone had cleared a path through the charred wood and other debris to stairs leading to the upper level of what remained. He grabbed a flashlight from Officer Humana and made his way upward.

As Koa climbed, the heat became stifling and a rusty, metallic smell grew stronger. The smell told him whatever awaited at the top of the stairs would be drenched in blood. Mo's words—nightmare screams in the night—ricocheted in Koa's mind. He reached the top and entered a hallway that had once run the length of the house, but now ended in a jumble of burned framing. The flashlight revealed a single door to his left. He gently pushed the door open. Darkness. No light emanated from the space. The overpowering smell of blood filled his nostrils. He pointed the light down, checking the flooring. He didn't want to step into a hole and fall through to the ground below.

Satisfied the floor would hold, he stepped inside the darkened room and was hit by a heat wave. The temperature in the confined space had to be 130 degrees. Sweat poured from his face and ran down his chest. He played the light over a bizarre scene. Heavy black plastic sheeting, nailed to the walls, covered the windows. Rough wooden planks, a shoulder-width wide and six feet long, sat on sawhorses occupying the center of the otherwise unfurnished space. Leather straps nailed to the wood, such as might tie a man down, hung from either side of the planks. Dark reddish-brown and black stains saturated the planks and formed dried pools on the floor. Dozens of cigarette butts lay scattered around the room. In the center of it all, a severed human hand—a left hand—had fallen to the floor.

"Damn!" he swore. Now he, too, would see nightmare screams in the night. He needed to get the crime-scene techs out here, and fast. He called down to Basa to get them started.

CHAPTER SIX

THE CRIME-SCENE TEAM searched the Campbells' remote artist's studio. They collected DNA samples from bed linens, a woman's hairbrush, Q-tips, cosmetic swabs, and a man's comb. Dozens of fingerprints throughout the house belonged to two people, presumably Gwendolyn and Arthur Campbell. A ledger, found in a drawer under one of the worktables, revealed that Gwendolyn Campbell had sold drawings and paintings for the last decade at prices ranging from $50 to $3,000. The absence of ID bothered Koa. There were no letters, no bank or credit card records, no tax returns, deeds, wills, Social Security cards, or other legal papers.

A Hawai'i records check failed to turn up any evidence Arthur Campbell had ever existed. He hadn't registered his handgun with the police department. The DMV had no Hawai'i driver's license for him. The Department of Finance had no tax returns. Property records revealed no real property held in his name. Police canvassing the neighborhood failed to turn up anyone who knew much about Arthur Campbell. He didn't frequent local shops. He didn't eat out in any of the handful of Volcano restaurants. His neighbors rarely, if ever, saw him. When acquaintances inquired, Gwendolyn described Arthur as a retired recluse. According to local merchants,

Gwendolyn did all the shopping, most of it at the Volcano General Store, and always with cash.

More sophisticated inquiries produced more mysteries. County tax records revealed that Hansel GmbH, a Lichtenstein trust, owned, and paid taxes on, the Campbell property, encompassing ten acres of forestland, the decrepit house, and its outbuildings. In a dozen years on the police force, Koa had never heard of a Lichtenstein trust and doubted such a trust held any other property on the island. He sent Interpol a request for information on Hansel GmbH, but doubted he'd get anything back.

* * *

Koa's mind drifted to Escher's *Reptiles* drawing on his office wall. He'd bought the image to remind himself of his darkest secrets. After killing Hazzard, he'd sat alone in the remote cabin, contemplating what he'd done. Feelings of fear—of punishment and what his friends and family would think—consumed him. Fear morphed into guilt. He hadn't meant to kill Hazzard, but the deed was done. As realization sank in, he became angry at his own stupidity. He'd ruined his own life.

Koa knew the police would conclude he'd tracked Hazzard for revenge. Although low sugar prices and foreign competition were forcing the plantations out of business, sugar barons still controlled the police and the courts. They would see Koa charged, convicted, and locked away.

Desperate for a way out, he considered how he might hide his crime. He'd never shared his suspicions of Hazzard's complicity in his father's death, and no one knew he'd tracked Hazzard into the mountains. His family thought he was off on a fishing trip. Not the best alibi, but it might work.

He rejected the idea of planting evidence pointing to someone else. He couldn't think of another good suspect and didn't want an innocent to suffer. Instead, he settled upon faking a suicide. Sugar mills had been closing all across the island. Overseers and managers as well as workers were losing their jobs. Hazzard had come alone to the mountains and had been drinking heavily. Suicide might seem odd, but not impossible.

The mill closed following Koa's father's death, and days might pass before someone came looking for Hazzard. The isolated location of the cabin deep in the forest made it unlikely anyone would soon stumble upon the scene. It might be a long while before the authorities examined Hazzard's decomposing body.

Koa opened a bottle of whiskey, and poured more alcohol down Hazzard's throat, spilling it liberally over the man's clothes. People in remote cabins always kept a supply of rope, and he quickly discovered that Hazzard was no exception. Koa chose a badly frayed piece, hoping it would hold together long enough for his purpose. Fashioning a noose, he wrapped it around Hazzard's neck, and looped the rope over one of the ceiling beams. He struggled to haul the mill manager's body up, but the rope held, and he managed to get the dead man atop a small table before finally hoisting the body until it hung from the rafters with its feet barely touching the table.

Koa had downed a slug of whiskey to steady his nerves, before upsetting the table, like a man hanging himself might have kicked it away. The liquor bottle crashed to the floor. The corpse swung slowly, casting a weird moving shadow on the cabin wall.

Standing on a chair, Koa slowly sawed on the rope with a knife, scraping rather than cutting. Koa's arms grew sore before the rope split, allowing Hazzard's body, the noose still around his neck, to tumble to the floor. Koa moved the chair away and placed the metal poker under Hazzard's head with its overturned stand nearby. He hoped he'd staged a believable suicide-hanging where the rope had failed, causing Hazzard to fall on the metal fire tools, explaining his head injury.

Koa considered setting the cabin on fire but thought better of it. Smoke would only bring instant attention to the scene, and he wanted the body to rot. Instead, he propped the cabin door open, knowing that animals would soon scavenge the place. He'd seen the island's army of wild pigs gnaw away at all kinds of dead meat, including rats, birds, and cows. Given a little time, animals and insects would make it difficult, if not impossible, for the authorities to reconstruct what had happened.

He eventually left the cabin, fearing it would only be a matter of time before the police arrested him. He found himself looking over his shoulder and struggling to act normal. He'd worried about all the mistakes he might have made. Would the cops figure out that he'd cut the rope? Had he left fingerprints? One sleepless night followed another. For twelve days, he heard nothing. Then the *Hawaii Herald Tribune* reported that hikers had found a horribly ravaged and decomposed body in a remote Kohala cabin. Although the paper didn't print the details, Koa guessed pigs had feasted on Hazzard's remains. A month later, the newspaper recounted that authorities, with the aid of a local doctor who acted as coroner, had concluded that the former mill manager had hanged himself.

Koa's ruse had worked, but it did nothing to salve his conscience. Every day he relived what he'd done. He saw Hazzard's face in strangers on the street, and in the cloud formations overhead. He had trouble sleeping, and some days the guilt was unbearable. He thought about turning himself in, but never found the courage.

Like the amphibians emerging from reptile land in Escher's drawing, there were missing pieces, clues hidden beneath the surface, not only in Koa's life but also in Arthur Campbell's past. Koa couldn't picture the man's history. Maybe Arthur, like Escher's lizards, had disappeared and reemerged a changed man. Koa wanted to know what he'd been doing in Volcano Village and how he'd supported himself. Koa had Piki put the fingerprints found at the Campbell house into the FBI's IAFIS, Integrated Automated Fingerprint Identification System. He'd know soon enough whether Arthur Campbell was a chameleon.

* * *

As was his habit, Koa headed back to the Campbell property after the crime-scene team departed. As he wound his way through the forest in the late morning sunlight, he expected to find little or nothing. The crime-scene team had undoubtedly been thorough, but an inner compulsion drove him to look for the most obscure of clues. It was his way, one of the traits that made him a good detective.

His investigation skills traced back to his own crime. After becoming a detective, he'd dug out and studied the old police file on Hazzard's death and learned a great deal about how not to conduct an investigation. The investigators on the case had been taken in by superficial impressions and jumped to conclusions. According to the file, the investigators had never closely examined the ends of the rope, but just assumed it had come apart under Hazzard's weight. Nor had they matched the position of the poker on the floor to Hazzard's head injury. They had found unknown fingerprints but hadn't been able to identify them. They never ferreted out a satisfactory reason for Hazzard to take his own life, and one of the old cops had been skeptical of the suicide theory, but nothing had come of it.

The Hazzard killing had given Koa insight into the criminal mind, the guilt and fear at having taken a human life, the elation of getting away with it, and the ever-present worry that the past might rear up at any moment. The police file had taught him not to get sucked into initial impressions and to look at a crime scene from every conceivable angle. He'd become paranoid that he'd get snookered, just like he'd fooled the cops who'd investigated Hazzard's death.

To bring these instincts to bear, he needed to get inside the victims' lives, see their homes, feel their vibrations, and meet their ghosts. All places harbored *lapu*—ghosts—telltales of the people who'd lived, loved, and fought there. He could sense those phantoms only if he was alone, surrounded by the victims' possessions, walking where they'd walked, breathing the air they'd breathed.

He started inside, trying to get a feel for the victims' lives. Neat or cluttered, airy or cavelike, surrounded by pictures and plants, or barren. Each little detail hinted at personality and habit. These tidbits sometimes turned up clues to the mystery of a victim's demise, but more importantly they gave Koa a connection to the deceased, to think as they might have thought. Life's little details also fueled his empathy for the victims, reinforcing the commitment he'd made after Jerry's death.

The house bulged with so much stuff the task seemed hopeless, but he plowed through pile after pile of books, papers, and other assorted junk. The art books, paintings, and drawings reinforced his impression of Gwendolyn as a struggling artist. She'd made countless sketches of native birds, often in scenes of ancient Hawaiian *heiau*, or temple platforms.

His search through the hundreds of books and objects in the studio told him nothing about Arthur. Nor did the eclectic collection in the downstairs bedroom enlighten him about the reclusive man who appeared to have lived in the house without leaving much of a trace. For all he could glean from the ground floor, Arthur had spent his life tossing darts at an old Nihoa campaign poster. There had to be more to this apparition of a man.

He climbed the stairs and entered the master bedroom. The orchids near the window and on the balcony caught his eye. What had Gwendolyn's friend Ryan Chang said? Arthur spent "much time in forest with orchid." She couldn't have meant these orchids. No man spent his days in the company of twenty-some orchid plants.

He sat down on the end of the bed, examining Arthur's picture, trying to coax some new revelation from the image. It had a flatness, lacking the three-dimensional quality that made portraits vivid. He guessed Gwendolyn painted this likeness. He imagined waking up every morning to look at this dull, lifeless self-image and found the thought depressing.

The portrait stuck out from the wall. He touched the frame, trying to shift the portrait. It didn't budge. Whoever hung the picture must've anchored it to the wall. He tried to look behind it but saw no gap. He moved to the other side of the portrait, the side away from the hallway door, and noticed a dark patch on the edge of the frame, as though someone had smeared a dab of grease on it. He touched the patch, and it gave a bit under the pressure of his finger. He pressed harder.

The painting came unlatched from the wall and swung out like a closet door, hinged on the side opposite the latch. When Koa swung the portrait away from the wall, he saw, hidden behind it, a television screen. He had a fleeting image of the Campbells watching television from the bed, but almost immediately dismissed the thought. While the house had generator power, it had no cable connection, and he'd seen no satellite dish. There was no over-the-air reception in Volcano Village.

He examined the controls and pushed the power button. Nothing. The crime-scene team had shut down the generator. That problem was easily solved. He walked out to the shed, checked the fuel, and pressed the starter switch. The machine roared to life, a green light illuminated, and the gauges showed 110 volts.

Koa returned to the master bedroom and once again pumped the power button on the monitor. The screen came alive. At first, the image confused him. Then, slowly, he identified a forest scene in black and white. A trail meandered away from the viewer through dense, overhanging forest. A bird flying through the picture startled him; he was watching a live feed from a remote camera. The picture switched to a different camera view of another forest scene. Soon the picture changed again . . . and then again.

After several minutes, he figured out the sequence—eight cameras or camera angles and eight different forest scenes. Arthur Campbell had rigged up a surveillance system. Where, Koa wondered, were the cameras? What did the system protect? Most likely, the images came from the forest surrounding the house, but the cameras could be elsewhere. He'd seen no wires running off into the forest, and guessed the system used wireless technology to transmit images. The cameras would be hard to find. He turned off the television and returned the portrait to its closed, latched position.

He ventured out into the steamy, bug-infested area surrounding the house. After shutting down the generator, he crawled into the space beneath the building, but found only carcasses of dead birds, probably killed by the cats. The underside of the joists revealed only electric wiring from the generator and plumbing, connecting the building to a well and a cesspool. He checked for wires supporting the security system, but the absence of hard wiring didn't surprise him.

Crawling out from under the house, his foot caught on a board covering the post where the generator wires hooked to a fuse box. A board fell away, revealing a small space containing a military ammunition box. He pulled the box out of its hiding place and un-latched the lid, finding a second Heckler & Koch HK45, along with three fully loaded clips of ammunition. This weapon, like the one he'd found in the bedroom, had a round already chambered. Arthur Campbell must have stashed the weapon in case he couldn't get to the one in the bedroom.

Many island residents kept guns. Some surrounded themselves with firearms. Koa knew many of those guns weren't registered, but few gun nuts owned expensive, military-grade handguns like the Heckler & Koch HK45. And most gun owners took care with loaded weapons. The prepositioning of loaded military-grade hand-guns, ready for instantaneous carnage, suggested Arthur Campbell feared an assault on his life. Koa wondered what would frighten a former Special Forces operative.

He made short work of the carport. It consisted of little more than canvas stretched across a frame supported by four poles. That left the generator shed, and it contained only a generator, a gas can, some tools, and the massive Boss Hog motorcycle. He checked the storage compartments on the big machine. Empty.

Koa circled the edge of the forest around the house, checking for the surveillance cameras feeding the monitor in the bedroom. He found nothing and was about to give up when he noticed a single tire track made by the Boss Hog. It led not to the drive, but into the forest.

Swatting away mosquitoes, Koa entered the jungle-like forest, fol-lowing a narrow, twisting path. Water dripped from tree branches. The elevation increased as he ventured deeper. Puddles and muddy patches made the trek messy; mud soon covered his shoes. Sporadically, he spotted the Boss Hog's tread marks. After twenty yards, he came to a fence blocking the path. *Kapu*—forbidden—and no-trespassing signs on a gate warned against entry. He guessed he'd reached the property boundary, but the tracks of the Boss Hog continued past the gate.

He let himself through the gate and picked his way cautiously up the trail. A bird screeched and arced overhead. Koa stopped dead, remembering the black-and-white image on the bedroom monitor. He pictured the forest ahead of him in black and white. Slowly he swiveled around, searching the trees behind him, trying to recall the camera angle. Nothing. He looked higher, sweeping from right to left, and spotted the camera, a tiny box twenty feet off the ground. Arthur Campbell's security system protected this trail.

He moved farther up the path, passing more places where the motorcycle's tires had left tracks. He paused often, checking the trees for more cameras—nothing. He navigated around more muddy areas and came upon new, narrower tracks, perhaps those of a bicycle. After another quarter mile, Koa arrived in a clearing covered with camouflage netting hung on ropes strung from the surrounding trees. Mist hovered in the dank air. Long rows of greenhouse tables filled the open space.

Thousands of orchids. Koa recognized the intricate plants even before he reached the first rows of growing racks. The array of blossoms made him think of Nālani, and he smiled, remembering one of their first hikes into the rain forest. He pictured her happy, engaged face in the mottled sunlight of the deep forest where she'd discovered a rare epiphytic orchid with its aerial roots extending several feet. She'd shared her deep knowledge of the unique plants.

As the son of a native healer, he'd grown up with herbal blossoms and flowered *leis*, but never had much interest in horticulture. Nālani had changed that. She'd taught him about an ecological world, populated with over twenty thousand species of orchids. Lacking her scientific background, he'd never mastered the Latin names, but she'd taught him to recognize the most common varieties. He'd learned enough to realize that Arthur had many prized specimens. Koa spotted pure yellow, star-shaped red, and hairy green orchids. Pulling out his cell phone, he snapped pictures of the more exotic varieties for Nālani to identify.

He counted the growing benches—ten, twenty, more than thirty tables covered with plastic racks holding thousands of plants. Some benches held cuttings, each carefully labeled with a plastic tag, while others sported mature plants. Potting stands, misters, and other equipment evidenced a professional operation. Arthur Campbell had been an orchid grower and not just an ordinary one. He'd amassed an extensive collection of carefully tended plants. His orchid obsession explained where he'd spent his days and why his neighbors hardly knew him.

Arthur must have spent countless hours in these clearings. Koa figured Arthur had likely stashed guns here, too. Dropping to his hands and knees, he examined the underside of the nearest growing table. He saw no weapon, but as he scanned the other tables he saw something taped to the underside of the third table in the row: another Heckler & Koch HK45, fully loaded and ready to go, just like the other two semiautomatic pistols.

Koa continued to snoop. The scope and sophistication of the orchid-growing operation became clearer. A small aqueduct carried water from a spring to an elevated tank feeding the watering system. Clock-controlled misters above the growing tables irrigated the plants. A shed bulged with wheelbarrows, stacks of planting containers, dozens of bags of fertilizer, sprayers, moss, bark, and other growing paraphernalia, along with shelves of tools and ancillary supplies. A homemade cart with bicycle wheels explained the narrow tracks along the forest trail. The equipment alone cost tens of thousands of dollars. He couldn't imagine how Arthur had managed to get the equivalent of a half dozen greenhouses to this remote forest location. And where did Arthur get the money to support his expensive operation?

Orchid farms abounded around Volcano, but no one located them deep in a rain forest. The ramshackle house stood in sharp contrast to this sophisticated orchid-growing operation. Arthur had chosen an impoverished front for a classy operation. The county land records showed he held no title to any land. He must have made some arrangement to use this property. He couldn't be an uninvited squatter with this kind of investment. The tax records, Koa knew, would at least tell him who owned the property.

The size and complexity of the facility suggested a business, but Koa found no access road. There was no way to get supplies in or orchids out except along the twisting, muddy trail where Koa had entered. Campbell couldn't have managed the sale of orchids in commercial quantities using only the motorcycle and the small cart for transportation. So he must have been raising the plants for himself. Arthur Campbell had been a reclusive connoisseur, obsessed with a most expensive hobby.

A tiny alarm triggered in Koa's subconscious. He sensed a presence and felt eyes watching him. He'd known the same feeling in Somalia and learned not to ignore it. By affording him a few seconds' warning, his instinctive sixth sense had saved him from a sniper's bullet not once but twice. It'd also gotten Jerry killed. He glanced around casually, careful not to alert the unknown watcher. He saw no one, but he had no doubt. Someone had him under observation.

As in Somalia, his first concern was for his safety. He was alone in a remote forest, miles from his nearest colleague. He doubted his unknown watcher would take hostile action. It had been years since a Big Island police officer had been killed in the line of duty, but it still made sense to take precautions. He'd set his iPhone up for just such a situation.

Moving casually, he slipped his Bluetooth earpiece into place and used its built-in software to call Basa. When the police sergeant picked up, Koa softly reported his location, requested backup, and asked Basa to stay on the line to monitor his situation.

He focused on the intruder, curious about his or her identity and connection to the killings. He circled the site, darting looks into the forest, around the benches, and back toward the house, trying to spot watchers and cameras, but they remained hidden. Still keeping an eye out for an intruder, Koa explored several footpaths leading away from the orchid farm. One led to a compost pile. Another followed the aqueduct up to the spring fifty yards behind the greenhouse tables. Along this path, not far from the spring, he spotted another camera, this one pointed up the trail leading away from the orchid farm. He guessed the other cameras protected other approaches to the farm.

A third trail led off into the forest. Narrow, twisting, and rarely used, it seemed to peter out in places, only to reestablish itself. Koa found no sign of motorcycle tracks or any other evidence of recent human passage. The elevation increased. He climbed over a fallen tree. As he got farther up the trail, the prickling sensation of being watched faded, and he was once again alone. He was thinking about abandoning the trek when the vegetation grew thinner and he came upon ruins.

He stopped short and stared at a stone platform. He'd found a remote *heiau*, an ancient Hawaiian temple, where his ancestors had paid homage to the gods who ruled their lives. He felt a shiver run down his spine. All manner of superstitions surrounded such temples. Some had been built by the *menehune*, mythical little people who worked only at night, while ghosts inhabited other *heiau*. Evil luck befell those who entered without proper ritual. Had the murdered couple wandered up the little-used trail and found this *heiau*? For a moment Koa wondered if the gods who'd once presided over the platform had cursed the deceased, but quickly dismissed the idea.

The place carried Koa back to his youth. He'd been a young teen when his mother had first taken him to the *heiau* at Pu'uhonua, beside the ocean. Māmā had looked out over the waves. "There were once many *heiau* on this island built to honor the old gods—the gods of farmers, fishermen, and priests. There were *luakini heiau*— bad places—where priests performed human sacrifices. But this is my favorite of all the *heiau*. This was a place of refuge—a place of safety for the sick, for *kapu*-breakers who violated taboos, and even for defeated *ali'i* or royalty. It, like all *heiau*, is a sacred place, but a good one." Even back then Koa had understood his mother's attachment to Pu'uhonua. As a native healer who tended her neighbors' spiritual well-being as well as their physical injuries, she found comfort in a place that protected people from their troubles.

He looked again at the *heiau* in front of him. Compared with the massive platform at Pu'uhonua, it was a relatively small temple—probably connected to some daily ritual. It didn't have the forebodingness of a *luakini heiau*. Still, he refrained from climbing onto the platform. Whether out of respect or superstition—he wasn't sure.

Most *heiau* had been vandalized after the ruling class abolished the old *kapu* system of taboos in 1819, and the missionaries converted many Hawaiians to Christianity. Others had been ravaged for building stones, but this one appeared to be in excellent condition. He wondered why this particular *heiau* had escaped the fate of so many other sacred places. Perhaps its isolation protected it.

Koa's thoughts returned to the watcher. He walked back to the orchid farm and headed toward the Campbell house. Someone had been watching him as he explored the orchid farm, but lost interest or fled when he'd wandered up the trail toward the *heiau*. He wanted to know who and why. He checked the ground along the trail, around the house, and along the drive, but found only his own footprints and no unknown tire tracks. Perhaps the watcher was an expert tracker, but more likely, he or she had entered the orchid farm from a different direction.

* * *

In his office, Koa located a high-resolution satellite map of the Volcano area and identified an obscure fire trail ending about three-quarters of a mile from the orchid farm. He asked Sergeant Basa to join him, and they headed back toward Volcano. "You look beat," Koa commented as they drove south.

"That damned sovereignty socialist has fucked up my life."

Koa heard the anger in Basa's voice. "Nāinoa Nihoa?"

"Yeah. I've never seen a politician generate so much hate. We've got vandals painting vile messages on county buildings. The public school teachers are threatening strikes. Hell, some of the county employees are talking about sick-ins and work stoppages."

"He's got a lot of supporters and some good ideas," Koa observed. "The public education system is a disaster."

Basa frowned. "You support turning the clock back to 1893?"

"No, and I don't support cutting the police budget."

"You think the chief is cutting jobs to curry favor with Nihoa because he's leading in the polls?"

That was exactly what Koa thought. "Is that what they're saying around the station?"

"Yeah. That and a lot of stuff you don't want to hear. The cops are angry, along with the teachers and the state workers. There'll be a riot at this damn rally next week."

Koa's job didn't include public safety, but violence of any kind would mean more crimes to investigate, and mass violence would be a nightmare. "I sure hope you're wrong."

The two men fell silent for a while, contemplating the upcoming rally. Koa had a double homicide on his hands and didn't want manpower diverted because some politician liked the sound of his own voice.

They found the fire lane and parked. Koa observed crushed grass and broken branches where a vehicle had recently passed. They'd walked nearly half a mile before a fallen tree blocked their path. The grass had been crushed sideways and the bark had been scraped off a tree on the edge of the forest, probably by a vehicle turning around to exit the narrow lane. Koa rubbed his fingers over the raw wood. It was slick with sap. Koa guessed whoever had been spying on him had driven up the lane, parked, and slipped through the forest to the orchid farm. He was going to need a lot more than crushed grass and a damaged tree to find out who it'd been.

* * *

That night Koa told Nālani about the orchid farm with thousands of plants deep in the rain forest.

"You're kidding. An orchid farm buried in the forest with no road access? What varieties?"

"Many of the common varieties, ones you've shown me," he said, "but dozens I've never seen before."

"Can you describe them?"

"I can do better. I have pictures." He found his phone, pressed the gallery icon, and handed it to her.

She identified the pure yellow orchids as *bulbophyllum* and the hairy green ones as *dendrobium macrophyllum*. The one with red star flowers stumped her. She pulled a reference book from a shelf and leafed through it before identifying the red orchids as a rare type of *catteya araguaiensis*. She paused, thinking. "I can understand this guy, this recluse, raising exotic varieties and maybe breeding hybrids, but why so many plants? Was he possibly selling them by mail?"

"Doesn't that require state inspections?"

"Absolutely. The Hawai'i Department of Agriculture has an orchid growers' certification program for mainland shippers."

"I don't think Arthur invited officials to his little orchid preserve. He seems to have avoided all official contacts."

"I don't know, Koa," she said. "You don't grow so many plants unless you plan to sell them. From what you told me, those sales could well be what kept the Campbells going all those years."

Nālani was right about the number of orchid plants, but Koa had seen no evidence of sales or even a feasible means of commercial transportation. Still, Arthur Campbell had somehow obtained the considerable funds needed to support his obsession. How? Koa pondered that mystery as he drifted off to sleep.

CHAPTER SEVEN

As chief detective, Koa chafed under many handicaps, but none more aggravating than the lack of a decent coroner. Shizuo Hiro bungled nearly every case, delighting defense counsel, who mocked him unmercifully during cross-examination. Koa sometimes laughed inwardly at the irony. A bungling coroner had saved him from the consequences of killing Anthony Hazzard, and now an equally incompetent pathologist complicated his work. Only, it wasn't so funny. Shizuo's report that the victim had been "tossed in a pit and half-burned by an advancing lava flow" told Koa nothing he didn't already know.

"What about the burns?" Koa asked Shizuo.

"They look like cigarette burns."

"Yes, I saw them, remember? What's your professional opinion?"

"They're cigarette burns, third degree in the center, lesser in the peri-ulcer around the circumference. No evidence of lava particles. Tobacco ash present in some of the ulcers."

"Premortem?"

"Yes, the inflammation surrounding the ulcers suggests premortem, or in detective-speak," Shizuo said in a condescending tone, "some of the wounds started to heal. That can't happen postmortem."

"Cause of death?"

"Don't know. The heat from the lava would have been fatal, but even with the heat, the weight loss is exceptional, perhaps 50, maybe 60 percent. It's more like hypovolemia than dehydration—"

"Hypovolemia?" Koa interrupted. "Translate that to detective-speak."

"Blood loss."

"So the victim bled to death?" Koa asked.

"Well, hypovolemic shock would be consistent with the condition of the corpse, but I found no open wounds."

Koa thought of the severed hand on the floor of the blacked-out room at Royal Gardens. "You checked the hands?"

"The fingers on the right hand were all messed up."

"How?" Koa asked.

"Missing nails and twisted, broken bones," Shizuo said.

"All five digits?"

"Yes, and the thumb was nearly severed."

Jesus, Koa thought. Cigarette burns on the chest and groin, ripped-out fingernails, and snapped finger bones pointed to prolonged torture. Koa tried to imagine the agony the man had gone through. Severe torture and premeditated murder. He wanted to hammer the assholes who'd done it and take them out of circulation for the rest of their lives. "What about the left hand?"

"The left arm was encrusted in lava from the elbow down."

"Tell me about the condition of the left hand."

"I don't know. I'd have to cut away the lava." Shizuo sounded defensive.

Koa sighed. Shizuo hadn't bothered to check the left hand. How could a coroner perform an autopsy without discovering a missing hand? And the missing hand could explain the blood loss. "You've got to examine the left hand," Koa insisted.

"That's a big job. It'll take time, and I've got patients to see."

"I also need to know whether there are other marks on the body."

"Tomorrow, end of the day tomorrow."

Slamming the phone down, Koa turned to a report from the crime-scene technicians. Chip Baxter and Georgina Pau had gone over the upstairs room at the abandoned Royal Gardens house like jewelers evaluating diamonds. They'd confirmed the existence of human bloodstains, estimated the volume at just under a gallon, and matched the blood type to the body found in the lava field. *Christ*, Koa thought. A gallon of blood. That's three-quarters of the blood in a human body. The Royal Gardens victim must indeed have bled to death.

Georgina found only one fingerprint, a partial thumb impression lifted from the doorjamb in the upstairs room. Critically, the print showed traces of the victim's blood. That made it potent evidence, if they could identify the owner of the print. It didn't match the prints recovered from the Campbell house, or any prints in the Hawai'i fingerprint database. That print, like the Campbell prints, had gone to the FBI's IAFIS fingerprint database.

Analysis of the numerous cigarettes butts collected from the floor of the upstairs room in the half-burned Royal Gardens house showed traces of burned flesh. Chip had examined the severed hand and reported all four fingers, as well as the thumb, were bent backward and broken. Koa closed his eyes and forced his mind back into the superheated, blacked-out room. Arthur Campbell had been tortured, probably for hours, maybe days, in that hellhole in the middle of *Pele*'s excreta. Had his torturers, Koa wondered, gotten the information they sought and let the man bleed to death? Or had they been overzealous and bled him out before he revealed his secrets?

Hawai'i County had a crime lab, but it lacked the accreditation and sophistication to perform DNA analysis. They sent DNA samples to the Honolulu Police Department Crime Lab for analysis and comparison in CODIS, the national Combined DNA Index System, with over eleven million DNA profiles. The lab purified and amplified the DNA samples found in the Campbell house, the remains of the two bodies, and the blood in the "Chinese house" using FBI-approved STR DNA analysis techniques.

DNA from a woman's hairbrush at the Campbell house matched DNA from the body parts in the shredded brown Honda Civic. DNA from the pooled blood in the "Chinese house" matched DNA from the body found in the lava field and DNA from the male implements in the Campbell house. As Koa had guessed, Arthur Campbell died at Royal Gardens and Gwendolyn Campbell died in the bizarre accident with the county dump truck. But the lab reported no match in the CODIS database.

Koa kept returning to one extraordinary fact. Although many largely invisible people lived on the Big Island, none of them lived in a house owned by a Lichtenstein trust. He reminded himself that Arthur Campbell's orchid farm hadn't been located on the same ten-acre property as the dwelling. Time to see who owned that property.

Koa walked down the street to the finance department and found Betty Kim, a records clerk who'd once worked for the police department. A chubby, cheerful woman, Betty pulled out a tax map for the Volcano area, and Koa located the large parcel adjacent to the Campbell house.

"Here, Betty." Koa pointed to the parcel and read off the tax identification number. "Who owns this parcel?"

Betty punched the numbers into her computer. "It's 240 acres, owned by Gretel GmbH, a Cayman Islands trust."

Hansel and Gretel—like the fairy tale—Koa thought. The two Campbell properties were plainly connected, but whoever had set up the ownership structure had tried to camouflage the connection by titling the two parcels in different tax havens. Koa pondered how Hansel and Gretel, two offshore trusts, in different offshore venues, had come to own adjoining parcels of land used by Arthur Campbell. Koa wanted to know when and from whom the trusts had acquired the property—information available only at the state level.

After more than an hour on the phone with the State Bureau of Conveyances, Koa learned the Hansel and Gretel trusts had purchased the two land parcels in August 1999 from South Mauna Loa Farms Inc. State records showed prices of $7,000 for the ten-acre Hansel property and $168,000 for the 240-acre Gretel property. The information surprised Koa. Ranchers on the Big Island rarely sold off their land, and never for $700 per acre. Hell, even the decrepit Campbell house had to be valued at multiples of $7,000.

Koa knew of South Mauna Loa Farms only as a large landowner with property along the eastern and southern flanks of Mauna Loa, so he asked Piki, his Internet wizard, to dig up everything he could find on the ranch and its owners. The young detective returned an hour later with a raft of printouts. The first article identified Raul Oshoa as the owner of South Mauna Loa Farms. Oshoa managed privately held agricultural properties in Indonesia, South America, Colorado, and Texas from his headquarters on the southern slopes of Mauna Loa. According to a profile in the *Honolulu Advertiser*, Oshoa, the billionaire doyen of a wealthy Cuban family, had escaped Cuba in 1960 during the Fidel Castro–led revolution. Oshoa's brother had died and friends had been humiliated in the failed Bay of Pigs invasion, leaving Oshoa an outspoken anticommunist.

The *Advertiser* profile focused on Oshoa's political role as a major fund-raiser for Republican candidates for national, state, and local office. The newspaper featured pictures of Oshoa with Republicans in the Hawai'i legislature and with the state's single Republican senator. To Koa's surprise, he spotted Hawai'i County mayor Tenaka in one photograph taken at a fund-raising barbecue at the ranch. Raul Oshoa plainly ranked as a major political force in the state.

This picture of Oshoa left Koa puzzled. He couldn't understand why the man would sell land to Arthur Campbell, let alone for $700 per acre, far less than its value. Like most police officers, he assumed people used offshore trusts to hide assets, evade taxes, and for other nefarious purposes. Putting those mysteries aside, Koa turned to a more immediate roadblock—how to interview a well-connected political moneyman like Oshoa. Politicians and their financial backers occupied a foreign world, a universe with hidden agendas and strange alliances, a realm where people promised one thing and did another.

Koa had grown up poor in a gritty neighborhood. Although he made small charitable donations to his alma mater, the Kamehameha Schools for children of Hawaiian descent, he'd never made a political contribution. He and his fellow officers in the elite Fifth Special Forces Group had been wary of politicians, especially after President Bill Clinton ordered a pathetically inadequate U.S. force into Mogadishu, leading to the catastrophe in which Jerry and another of Koa's men had died. And throughout his tenure in the Hawai'i police force, he'd avoided politics. He understood and related to real people, not politicians.

Yet, politics infected Koa's relationship with Chief Lannua, who for all his good character traits owed his job to the mayor. They were political cronies, and Oshoa financed the mayor's campaigns. Koa dared not interview Oshoa without the chief's blessing; as a realist, he suspected he'd be unlikely to get to Oshoa without the chief's help. But Mayor Tenaka would be protective of his financial backers, and Chief would be reluctant at best, and more likely hostile, to do anything to antagonize the mayor.

Koa stood up from his desk and raised his arms high to stretch. This strange case was now leading into the murky waters of political fund-raising. The last thing Koa wanted to do—confront Raul Oshoa—had to be his next step.

CHAPTER EIGHT

KOA HAD A bad feeling as he walked upstairs to the chief's office. His boss wasn't going to like his request to interview Raul Oshoa. In the outer office, the chief's assistant told him the chief was on his way back from visiting Mayor Tenaka and suggested Koa wait in the chief's inner office. Koa wondered if the chief had been talking politics or police business.

Blessed or perhaps cursed with a policeman's eye for detail, Koa noticed a "Nihoa for Governor" campaign button on the chief's credenza next to pictures of the chief, his wife, and their twenty-year-old son. Koa wondered just how deeply the chief had involved himself in Nihoa's campaign.

"What's the story on the county dump truck? We going to get sued?" the chief asked when he returned ten minutes later.

"I don't know, Chief. It looks like a staged accident. The perps stole the truck from the Kurtistown yard and lay in wait for the victim, Gwendolyn Campbell. Her companion, maybe her husband, was tortured and killed sometime shortly before the accident."

"Christ," the chief erupted. "Any kin come forward?"

Typical, Koa thought. He's more worried about a lawsuit than two murders. "Not yet, and there may not be any kin. The Campbells seem to have been a couple of loners."

"We should be so lucky." The chief looked up, almost as if he were asking God to make it so.

Koa explained the weird ownership of the Campbell property and the land transactions with South Mauna Loa Farms. "So I need to talk to Raul Oshoa," he concluded.

The chief's face hardened at the mention of Oshoa's name, and Koa could see a storm brewing. "Oshoa's one of the island's true power brokers," the chief began, "and right now we got a sensitive situation with this Nihoa rally coming up."

Koa didn't see the connection. "What's the Nihoa rally have to do with investigating two murders?"

"Nothing, but Oshoa's a major force in Nihoa's campaign, and I don't want you rocking that canoe."

"Chief," Koa protested, "I can't get to the bottom of this hit-and-run accident without talking to Oshoa." Koa tried to appeal to the chief's desire to avoid liability to the county.

"Yeah, well that's not so important if there's no next of kin waiting to sue."

"Chief, we've got two murders. Oshoa could be the key to solving them."

"And we've got the largest political rally in Hilo history. We need to keep our eye on that ball."

"Okay," Koa conceded, "so I talk to Oshoa after the rally."

"Not till I give the okay, and you're going to have to show me why it's necessary . . . why you can't get the information any other way."

They'd reached this point only a couple of times before, and Koa had always stood his ground. "Chief." He lowered his voice. "I'm going to investigate these murders."

The chief stared at him with hard eyes. "Okay. That's your job, but stay away from Oshoa till I give the okay. Understand?"

"And when will that be?" Koa demanded.

"I'll let you know." The chief turned to the paperwork on his desk, signaling the end of the discussion.

Koa thought about raising the Smithy issue but didn't. The Oshoa discussion had put the chief on guard, and he wouldn't take kindly to being questioned about Smithy. Koa would find a better time.

Fuck, Koa thought as he left the chief's office, *I struck out*. The chief had stalled and would ultimately block the interview with Oshoa. Still, Koa searched for an alternative. The chief might not like it, but Koa would find a way.

* * *

Nālani called at five o'clock to remind Koa of their dinner at the Kīlauea Lodge. He arrived a little after five forty to a raucous chorus of "Surprise!" and "*Hauʻoli lā hānau!*" Happy birthday. A who's who of friends piled birthday *leis* of *maile* leaves and orchids around Koa's neck until he resembled a walking flower boutique.

Many detectives attended along with a third of the off-duty patrol force. Even Chief Lannua put in an appearance. The throng of carousers scarfed down *kālua* pork tidbits, *ʻahi* poke, Black Sand Porter, and Bikini Blonde Lager. One guest after another clapped him on the back and joked about his advanced age. The chief appeared to be in a good mood, and Koa decided to raise the Smithy issue.

"Can I have a quick private word?" The chief nodded and they moved to a corner. Koa wasn't sure how to broach the subject, so he decided to get right to the heart of it. "You know, there's a lot of discontent on the force about layoffs. I'm getting questions."

The chief's face stiffened. "You have to understand. The mayor and I are trying to get ahead of the curve. Nihoa is way ahead in the governor's race, and austerity budgets are coming for sure. We're aiming to cut the department 5 to 7 percent."

"But, Chief, we're already short of manpower and way behind where we need to be on the technical side."

The chief wasn't to be budged. "Sorry, Koa. We've got some tough decisions to make."

Koa lowered his voice. "Including Smithy? You can't fire Smithy."

The chief bristled. "You're out of line. Stick to running your operation." He turned abruptly and walked away, out of the party.

That went well, Koa thought ironically. The chief always had an eye for what feathered his own nest, and if that meant shoving a crippled man aside, so be it. Well, the chief had made a mistake. Koa vowed he wouldn't give up. Not on Smithy, who didn't deserve to be sacrificed on the altar of political expediency.

After dinner, Koa's friends and colleagues offered round after round of toasts, and Piki presented Koa with a Gillespie Hybrid Power Surge paddle as a gift from the detectives. "Paddling an outrigger canoe takes a lot out of an old man, especially with those heavy wooden paddles. So, boss, we all figured, being so old and creaky, you needed a lighter one." Piki waved the carbon fiber paddle high in the air, and the crowd yelled, "Hear, hear!"

Koa forced a grin as he stepped forward. His people had chosen a magnificent gift, but it carried depressing symbolism. The Canoe Racing Associations allowed only wooden paddles in the big races like the Moloka'i Hoe. His neck surgery the previous year had robbed him of the ability to compete in the great open-ocean races, and now this paddle symbolized a further retreat.

He was still mulling over this unpleasant fate as Nālani, outfitted in an elegant white dress with matching *pīkake lei*, took the floor. The white against her flawless golden-brown skin made her look like an angel—at least in Koa's eyes. An easel holding a cloth-covered picture miraculously appeared next to her. Someone rapped on a wineglass, and all eyes turned to Koa's girlfriend. Even after their time together, he never failed to be surprised by her grace, beauty, and poise. "*Kū i ka poholima ua mea he wahine maikaʻi . . .*" The words came automatically to Koa from his heritage. Nālani aroused the desire to caress. That's exactly what he planned to do when they got home.

"*Aloha*," she began, and the group responded in unison, "*Aloha.*"

"Thank you for honoring the love of my life on his forty-fourth birthday. As you know, Koa solves cases by studying the two lithographs on his office walls." A chuckle rippled through the group. "In his world, humans often morph from one shape to another, as in M. C. Escher's *Reptiles*, and their behavior can be as confusing as the twisted stairways of Escher's *Relativity*." Nālani paused as Zeke Brown, the county prosecutor, and Hook Hao, a longtime police informer—now two of Koa's closest longtime friends—came forward to stand next to the easel.

"To inspire Koa to even greater success and to celebrate his birthday, Zeke, Hook, and I"—Nālani held out her arms to acknowledge their friends—"have a gift for him." Nālani stepped to the easel and pulled the cover from M. C. Escher's 1955 lithograph *Convex and Concave*.

The gift stunned Koa. He'd had an emotional attachment to Escher's enigmatic drawings since he'd first seen them. *Reptiles* symbolized his secret past, and *Relativity* mirrored the twisted path his own life had taken since he killed Hazzard, fled into the military, experienced an epiphany when his buddy Jerry died, and his own strange resurrection as a cop.

"Speech! Speech!" came from those gathered around. Koa suppressed the emotions welling within him and stepped forward to kiss Nālani and shake hands with Zeke and Hook. They had no way of knowing how deeply the gift touched him.

"I've loved M. C. Escher's works since I first saw them while attending Kamehameha Schools," Koa began. "I've long coveted *Convex and Concave.*" He waved a hand toward the lithograph. "It not only depicts an inside-out fantasy but also an upside-down world where people are hidden." Koa carefully turned the image upside down, revealing a different world with a host of new figures. As the oohs and aahs faded, Koa continued. "As y'all see every day on our streets, people have ever more ways to hide their evil deeds." He didn't say that he himself was an expert in hiding evil deeds.

As the festivities wound down, Koa grabbed Zeke Brown for a private conversation. As county prosecutor, Zeke held one of the most powerful positions in county government, and by sheer force of will and unstinting integrity, he'd built a legendary reputation. Fiercely independent, straight-talking, often crudely so, and friendly, he'd been elected to his sixth four-year term, making him the longest-serving elected public official in the county.

Every politician around feared, respected, and courted Zeke Brown. Koa often sought Zeke's legal guidance on difficult investigations and worked with him on arrest and search warrants, as well as prosecutions. The two men had forged a deep and lasting friendship. Recently Zeke had been instrumental in helping Reggie Hao, the son of Koa's old friend, Hook Hao, avoid criminal prosecution.

All too familiar with Zeke's booming voice, Koa led him to an outdoor gazebo far away from the other guests before detailing developments in the Campbell deaths. He described the torture and death of Arthur Campbell and his digging into the land holdings. Raul Oshoa's sale of prime forestland to offshore trusts for a fraction of the market price surprised and intrigued Zeke.

"That's goddamn odd," he shouted and Koa looked around to see if anyone was listening.

"You're right. The whole case is convex and concave." Koa grinned.

Zeke chuckled. "We surprised you, huh?"

"Did you ever!"

"Tell me about this house. What kind of house is owned by a Liechtenstein trust?"

"Maybe fifty years old, two stories, deep in the forest, off the grid, not falling down, but in pretty bad shape."

"So the land sale to this Lichtenstein trust included the house for $7,000?" Zeke sounded incredulous.

"That's what the folks in the Conveyances Bureau say, and the back parcel is just as weird." Koa explained the isolated orchid farm with the camera system monitoring it.

"They reported the $700-per-acre price to the state Bureau of Conveyances?" Zeke asked.

"Yes. Why's that important?"

"The transfer tax. Underreporting the price defrauds the state of its rightful percentage. But it's done all the time. Fuckin' tax cheats."

"That might be useful if Oshoa decides not to talk," Koa responded.

"Jesus, I'd say Mr. Oshoa's got some explaining to do."

"But Mayor Tenaka will shit a brick," Koa warned. "Oshoa's got money and writes campaign checks. Mayor Tenaka's been to Oshoa's barbecues. There's a picture of them together in the *Advertiser*. Hell, Oshoa's got to be one of the mayor's biggest money angels."

"So fuckin' what?"

"So the chief won't let me talk to Oshoa. I asked him this morning. He put me off until after the Nihoa rally."

"What's the fuckin' rally have to do with interviewing Oshoa?" Zeke barked.

"Beats me, but the chief insisted, stalling until after the Nihoa rally, and he's not going to relent. We've talked about this before. The chief supports the force until things get political, but he won't buck the mayor or the council."

"Tough shit! I don't care if Oshoa owns the whole West Coast and plays poker with the pope. If he's got evidence, I'll haul his ass before a grand jury."

"So how should I handle the chief?" Koa asked.

Zeke thought for a minute. "Give me the morning. I'll fix it with the mayor. Then you talk to your chief."

"That would be great. On another topic, you heard about the layoffs in the police department?"

"Yeah, I've heard," Zeke responded with a dour expression. He sat atop an incredible network of informants. Hardly anything in county government escaped his notice.

"The chief says he and the mayor think Nihoa is going to win and they're preparing for an austerity budget."

"Baloney. Mayor Tenaka has nothing to do with it. Chief Lannua is angling for a job in the new governor's office."

Koa stiffened at this new revelation. "You're kidding. He's gonna can Smithy for a lousy political job in Honolulu?" Even as he asked the question, Koa knew Zeke had it right. The layoff notices hadn't come out of budget reviews. They'd all come straight out of the chief's office, and the chief had gotten his back up when questioned about the cuts. Besides, Zeke had irrefutable sources throughout the state. The chief fell several notches in Koa's esteem.

"Pretty shitty, isn't it?"

"You got that right, but thanks for the intel and the birthday present." He gave Zeke a clap on the back before they both went back inside.

*   *   *

"*I mānia kāu. i pua hoʻi kui ʻia ka makemake a lawa pono* . . . yours the *lei*-making needle, mine the flowers . . . let us do as we wish," Nālani whispered as they arrived home. Koa needed no further invitation. "My *ipo*, my love . . ." he murmured as he lifted the *pīkake lei* from around her neck and undid her dress. The sweet smell of jasmine lingered on her skin as his lips made their way down her neck to her breasts. His left hand drifted lower and his fingers found the soft indentation around her naval. He loved to touch her there; it was one of his fetishes, and it never failed to make her giggle. This time was no exception.

They left a trail of clothes on their way to the bedroom, where she eventually pushed him down and climbed on top. "I'll take charge from here, birthday boy," she whispered as her breasts brushed his chest and her fingers combed through his thick black hair. She moved slowly, teasing him mercilessly. Lost in Nālani's intimate embrace, the details of the murder cases evaporated from Koa's mind. A single question filled his mind: How had he, the son of a lowly sugar worker, found such a lover? Her body became his most precious birthday gift.

Afterward, as they lay together in bed, the glow of their intimacy faded. After a while Nālani touched the bruise on his shoulder. "That's a nasty bruise. What happened?"

He'd already told her about the accident, the explosion, and the driver's death, but not about getting knocked down. He wasn't sure how she'd react, but responded, "When the car exploded, a piece of debris hit my shoulder." He paused, before adding, "I was lucky. One of the firefighters got pretty badly banged up."

"Is he alright?"

"It was Mike Tolman. You met him at the fund-raiser for the fire department a couple of months ago. He's in the hospital, but he should be out in a day or two."

"I remember Mike," she responded. "Big guy with infectious grin."

"That's Mike."

"We should go see him."

CHAPTER NINE

KOA DIDN'T KNOW what magic Zeke Brown worked, but Chief Lannua not only agreed to let him interview Raul Oshoa but arranged an appointment. Maybe, Koa thought cynically, Oshoa's campaign contributions weren't so big last time around. Koa drove down the southeastern side of the island to Pāhala, a former sugarcane town, before turning inland and up private roads to Oshoa's ranch. Oshoa's home and headquarters occupied the western slope of a broad bowl-shaped valley, where cattle grazed on emerald-green grass. A tall fencepost of a man with hard black eyes, wearing jeans and a *paniolo* shirt, met Koa at the door to Oshoa's magnificently renovated turn-of-the-century plantation house, introducing himself as Jorge Chavez, head of ranch operations.

"Raul is a very busy man." Chavez spoke softly with a slight Spanish accent. "You could save everyone a lot of time by letting me answer your questions."

Subordinates frequently tried to protect their powerful employers from the police, and rich men liked to pawn the cops off on underlings. Koa wanted none of it. "We don't work that way, Mr. Chavez."

"Then keep it short." He turned his back on Koa and led him along a walkway to a modern building largely concealed behind a row of ironwood trees. "Don't waste his time," Chavez warned.

They climbed a set of wide stairs to the second floor, turned down a corridor, and walked past a row of small offices. As he went by open doors, Koa noted orchid plants in almost every office. Without entering the offices, he couldn't be sure, but the flowers appeared to be the same rare varieties he'd seen at Campbell's place. Campbell must have been selling orchids to Oshoa. There was more to the Campbell-Oshoa connection than he'd first imagined.

Chavez led him to Oshoa's huge, luxuriously appointed study. "He's busy. It'll be a while," Chavez announced and abruptly left.

Typical, Koa thought. *The servant borrows the airs of the master.* Tomorrow might be different—Koa might need to interview Chavez. *Then*, he thought, *we'll see if he's such a big man.*

Large arrays of orchids, each composed of several plants, adorned a conference table, the credenza behind Raul Oshoa's desk, and stands in corners of the room. The arrangement on the table featured multiple hairy green *dendrobium macrophyllum* orchids, and across the room a half dozen red star-shaped *catteya araguaiensis* orchids branched in another spectacular display. It couldn't be a coincidence, he thought. These orchids must have come from Arthur Campbell's farm. Was Oshoa, Koa wondered, the financial angel behind Campbell's orchid obsession.

Looking around the elegant space, Koa took in a museum of sorts. One wall, covered with photographs and framed press clippings, presented a pictorial history of the Bay of Pigs fiasco, starting with photographs of the CIA-sponsored training camps in Mexico. Koa remembered Oshoa's photograph in the *Honolulu Advertiser* profile, and recognized a young Raul in picture after picture, posing with his comrades-in-arms. Additional images depicted the loading of boats and nighttime shots of the sea crossing to Cuba, followed by a dozen pictures on Cuban beaches and war photos taken as the ill-fated force moved inland. Toward the end of the display, the photographs turned bloody with close-ups of wounded men and dead bodies.

Koa walked across the room to a row of vitrines along the opposite wall. The cases held an astounding variety of political memorabilia from several presidential campaigns. Photographs on the wall above the cases depicted Raul Oshoa with President Reagan and both Presidents Bush, as well as numerous other Republican dignitaries. Several of the pictures appeared to have been taken at the White House. Koa studied the pictures, and then looked around. *Interesting*, he thought. Oshoa had decorated his office like the Oval Office with Frederic Remington bronzes, a bust of Thomas Jefferson, and portraits of George Washington and Ronald Reagan.

Among the political mementos, Koa spotted pictures of several prominent Hawaiian politicians. Oshoa stood beside the governor in a picture taken at the *'Iolani* Palace in Honolulu. Another image showed Oshoa with Hawai'i County mayor Tenaka at some official function. Several photographs featured various barbecues, picnics, and even a rodeo at South Mauna Loa Farms, attended by a who's who of Hawaiian politics, including, Koa noted, Nāinoa Nihoa, the current Republican candidate for governor.

"Good afternoon." Koa turned to face a handsome man with dark Cuban features and bushy eyebrows. Oshoa had to be well into his seventies, given the Bay of Pigs photos, but he appeared to be ten years younger. "You were involved in that observatory business," he said, referring to Koa's recent role in solving the murder of a young astronomer. "Chief Lannua speaks most highly of you." Nice words, but, Koa thought, the rancher might also be signaling a close relationship with the police chief in an effort to intimidate.

"That's nice to know. Thank you for seeing me."

"Have a seat. I asked Chavez, the head of our ranch operations, and Rachael Ortega, my aide-de-camp, to join us." Jorge Chavez entered, followed by Rachael Ortega. Maybe forty-five years old and twenty-five pounds overweight for her five-six frame, Rachael had deep crow's feet around small eyes in a pockmarked face. Ribbons of gray streaked her short black hair. Except for the mascara and false eyelashes, she might have passed for a battle-scarred aide to a military tank commander. Attractive she was not, and her makeup seemed out of place to Koa. In his experience, ranch women didn't wear makeup.

Koa wanted to talk to Oshoa alone, but given the political delicacy of the interview, chose not to press the point. They sat in chairs grouped around the conference table.

Koa took the initiative. "I'm here to talk about Arthur Campbell."

"I don't recognize the name." With his chair at an angle to the table, Oshoa appeared relaxed. He spoke with only the slightest trace of a Spanish accent.

"He lived on a parcel of land up behind Volcano I believe you sold in 1999."

"You used the past tense. Did something happen to this man, this Arthur Campbell?"

He's smooth, Koa thought, and he listens to every word. He's already asking questions, and it's my interview. Still, the chief had instructed Koa to go easy on Oshoa, so he answered. "Yes, we believe he was murdered."

"Believe?" Oshoa cocked his head.

"There's not much doubt, but we haven't completed the identification process."

"I see." Oshoa seemed unaffected by the news.

Koa glanced at Chavez and Ortega, but neither showed any emotion. "He lived, apparently rent-free, on property you sold to Hansel GmbH in 1999. Could you tell me about that transaction?"

Chavez answered before his boss could speak. "Lawyers handled that transaction."

Koa wanted answers from Oshoa, not his minions. "Is that correct?" Koa looked Oshoa in the eye as he asked.

"Yes."

"Who negotiated for the purchaser?" Koa again stared at Oshoa, determined to control the interview without interference from subordinates.

"A German firm of lawyers handled the transaction for the purchaser."

"How was the sales price established?"

"I gave my lawyers discretion over the arrangements." Oshoa appeared completely at ease.

"Why would you sell prime forestland to a Liechtenstein trust?"

"Why not?"

"For $700 per acre?"

"Land prices fluctuate."

Koa frowned. He didn't like Oshoa's evasive, condescending attitude. The man appeared too cool, too detached, too unaffected by Koa's questions.

"Isn't $7,000 for ten acres with a three-bedroom house well outside the usual price fluctuation?"

"Land transactions are negotiated between a willing buyer and seller. It's the free market." Once again, Oshoa displayed studied casualness.

Koa sharpened his tone. "Did your lawyers also handle the sale of the adjoining 240 acres to Gretel GmbH, a Cayman Island trust, at about the same time for the same per-acre price?"

Koa had trained himself to catch fleeting changes in a person's facial muscles, often tiny tells to a person's thoughts. He caught the merest flicker in Oshoa's expression and guessed he'd surprised the man.

"You've done your homework," Oshoa said.

"We'd greatly appreciate your help in understanding these transactions." Again, Koa bore down directly on Oshoa.

"We?"

"Yes, the police department and Zeke Brown, the county prosecutor."

"You've already spoken to the county prosecutor?"

Again, Koa thought he detected just the slightest hint of uncertainty in Oshoa's eyes, but he couldn't be sure. The man was devilishly hard to read. "Yes, Mr. Oshoa. No doubt you would like to help us avoid a grand jury investigation with all the attendant publicity—"

"Are you threatening us?" Chavez interrupted.

"No, Mr. Chavez. I just want Mr. *Oshoa's* assistance."

"Why would a grand jury be interested in these land transactions?" Oshoa asked.

"There might be several reasons." Koa spoke in measured tones. "The names, Hansel and Gretel, the timing and prices of the sales, and the fact the Gretel parcel can only be easily accessed through the Hansel parcel suggest a common purpose. Then we have the matter of price. Based on fair market value in 1999, one might think the seller dramatically underpaid the state conveyance tax. And finally, the grand jury might want to know whether Arthur Campbell's rent-free arrangement relates to his murder."

Koa caught no sign of emotion in Raul's face, but Ortega shifted uneasily in her chair.

"You're seeing ghosts where there are none," Oshoa said.

"I'll be the judge of that," Koa responded.

"Raul." Chavez now addressed his boss. "This has gone far enough, don't you think?" Again, the ranch foreman shot Koa an unfriendly glare.

"It's okay," Oshoa said. "As I said, there's nothing to this. I did a favor for a dear friend, for a comrade-in-arms from the Bay of Pigs days. He asked me to meet with Elian Cervara, the son of another comrade, and help him get settled on the Big Island."

"And you met this Elian . . . Elian Cervara?"

"Yes, he came by the ranch. An odd, taciturn man. I tried to engage him about his family. I knew his father like a brother, but Elian said little. *La oveja negra de la familia.*"

"Pardon?"

"A black sheep. Elian seemed to be the black sheep of his family. And his accent left me puzzled."

"In what way?" Koa asked.

"His family comes from Catalonia, but Elian spoke a Cuban, or perhaps a Caribbean, Spanish. I wondered why he hadn't been educated in Barcelona along with his brothers."

"Okay. Tell me how the land transaction came about."

"Elian had chosen three parcels, three different parcels, each on the edge of my Mauna Loa ranch property, ranked in order of preference."

"The Volcano property was his first choice?"

"No, not at all. It was his last option. The other properties encompassed historic sites, and I wasn't comfortable letting Elian choose them."

"Why not?"

Oshoa leaned forward, placing both forearms on the tabletop. "I've worked hard to maintain relationships with native groups. I didn't want to offend them by relinquishing control of historic sites I'd agreed to protect."

"Can you identify those other properties?" Koa doubted his question would lead anywhere, but he suspected that Arthur Campbell and Elian Cervara were one and the same. He was intensely curious about Arthur Campbell. Any clue to the man's thinking might help him understand.

"Rachael, can you show him the parcels on a map after we finish here?" Oshoa nodded toward his aide-de-camp.

"Of course," she responded in the raspy voice of a heavy smoker.

"How did you negotiate the terms?" Koa asked.

"As I told you, once we agreed on the property, I instructed my solicitors and gave them discretion."

"And the price?"

"It may be hard for you to believe, but I viewed the price as irrelevant. I accommodated Elian as a favor to my comrade-in-arms."

Some favor, Koa thought. "And the offshore trusts?"

"My solicitors handled the details."

"You didn't know the details?"

"Not until afterward when I saw the final documents."

There was no way to disprove any of these statements, Koa thought with a sinking feeling. "Did the offshore trusts surprise you?"

"More displeased than surprised. Sophisticated businessmen routinely use offshore accounts for all variety of purposes, but such accounts tend to attract unwanted attention in American political circles. I try not to embarrass my political friends." Raul smiled.

The man was far too slick for the usual interview approach. "I appreciate your help, Mr. Oshoa. Just a couple more questions. Can you describe Elian?"

"Maybe five feet ten inches, medium build, swarthy complexion, kind of a pointed jaw, heavy lower lip with a double gap in his front teeth."

Koa instantly visualized the face. He'd seen it twice before—in the lava near Royal Gardens and in the portrait hanging in Arthur and Gwendolyn's bedroom.

"If I were to show you a picture, you would recognize him?"

"Of course."

Hoping to shock Oshoa into some revelation, Koa handed Oshoa a crime-scene headshot of the corpse in the lava field. "Is this the man you knew as Elian Cervara?"

"*Ay dios mio.*" Raul's thick eyebrows shot up. "*Dios tenga en su gloria.*"

"That's the man you knew as Elian Cervara?"

"Yes."

"Did you have further dealings with Elian after the land transactions?"

Raul shrugged. "I met the man only once when he showed up at my ranch."

Koa turned to Chavez. "And you, did you communicate with Elian?"

The foreman looked annoyed at the question, but answered, "Just that once when he met with Raul."

Koa turned to Rachael. "And you?"

For the tiniest moment, the woman's eyes went wide. "No, never. I wasn't working for Mr. Oshoa when these transactions took place."

Something in this whole arrangement, Koa thought, was amiss. He would bet his brand-new carbon fiber canoe paddle the hairy green *dendrobium macrophyllum* orchids on the conference table in front of him had come from Arthur Campbell's farm. What were these people hiding?

He turned back to Raul Oshoa. "What did Elian Cervara, alias Arthur Campbell, do with the land?"

"I heard somewhere he grew orchids, but I don't know for sure."

"Did you buy orchids from him?" Koa asked.

Raul Oshoa flipped his palms up in a how-should-I-know gesture. "Housekeeping handles the flowers." But Koa didn't miss the fleeting glances exchanged between Rachael and Jorge.

Koa figured he'd gotten as much as he was going to get from these people. "Thank you, Mr. Oshoa. Just one last question. What is the name of the old comrade who requested this favor of you?"

"Ahh, for that, your prosecutor will have to convene the grand jury, and my lawyers will erect every available legal roadblock." Raul held out his hand. "Give my regards to your chief." The interview had ended. "Rachael will show you the map."

Chavez didn't bother saying goodbye. Ortega said nothing while she led Koa down the hall to a small office.

"How long have you been with Oshoa?" Koa asked.

"Many years." Her words came out clipped and hard.

"What does he raise here besides cattle?"

"Nuts, papayas, bananas, avocados, coffee."

"Tell me, where are you from?"

"The mainland." She opened a drawer in a large map cabinet and searched through a pile of U.S. Geological Survey maps.

Many people were suspicious of the police and reluctant to talk, but this woman seemed more reticent than most, and Koa didn't understand why. He tried a different approach. "What brought you here to the Big Island?"

She turned from the cabinet to look at him, and he saw sadness in her hazel eyes. "Something happened, and I needed to change my life."

Koa sensed he'd entered dangerous territory, but, as was his habit, he forged ahead. "What happened?"

"My baby brother, my only family after my parents passed, was killed by the police."

Sorry he'd asked, Koa at least understood her tight-lipped reaction to him. He said the only thing he could. "I'm sorry for your loss."

A tear formed in the corner of her eye, and Koa thought she might break down, but she turned back to the cabinet and seemed to get control of herself. She found a large-scale USGS map with the boundaries of South Mauna Loa Farms overlaid in heavy black ink and placed it on the table. She drew two circles on the map. "There. Those are the parcels. You can take the map."

CHAPTER TEN

"WE'LL GET FLOWERS," Nālani said as they headed toward the hospital to visit Mike Tolman. "At Auntie Anna's." Auntie Anna had one of the largest flower farms around Hilo. Nālani had known her since childhood and introduced Koa shortly after they'd met. He'd been charmed by the grandmotherly woman. Auntie Anna knew more stories of old Hawai'i than most historians and told them with a flair that put Aesop to shame.

Auntie Anna's flower farm lay tucked away at the end of a lane in the hills just southwest of Hilo. After navigating their way through a maze of gardens, they found Anna in her open-air workshop, protected from the sun by a tin roof. The women exchanged hugs, and Nālani explained Mike Tolman's situation. Auntie Anna turned to the shelf behind her worktable to retrieve a copy of the *Hilo Tribune*. "Here. This story." She pointed to an article. "So terrible about Gwendolyn."

Koa couldn't conceal his surprise. "You knew her?"

"Only a little. She was an artist. Someone told her about my flower farm, and she came to paint my gardens, maybe a dozen times. Sat right over there." The old woman pointed a gnarled finger and gave a little shake of her head. "She was no Madge Tennent, but she worked hard at it." Madge Tennent was one of Hawai'i's most accomplished modern artists.

Koa couldn't quite believe the coincidence. "Strange you should have known Gwendolyn."

"Not so unusual," Anna responded. "Lots of artists and photographers come up here. I think the farm is listed on one of those computer things . . . you know . . ."

"Blogs," Nālani suggested.

"Yes, one of those blog things for artists."

"You remember anything about her, anything she said?" Koa asked.

"Just the orchids. She brought a dozen or so orchid plants every time she came. Beautiful plants. I offered to pay her, but she wouldn't take money."

Recalling their conversation about Arthur Campbell's possible sale of orchids, Koa exchanged glances with Nālani. If Gwendolyn was giving away orchids by the dozen, it seemed unlikely the Campbells supported themselves through sales of the plants. The case was getting stranger.

With a beautiful bouquet of haliconia, protea, and ginger flowers from Auntie Anna's gardens, Koa and Nālani said their goodbyes and left for the Hilo Burger Joint. Flowers might be the tradition, but if he were in the hospital, Koa would want a supersized, grass-fed, double-decked burger with a triple order of fries. Too bad the hospital didn't allow beer.

Soon they were sailing through the main entrance of Hilo Medical, waving hello to Nancy Kenoi, one of the hospital volunteers at the reception desk whom they both knew, before heading for Tolman's room. The smell of antiseptic permeated the hallways, reminding Koa how much he hated hospitals. Maybe, he thought, with a wry smile, he'd inherited his dislike from his mother, who refused all forms of *haole*, or Western, medicine. The fact that Shizuo Hori, the makeshift county coroner, worked out of the building only added to Koa's own disdain for this particular facility.

They found Tolman with a broken leg, multiple abrasions, and a concussion. His head wrapped in bandages, he lay propped up in bed reading an arson investigator's textbook. Clearly in worse shape than Koa had imagined. Still, Tolman had recovered enough to be working.

Koa greeted the firefighter. "Hey, Mike, how you feeling?"

"Koa! Nālani!" Tolman's brown eyes sparkled at the sight of his visitors. "*Mahalo* for coming. And, Nālani, it's a real treat to see you." He paused. "My head still hurts like a busted watermelon, and my ears ring like I spent a week at a rock concert, but the doctors say I'm gonna live."

"We brought you some food. Thought you might want a break from hospital grub." Koa handed over the Burger Joint bag.

Tolman grinned. "Wow. Thanks. The coroner works in the kitchen here."

Koa didn't want to think what Shizuo could do to a meal. "Glad you're on the mend. You had a close call."

"I hear you got knocked down, too," Tolman responded.

A quizzical look flashed across Nālani's face. In explaining his bruise, Koa had neglected to mention anything about getting knocked down or how close he'd come to being in Mike Tolman's shoes. Realizing that he should have given Nālani a more fulsome description, he tried to make light of the incident. "I popped right back up like a Jack-in-the-box."

Then Tolman made it worse. "That's not the way I got the story, brah. One of the boys told me a runaway fire hose nearly took your head off."

Koa suddenly regretted having come at all, or at least having brought Nālani. He tried to change the subject. "Word in the office has you outta here and back home in a day or two."

Tolman didn't pick up on the change and continued to talk about the accident. "I've never seen a car go up like that, not even in training films." He shifted on the bed, trying to get more comfortable. "Musta been a bomb—something right out of Kabul."

Koa glanced at Nālani. She wasn't smiling, but didn't look upset, so Koa gave up trying to redirect the conversation. "Sam Ikeda's looking into that possibility as we speak."

"I hear the driver didn't make it," Tolman said. "Sounded like a woman. You identify her?"

"Yeah. Gwendolyn Campbell," he responded. "An artist living off the grid in the hills up the road from the accident scene."

"You say she was an artist?" Tolman pulled himself up in the hospital bed.

"Yes. Is that significant?"

"I don't know, but I'm pretty sure I've seen that brown car a bunch of times. I mean, before the accident."

"Where?" Koa asked, wondering how anyone could have recognized the crumpled car halfway under the county dump truck.

"Where I live . . . I've seen it going down toward a glassblower's place at the end of my street," Tolman responded.

"There are a lot of 1994 Honda Civics still on the road. How could you tell it was the same car?"

"Can't be positive, but when I was fogging water on that wreck, I saw this big black decal with the word 'ARTIST,' just like on the brown Honda going by my house. Can't be too many brown Hondas with a decal like that."

Koa nodded. An artist going to visit another artist wasn't much of a lead. "I'll check it out."

Tolman was on a roll. "You know," he continued, "I've got a weird memory. After the scream—I remember the scream—I heard gunshots . . . bam, bam, bam. I'm sure I heard gunfire."

"That's interesting, Mike." Koa wondered briefly if gunshots had somehow triggered the explosion.

Nālani was quiet and Tolman looked tired, so Koa figured it was time to go. He pointed to the bag of food. "We brought you a burger and fries from the Hilo Burger Joint. You should probably dig in before they get cold."

Mike reached for the wallet on his hospital table, but Koa stopped him. "On me, dude."

"*Mahalo nui* and *mahalo* again for coming, Koa. You, too, Nālani."

Nālani said nothing as they left the hospital room. They walked outside and down the path behind the hospital toward Rainbow Falls. She stopped at the guardrail overlooking the falls and stood watching the changing colors of refracted light in the torrent of water. He stood beside her. Neither spoke for some time.

Then, turning to face him, her arms folded across her chest, she said, "You weren't straight with me. You said you got hit by some debris. You didn't tell me you got knocked down and nearly decapitated by a runaway fire hose."

"I didn't want to upset you."

He saw a sudden flare of anger. "I know you're a cop. I know there are dangers. I can deal with it, so long as you're careful and think about us when you're out there, but don't hide things from me." She paused, and he opened his mouth to respond, but she continued before he could say anything. "Growing up, my mother told me she'd married my father and he'd died in a car accident. I was in college before I learned it was all a lie . . . that they'd just shacked up and he'd died in a gang fight in prison. I've never forgiven her lying to me. Honesty is important to me. Can you understand that?"

He hesitated, surprised he'd gotten it backward. "I'm sorry. I thought it was the right thing to do."

"Well, you were wrong."

Hands on the guardrail, he stared at the water tumbling over the falls, not sure what more to say. Confident at his job, he felt unsure of his footing in this emotional jungle. Still, he knew he wasn't going to be able to talk his way out. He had a weak hand and was enough of a poker player to know when to fold. Turning to face her, he said, "I'm sorry. It won't happen again."

Half a million gallons of water cascaded over the falls before she reached for his hand.

CHAPTER ELEVEN

KOA WAS IN a foul mood when he reached Pete's Hog Shop. He strolled among the new Boss Hogs, Harleys, and Suzukis, constantly giving Pete the eye, while the proprietor finished with a customer. The high price of gas—about a dollar a gallon more than on the mainland—made Hawai'i big motorcycle territory.

Pete turned to Koa when the customer finally left the shop. "You interested in a bike? We've got a discount program for the police."

"Sorry, Pete. I'm looking for some information."

Pete responded hesitantly. "Like what kind of info?"

"You know Arthur Campbell?"

"Ahem." Pete cleared his throat. "Name don't mean nothin'."

"You sold him a Boss Hog, a big LS445. A really hot machine. It's got one of your Pete's Hog Shop emblems on the fender. Can't be more than a couple of years old."

Pete chewed his lower lip. "That's a pricey machine. We don't sell a lot of LS445s."

That's why, Koa thought, you should remember the customer. "It's got no license plates," Koa added. "Probably went out that way."

Pete cleared his throat a second time. "That's odd, but it might have been a transfer. Sometimes owners want to keep the same plate, especially a vanity plate."

Pete didn't look him in the eye, and Koa sensed he was holding something back. "Can you go through your invoices checking for a buyer named Arthur Campbell?"

"I guess. It'll take a while. I keep paper records, the old-fashioned way. When do ya need it?"

"Now."

"Jesus. There must be two hundred invoices."

Pete's response only heightened Koa's suspicions. Pete was hiding something. Koa was sure of it. "Two hundred shouldn't take long," Koa responded.

Grudgingly, Pete went in back to his cluttered office, opened a file drawer, and removed a folder of invoices. He went through them one by one, taking his time, almost as if he were stalling. Koa wasn't surprised when Arthur Campbell's name didn't appear on any invoice.

"Is that every sale in the past two years?" Koa asked suspiciously.

Pete cleared his throat again. "Gee, I'd think so."

Koa's own experiences made him suspicious of everyone, and Pete's lack of a direct answer reinforced Koa's doubts. The man was definitely holding out. "You have a list of the VIN numbers on machines shipped to your shop?" he asked.

"Yeah."

"Get it."

"Look. I got a business to run."

"You want a subpoena or maybe we should get a search warrant and tear this place apart."

"Okay, okay. I'll get the VIN numbers." Pete went back to the filing cabinet for a thinner folder.

Koa found the matching VIN number on the third invoice. He whistled at the manufacturer's suggested retail price. It cost nearly twice as much as his Explorer. Pete hadn't been kidding when he described it as a pricey machine. "Okay, Pete. This bike came in eighteen months ago, and now it's in Arthur Campbell's shed. You want to tell me how it got there?"

"Ma . . . maybe . . . he . . . he paid cash."

Koa understood Pete's reluctance. The man had cheated the governor out of the sales tax and probably failed to report the income as well. "Maybe he paid cash or you remember him paying cash. Which is it?"

"I kinda remember a cash customer," Pete said.

"Fifty-nine thousand bucks is a boatload of cash," Koa remarked.

Arthur Campbell must have been a high roller to afford a $59,000 motorcycle, but he'd lived in a dilapidated off-the-grid house deep in the forest. Koa couldn't put the picture together. A whole bunch of pixels had gone missing.

"Yeah, 590 Benjamins."

"So Campbell paid cash and didn't want the machine registered?"

"Yeah."

"And you saved a few bucks in taxes," Koa shot back. "So tell me about Arthur Campbell, all about him."

Pete apparently still didn't see the need to be cooperative. "There ain't much to tell. He bought an expensive cycle."

Enough of the comedy show, Koa decided. "You want the tax collectors in here? That's fine. I can arrange that for you."

"Okay, okay, okay. He came in here with an Asian hottie—"

"Describe her."

"Asian, a real looker, medium height, shoulder-length black hair. He called her Gwen."

Gwen, short for Gwendolyn. "Gwen?"

"Yeah, I mean, she's some kinda piece of ass."

"Save me the juvenile commentary. Just tell me about Arthur Campbell," Koa demanded.

"Okay, Campbell is ex-military. And he knew his fuckin' machines. Not just the specs. I mean, he could've stripped that Boss Hog apart an' put the sucker back together, probably with his eyes blindfolded."

"What else?"

"The dude had this awesome tat—"

"What kind of tattoo?" Koa demanded.

Pete used his finger to describe it. "It's a sword with this odd triangle that didn't connect at the top and this lightning bolt inside the triangle."

Koa knew the symbol, knew it well. He'd seen it many times in his Special Forces days. At last the pieces snapped together: military uniform, Heckler & Koch HK45, commando knife, and a singular tattoo. Arthur Campbell had been a Delta Force operative, part of the Army's most elite and secretive counterterrorist and special operations unit.

For Koa, this discovery added a bizarre twist to Arthur's murder. How could he possibly account for the torture and execution of a Delta operative who'd lived for a decade in isolation in the remote village of Volcano? Growing orchids. Something in the man's past had reared up and reached through time to sweep him to a horrific death, but Koa couldn't imagine what.

* * *

Koa drove back to Volcano and found the green house identified by Ryan Chang as belonging to Gwendolyn's teacher friend. Koa knocked, and a man, well muscled from weight training, answered the door. Koa identified himself and asked for Howie.

"I'm Howie Biaggio. Are you looking to buy one of my prints?"

"I'm afraid not," Koa responded. "We need to chat, Mr. Biaggio."

Koa sensed nervousness in Howie's jerky movement. He led Koa into a house filled with prints and drawings of ancient Hawaiian archaeological sites, villages, fish ponds, burial caves, canoe sheds, and *heiau*. When Koa asked about Gwendolyn, Howie turned pale like an albatross. "Why do you ask about Gwen?"

"You knew her?" For a moment, Koa thought the man would deny knowing Gwendolyn, but reason prevailed.

"Yeah, I knew her."

"Who's that, Howie?" a female voice called from a back room, and an Asian woman with pale skin and a mouth highlighted with neon red lipstick walked in. She could have been a Japanese movie star. Her presence explained Howie's reluctance to talk about Gwendolyn, and Koa's mind raced to find a way to talk to the man in private.

Howie, in a move revealing long practice, preempted his thoughts.

"It's all right, Yoko, this man is here about some drawings. We'll just sit out back and talk for a while."

Koa mentally applauded Howie's quick thinking while simultaneously judging him to be a skilled liar. They sat under a small gazebo in Howie's backyard, well out of Yoko's earshot.

"Sorry about that, but I can't piss off Yoko." He winked.

"Like Gwendolyn Campbell?"

"Oh, man. Gwen was one of a kind." Koa thought Howie might actually lick his lips.

"Tell me about her."

"Hot, fun, experimental. Really gifted in the sack."

"And her interests, Howie, her activities."

"We met at a little show I had. You see, I'm a teacher, but I buy and sell old Hawaiian prints on the side. She liked my prints, mostly the ones of old Hawai'i. You know, before Western contact, especially old *heiau*. The old temples. Said she was an artist and wanted to paint some of them."

"And you took her sightseeing?"

"Yeah, I took her around to *Kāneʻeleʻele, Keʻekū,* and a couple of the other old *heiau.* She made drawings. She'd sit there for hours, sometimes doing five or six drawings of the same *heiau,* trying to get her sketch to look exactly like the scene in front of her. I told her to loosen up, to take some artistic license, but no, she wanted a perfect copy of the real thing."

"And did you two do anything else?"

"Not outdoor activities." Howie grinned.

"You ever meet her husband?"

Howie reared back as if hit by 110 volts. "Jesus, that dude was her husband?"

"What dude?" Koa leaned forward.

"This dude, he needed a ride back from Pāhala. She called him a friend. Mean-lookin' man with a double gap in his front teeth. Scared the shit out of me."

"Cuban?"

"Don't think so. He said something to her in a foreign language. It wasn't Spanish, I know that. More guttural, like Russian or something Slavic."

The case kept getting stranger. "Where'd you pick him up?"

"In Pāhala by the post office, and I dropped him off right out front." Howie pointed toward the road. "He took off joggin' up the lane like a track star."

"You talk to him?"

"Not a word. The man made my skin crawl. Him sittin' in the back seat, lookin' around like gunmen were about to pop outta the asphalt and attack or something." Howie paused. "I don't need protection from him, do I?"

"No, he'll never bother you," Koa assured him. "You have a picture of Gwen?"

The simple question left Howie stammering. "I . . . I . . . I . . ."

"Get the pictures, Howie. All I have is a license photo. I need some pictures of Gwendolyn. It's important," Koa commanded.

Howie went into the house and returned a couple of minutes later with snapshots of Gwendolyn, all taken in a bedroom with an electronic flash and all showing a Chinese woman with jet black hair in a pixie cut with surprisingly large eyes, a mischievous smile, and full breasts capped with dark aureoles. Koa thought of Ryan Chang's words, "Gwendolyn very beautiful . . . man much like . . . many man."

"Howie, I didn't realize," Koa said dryly, "you're a real artist."

CHAPTER TWELVE

IN HUNDREDS OF interviews over his career, Koa had seen vast differences among witnesses. Some recited clear and detailed recollections. They saw the world through precision binoculars. Other gave sloppy, ultimately unreliable descriptions, as if they'd witnessed events in a funhouse mirror. Some understood reality; for others, objective truth didn't exist.

When Piki led him up the path to Marge Furgeson's house, the setting told Koa the woman who'd seen the dump truck idling before the accident would be an acute observer. The house, set well back from a dirt lane, had a large wooden platform attached to the upper story. Fields of 'ōhi'a trees, festooned with distinctive multi-needled red blossoms, bordered both sides of the unusual structure. Spikey red, yellow, and gold protea flowers exploded from bushes covering most of the large front yard. Koa spotted rich red 'apapane, rare Hawaiian honeycreepers, twittering in the trees and swooping in and out of the protea with an audible whir. Sitting in a wheelchair on the high wooden platform, Mrs. Furgeson used field glasses to watch the two policemen approach.

As they reached the front door, a cheery voice greeted them through an adjacent speaker: "Come on up." They found their way up a central staircase with a stair lift and emerged onto the deck, where the plumpish woman in the wheelchair waved them toward two small iron chairs. "Have a seat."

Their hostess, in her fifties, wearing a gray flannel shirt with a matching vest against the morning chill, had a roundish face with kindly gray eyes.

Koa introduced himself. "You have an amazing vantage point for spotting rare 'apapane, Mrs. Furgeson."

Her eyebrows lifted. "You know your birds?"

"A bit, Mrs. Furgeson. My girlfriend, she's a ranger at Hawai'i Volcanoes National Park. She taught me to recognize a few species."

"Please call me Marge. 'Mrs. Furgeson' makes me sound decrepit. They're my life, the 'apapane. I live to see them." Her face lit up. "I study them. I record them." She pointed at the headphones on top of an electronic contraption on the floor beside her chair. "And I write about them."

Koa looked out over the protea plants to the lane. 'Apapane were particularly fond of the nectar from the protea flowers, and this woman had a great vantage point, not only for the birds, but for the dirt roadway beyond the protea plants. "So you spend a lot of time up here with your binoculars?"

"Yes, indeed. The 'apapane are so much more interesting than that ridiculous *Survivor* reality stuff on TV."

Koa agreed. He didn't watch much TV, except news and sports. "I believe one of our officers spoke to you the other day about the accident up the street. You saw a county dump truck parked out front."

Her face darkened. "The day of that dreadful wreck down on the lane. I came out here to watch the 'apapane. It's their mating season. One of those big yellow county dump trucks stopped right over there," she said, pointing. "He had no business there. It's not a county road. You never see a county vehicle up this road."

"Is that why you remember seeing it, because it had no purpose there?"

"Not really. The '*apapane* are shy. The noise and the diesel smoke drove my birds away."

Birders did love their birds and hated anything that scared them away. "Can you describe the driver?" Koa asked.

"Tall and broad shouldered, age about thirty, black hair, heavy face, Asian eyes, thick lips, with a scar or blemish under his left eye and a small round gold earring in his right ear. Dressed like a field hand, jeans and a cowboy shirt, but he wore running shoes."

"How—" Piki started to ask when Marge held up her binoculars.

"I'm a bird-watcher. These are powerful image-stabilized Zeiss field glasses. I spend my life observing details." She smiled, like a teacher lecturing a slow pupil.

"Then what happened?" Koa asked.

"The truck just sat there belching smoke and making noise. The driver was out of the cab, leaning against the front, chain-smoking cigarettes for about forty-seven minutes."

"You timed it?" Koa couldn't suppress his surprise.

"I came out here at 6:25 a.m. The truck pulled up right away and just stood there idling until a Chevy Traverse, a black Hertz rental, driven by another Asian man, arrived a couple of minutes after seven."

"How do you know it was a Hertz rental?" Piki asked.

"Hertz rentals have a bar code on the lower left corner of the windshield. I think it's a control number. I got a good view with these." Again, she lifted her binoculars.

This woman was an extraordinary witness. "What happened when the car arrived?"

"An older man got out of the car. He huddled with the driver and they talked. The older man appeared to be giving instructions. Then he returned to the car and drove off."

"Can you describe the older man for us?"

"He was also Asian, about five-feet-eight or nine inches in height, medium build, maybe 155 pounds. A mature man in his late forties or early fifties, black hair, a triangular face, broad features, black eyes, no visible jewelry, also dressed in work clothes. I'm not sure about his shoes, except they were black."

Koa shook his head at her precision. Most witnesses didn't get the hair color right, and this woman faulted herself for missing the style of shoes. "This about seven in the morning?"

"About two minutes after. Then about ten minutes later, the truck driver used his cell phone, got into the truck, and took off, racing down the street. The truck really picked up speed, going way too fast for this road."

"That's when you heard the accident?"

"Yes, I heard the dreadful crash, but I couldn't see anything. Then maybe ten or fifteen minutes later I heard a terrible explosion."

"Mrs. . . . . Marge, your recall is fantastic. You remember anything else?"

"After the crash noise, but before the explosion, the truck driver came hurrying up the road, all dusty, like he'd rolled on the ground. The black SUV came back, picked up the truck driver, and sped away. They were gone before the explosion."

That explained the disappearing truck driver. "Thank you. You're a wonderful witness. We'll write this up and have you sign the statement. Is that okay?" Koa stood to end the interview.

"You don't want to hear the conversation?" Marge asked with a twinkle in her eye.

"The conversation?"

"I recorded their conversation. The older man giving instructions to the truck driver." Marge Furgeson picked up the electronics control box, which looked like a video game controller, beside her chair. She pointed toward what appeared to be a small satellite dish mounted on the corner of the deck. "It's a parabolic microphone. Joystick controlled. My nephew built it for me to record birdsongs."

"It can pick up a conversation on the street?" Piki, his eyes wide, couldn't hide his astonishment.

"Easily, if it's not windy, and the air was quite still that morning." She handed Koa a CD. "They spoke in some Asian language. It could be a Chinese dialect, but I suspect you'll figure that out, won't you?"

As he raced back to headquarters, Koa called Cap Roberts, the head of the police technical services department. By the time Koa walked into his office, Cap had a player set up. He popped the CD into the machine and they listened, but neither could make sense of the rapid exchanges in a foreign language neither of them recognized. Frustrated, Koa asked, "How long before you can get it translated?"

"Maybe a day or two. I gotta figure out the language first."

"It's really important, Cap. It could be the key to Gwendolyn's murder."

CHAPTER THIRTEEN

It took Cap Roberts less than a day to translate the CD. He waltzed into Koa's office the following morning. Cap, at sixty, was a first-rate scientist, and Koa fretted about what the department would do when the thin, balding tech services chief retired. "I don't believe the birdwatcher lady actually taped these dragons. From fifty yards, no less. I mean, it's bizarre. One chance in a million of somethin' like that. And the best part, these two Asian goons had no idea, nada, not a clue."

"So Crazy Mo may have been on to something," Koa mused.

"Crazy Mo?"

"A squatter out in Royal Gardens. He kept referring to the partially burned house as the 'Chinese house.' He probably saw one of these badasses out there."

"Oh, but they're not Chinese. The translator says it's an Indonesian dialect."

Indonesian? How did that compute? "You got a translation?"

Cap extracted two sheets of paper from his pocket. "Do I walk on water or what?"

"In your dreams, Cap."

The smile on Cap's face disappeared, replaced by hard lines around his mouth as the technician got down to business. "So here's the deal. They planned the whole thing. That poor woman never had a chance."

"The explosion?" Koa asked.

"Deliberate. To make sure they got her, obliterate the evidence, and maybe even kill the first responders. They're bad dudes."

"Damn! How? Sam Ikeda didn't find explosive residue."

Cap frowned. "I'm not sure how, but there're two references to a bomb."

A vision of the massive blast with Tolman on the ground came back to Koa. "We're lucky as hell. Tolman could have been killed in that explosion."

"It could've gotten you, too, from what I hear."

"Yeah, I guess."

"Sorry about that."

Koa reached for the papers, but Cap held them back. "The guy in the car wears the pants and calls the shots."

"Name?" Koa asked.

"Bambang."

Koa raised an eyebrow. "You're kidding me."

"I checked. It's a common Indonesian name."

"And the truck driver?"

"Not sure. Bambang only says his name once, but the tape's garbled at that point. Mister no-name rigged the bomb and drove the truck. Bambang promised to pick him up on the lane after he triggered the bomb."

"Any sign they were working with anyone else?"

"They weren't acting on their own. We found two references to 'kepala.' It's an Indonesian word that means chief or head, something like that," Cap responded. "In context, the chief or head wanted a clean job leaving no trails, no evidence."

"Any hint who this chief might be?"

"Nada." A look came into Cap's eyes, and Koa could see his mouth twisting to shape a new thought. "But changing the subject," he went on, "our glorious chief's going to be the death of me. Did you hear? He's cutting our budget by 10 percent."

Koa hit the desk with his fist. "Christ, you've already got a backlog, not to mention technology dating back to the seventies. What are you gonna do?"

"I'm thinking of looking for another job."

Cap's terse reply shocked Koa. It wasn't what he wanted to hear. The force could ill afford to lose Cap Roberts. If the chief kept going, he would destroy the department's effectiveness. Koa thought about what he'd heard from Basa, one of the patrol commanders, Zeke, and the chief himself. Koa wasn't worried about his own job, but what if the chief asked him to fire one of his people? He wasn't sure what he'd do. He sighed. He wasn't going to be able to change things within the department, but Zeke might be able to salvage something.

"Maybe things won't come to that," he said, feeling tired.

* * *

Cap had barely disappeared down the hall when Smithy rolled in with more grim news. Although in a wheelchair, the round-faced officer sat straight, his uniform pressed, his black hair combed, his brass polished, and his mustache neatly trimmed.

Koa closed the door and slid behind his desk. "Hey, Smithy. It's good to see you." *What wouldn't be so good*, he thought, recalling his conversation with the chief, *is what I have to tell you.* "How's your daughter? She still into art and drama?" Koa had met Smithy's wife and daughter at a police picnic and remembered Smithy's daughter had starred in a school play.

"It's good to see you, too, although I wish it were under better circumstances. My family's fine. Cindy's in another school play this month. Thanks for asking." He paused. "I guess you know I've been laid off."

"Sergeant Basa told me about it. I'm really sorry, Smithy."

Smithy sat rigidly in his wheelchair, his face expressionless.

Koa waited for Smithy to continue.

"I gave my legs to this police department, and every chief, four chiefs in the last eighteen years, has found a place for me. And it ain't charity. I pull my load better than most of the civilians down in dispatch.

"Well, I guess it's over. This chief"—Smithy spat the word and looked toward the ceiling as though he could see through to the chief's office—"doesn't see the need to look out for street cops who've given a lot for this county. He sent me my walking papers through the interoffice mail. That's his right, I guess, but you know what burns me?"

"You've got every right to be upset, Smithy," Koa said, finding the conversation painful.

"I got eighteen years and three months on the job. I need another lousy twenty-one months to draw a full pension, and I need that pension to support my wife, who's stayed with me all these years, and my little girl. I need that pension, Koa. I went up to the chief's office to ask him for another twenty-one months, twenty-one lousy months. And you know what he said to me?"

"No. Tell me."

"Nothing. Not a goddamn word. He wouldn't talk to me. He wouldn't look me in the eye."

Damn, Koa thought. This was even worse than he'd expected. Why, he wondered, hadn't the chief at least talked to Smithy? Then he remembered the chief's abrupt reaction when Koa had questioned him at the birthday party. It occurred to Koa that the chief was embarrassed by what he'd done. "I'm sorry. I—"

"I know you weren't part of this, and you probably can't change the chief's decision, but I'm asking you, please try. I need to work another twenty-one months."

Koa felt for Smithy. It wasn't right. And the chief's refusing to talk to Smithy made it worse. "Believe me, I'm going to try. You've no idea how hard I'm gonna try."

CHAPTER FOURTEEN

KOA DECIDED TO tap into the network of artisans in Volcano Village to see what more he could learn about Gwendolyn Campbell. Over a hundred local artists and craftsmen lived in the tiny bohemian community, which guarded the gateway to Hawai'i Volcanoes National Park, and sold supposed masterpieces to the two and a half million visitors who visited the park annually. Although Koa had lived just outside the village for a dozen years, he'd never met most of its artists. He started at the Volcano Arts Center, which occupied the former Volcano House Hotel, originally built in 1877 out of *naio* and *'ōhi'a* logs from the nearby forest.

He introduced himself to Allison Grace, who ran the gallery under a concession agreement with the National Park Service. Yes, she knew Gwendolyn Campbell, but not well. The Arts Center had never displayed or sold Gwendolyn's work. Allison suggested that Koa contact Betsy Galant, one of the organizers of the village's artists' *hui*, or syndicate.

Koa approached Betsy's extended A-frame through a grassy glade shaded by giant evergreen trees. The sulfur smell in the air from Kīlauea's vents reminded him that the lava field where he'd found Arthur's body was only a few miles to the east.

Betsy, a cheerful birdlike woman with a narrow face and a cascade of blond hair, showed him through her living quarters to a glass-louvered studio bathed in sunlight. A large block of *'ōhai*, monkey pod wood, slowly taking the life-sized shape of a voluptuous woman, stood on a pedestal, surrounded by carving tools.

"It's beautiful," Koa remarked, impressed with her delicate style.

"*Mahalo*," she chirped in a voice perfectly matched to her petite size. "She'll be *Poli'ahu*, the snow goddess of Mauna Kea, if I ever finish her." She stroked the *'ōhai* block as she talked.

The irony was not lost on Koa. In Hawaiian legend, *Pele*, the volcanic goddess, and *Poli'ahu*, the snow goddess, were jealous sisters locked in eternal combat, one with fire and the other with ice. This investigation had led him from one to the other. "I'm here about Gwendolyn Campbell—"

"Poor Gwendolyn," Betsy interrupted. "She struggled. Oh." Betsy brought her hand up to cover her mouth. "I mustn't speak ill of the dead."

Koa spent his life coaxing people to reveal what they would otherwise hide. "It's okay, I need an honest assessment," Koa assured her. "You say she struggled?"

"A sweet woman, she worked too hard at painting, so much so her ideas, brushstrokes, and images didn't flow naturally from her hands. Her paintings were forced, flat, uninspired . . ." Again, Betsy raised a hand to her mouth. "I can't believe I just said that."

Koa smiled inwardly. Betsy loved to gossip but pretended otherwise. "She belonged to your *hui*?"

"Oh, no, heavens no. Our syndicate members are all successful artists. None of them would sponsor Gwendolyn."

"Then how did you know her?"

"She came to most of our artists' fairs, trying to sell her work, without, I must say, much success. We chatted and she came by my studio a couple of times."

"Her paintings, the ones I've seen, are mostly of birds and *heiau*."

"Yes, yes, that's right. Anatomically correct birds," Betsy twittered, "like medical school texts. It's the Chinese education system, rigid and formulaic."

"So she wasn't successful?"

"Successful? No, not at all. I mean, she sold a few tourist canvases, but she didn't make a living as an artist. I'm sure of that."

"Then how did she support herself?"

"Well . . ." Betsy hesitated. "She had friends . . . male . . ." Once again Betsy's hand covered her mouth. "Well, there were rumors. Volcano is a tiny place. People talk. She . . . she didn't always sleep at home, if you know what I mean."

"What about her husband, Arthur? What was he—"

"She was married? Oh, my dear, oh, my."

"Did Gwendolyn have friends, people she—"

"Oh, yes," Betsy interrupted. "Yes, that bodybuilder fellow Howie and Michael and, well, there were others. It was, you know, like one of those doors that go round and round." She made a twirling gesture with her finger.

Koa suppressed a smile. Betsy didn't even do a good job of pretending to be shocked. "Michael?"

"Michael Olina. She spent a lot of time, a lot of time at Michael's. He's a glassblower. Really nice work. I mean, really nice."

"Where's Michael's?"

"On the road, back past the park."

"And Gwendolyn spent time there?"

"Oh yes, yes. I mean, she hung out there most days, hours and hours." Betsy covered her mouth. "Gwendolyn was very attractive, and, I mean, well, Michael has a reputation. And he's married, too." She shook her head in disapproval.

"Anything more specific?" Koa wanted hard facts and guessed she had a basis for her suspicions. In his experience women's intuition was more fact than guesswork.

"Well, once, I mean, when I walked into Michael's place they were . . . he had his hands on her . . . her body, and they were, you know, embracing. Yin and yang." This time, Betsy's hand made it only halfway up to her face. "There. I said it."

* * *

Koa had seen the signs for Michael's on the highway and had no trouble finding the place. He parked next to two other cars and entered a small warehouse building attached to what he assumed was Michael's home. The front part served as an artist's gallery. Elegantly shaped decorative bowls and vases in forest greens, burnt sienna, and yellow glass with irregular strands of copper, gold, and silver stood on shelves and display stands. Betsy was right: the pieces were stunning.

A well-outfitted glassblower's workshop occupied the back of the building, cordoned off from the showroom with a purple plastic chain. A handsome, muscular man, wearing goggles and a leather apron over a bare chest and shorts, stood in front of a furnace. As Koa watched, he used both hands on a long tube to gather a blob of glass from a vat in the furnace. He rotated the tube, moving it slowly in and out of the furnace, as he gathered more glass and began to shape it into a vase. Sweat drenched his face.

He pulled the glass from the furnace and rolled it on a steel-topped table, beginning to turn the blob into a cylinder. Then, it went back into the furnace to continue the gather. So intensely did the man attend to his craft that Koa went unnoticed.

A large garage door stood open at the left end of the workshop, presumably for shipping and receiving, guarded on one side by a bench with bubble wrap, tape, and other shipping supplies, and on the other side by a pile of broken crates and cardboard boxes. Koa guessed the broken crates once held supplies. Chinese characters caught his eye, and he spotted several wooden boxes bearing markings from the Dowlong Artistic Supply Company in Hong Kong, China.

A second man entered the workroom and walked over to Koa to introduce himself as Kaha'i, Michael's second. Koa asked to speak to Michael. Kaha'i exchanged words with his boss, then took over the blow tube. Michael removed his goggles and approached Koa.

"Chief Detective Koa Kāne." Koa extended a hand. "I'm here about Gwendolyn Campbell."

Michael wiped his sweaty palm on his shorts before shaking hands. "Damn shame about the accident."

"Yes." Koa took in the man's high cheekbones, straight nose, and easy smile. Michael's arms and chest were ripped. He hadn't developed those muscles handling glassblower's tools. Betsy was right. He could see how women might be attracted to this man. Thinking back to Howie, the bodybuilder, he guessed Gwendolyn Campbell had a fondness for muscular men. "What can you tell me about her?"

"Not much."

"Oh, I thought you knew her pretty well," Koa said. Although surprised by Michael's lack of knowledge, he was skilled at hiding his reactions and remained poker-faced.

A look of concern clouded Michael's face. "Where'd you get that idea?"

"She didn't hang around your shop?"

"She came in here a couple of times, but I didn't really know her."

It wasn't what Koa expected. Tolman had remembered seeing Gwendolyn's car going toward this glassblower's place "a bunch of times," and Betsy Galant had said Gwendolyn had spent "a lot of time at Michael's." Still, Koa let the interview develop at its own pace. He wanted to get a feel for this man before he started pushing. "Any observations might help, Michael."

"I'm not your source."

An attractive blond entered the shop and approached them. "Who's the handsome stranger?" She ran a hand through her hair. Koa noticed a wedding band set next to a diamond engagement ring. Koa figured she must be the reason for Michael's reticence to talk about Gwendolyn.

"He's a cop, Marcia, here about that woman who died in the car accident." The pair exchanged a look, communicating some message that escaped Koa, but he caught the odd use of "that woman" and tried to parse its significance. "This is my wife, Marcia."

"Mrs. Olina," Koa acknowledged her, "I am looking for information about Gwendolyn."

"Well, I wouldn't know anything about that woman," Marcia said with a flip of her hair. No love lost there, Koa thought. Betsy Galant was probably right about Michael's affair with Gwendolyn. And not surprisingly, Mrs. Olina didn't like "that woman."

Michael and Marcia plainly knew things they weren't willing to share, and Koa decided on an alternative approach. Promising to return, he left the shop, taking note of the license numbers on the two cars parked outside Michael's shop. One license plate bore a "combat veteran" designation. The county reserved those plates for owners who'd served in the armed forces during hostilities. A call to Sergeant Basa confirmed the other plate belonged to Michael's assistant, Kaha'i. Thirty seconds later, Koa had a text from Basa with Kaha'i's home address.

Koa visited Kaha'i that evening. Olina's assistant lived alone in a tiny house on the outskirts of Volcano Village. Kaha'i answered Koa's knock.

"Hello. What can I do for you?"

"We need to have a chat. Want to invite me in?"

Kaha'i stepped back, and Koa entered a room sparsely furnished with packing crates from Michael's workshop. Koa noted the Chinese markings he'd seen earlier. Elegant glass bowls and vases like those in Michael's showroom seemed out of place on packing boxes. The glass vessels, Koa noticed, had odd misshapen characters. Seconds, or perhaps thirds—mistakes from the glass shop, he surmised, although they radiated their own unique beauty—like Japanese pottery deliberately misshapen to enhance its appeal.

Kaha'i, a large Hawaiian man with bands of geometric tattoos around his neck and upper arms, sat on a green futon opposite Koa with a quizzical look. "What's this all about?"

Koa came to the point. "Did you know Gwendolyn Campbell?"

"The lady in the accident. Sure, I knew her." Kaha'i's widely spaced eyes met Koa's gaze with disarming directness. "She hung around the shop most every day."

"And her relationship with Michael?"

Alarm registered in Kaha'i's eyes. "Hey. You're not going to get me in trouble with Michael, are you? I need that job."

"This is between us. It won't get back to Michael," Koa reassured him.

Kaha'i hesitated. "Okay. Well, at first it was just business, but then, you know, it became something else."

"Business?" Koa leaned forward. "What kind of business?"

"I don't really know. At first, she came in for the packages."

Kahaʻi had Koa's full attention. "Packages?"

"Small boxes, wrapped in newspaper, like the other packing material in the shipments."

"I don't understand. What packing material? Give me some background."

"Okay. You see, Michael uses rare earth metals in his glass, stuff with names like lanthanum and cerium. That's what gives his glass pieces their metallic colors and makes them so popular. He gets the metals from China. It's the world's biggest supplier of rare earths. The shipments come in once or twice a month in crates like the one you're sitting on, but the Chinese don't use regular packing material. They use this crazy foam. It falls apart, so they wrap the foam packing material in newspapers, Chinese newspapers."

"And there were boxes for Gwendolyn in these shipments?"

"Right. There'd be a box in the shipment. She'd come by the shop, and Michael would give her the box."

"What was in these boxes?" The interview had developed a rhythm, as many successful interviews did, where the questions and answers flowed as the witness talked naturally.

"I've no idea. Michael wouldn't let me touch them. I'd pry the tops off, but he insisted on unpacking the crates himself."

"How big? How big were these boxes?"

"About the size of a Kleenex box, the family size."

"How heavy?"

"I don't know. I never held one, but it wasn't like lead or anything, the way he handed them to Gwendolyn."

Curiouser and curiouser. "How often did these boxes come?"

"I didn't keep a calendar or anything, but probably about once a month."

"Did Michael ever open any of them?"

"I think so, but I'm not positive. I didn't see him with the box open, but one day I went into his office, and it looked like he was just finishing rewrapping the box. I caught him with kind of a funny look on his face. I guessed he'd opened it."

"You said the relationship developed into something else—"

"Yeah, well, she was pretty hot. She knew it, really flaunted it, and Michael has a wandering eye. They spent a lot of time in his office, and they weren't blowing glass." He let out an awkward laugh. Koa had a good idea what kind of blowing had gone on.

"Michael's wife know?"

"Yeah, she knew."

"About the packages or the affair?"

"Both. I heard them talking about the packages, and she knew Michael chased skirts. Gwendolyn wasn't his virgin foray."

Koa remembered the combat veteran designation on one of the license plates outside Michael's. "Michael ex-military?"

"Yeah, some kind of Special Forces tour in Kosovo."

*　*　*

After leaving Kaha'i, Koa got down to business. He instructed Sergeant Basa to bring Michael Olina into the station. They left the glassblower alone in an interrogation room for forty-five minutes before Koa entered and sat opposite him with Piki at the end of the table. Koa liked to have a second person in his interrogations in case his subjects tried to claim police misconduct. Besides, Piki needed the training.

Koa began by reading Michael his *Miranda* rights, and watched expressions of shock, consternation, and fear float across the artist's face. "You lied to me." Koa hit him in a stern voice. "Obstruction of a police murder investigation is a felony."

"Gwendolyn was murdered?" Michael half-rose from his chair.

"Yeah, she was murdered."

"Oh, my God. That's awful."

Koa glared at the man. Koa had shaken him.

"Maybe I—I should call a lawyer."

Koa forced a smile, but his tone remained frosty. "We can proceed formally, if you wish."

"What'd ya mean?"

"It means I can file charges and deal with your lawyer. Or," he added after a pause, "you can answer my questions informally."

"And you won't charge me." Michael took the bait like a *pueo*, a Hawaiian owl, swooping in to pick up a rodent.

"That depends on what you have to say."

Michael considered his predicament for a long moment. "Okay, ask your questions."

"You lied to me once. Do so again at your peril. Understand?"

"Yeah, I understand. I haven't done anything."

"Tell me about Gwendolyn."

"Okay, she came on to me, and I screwed her." Michael stared at the table. "I just didn't want my wife to know."

"How charming, but I'm more interested in your business relationship with her."

Michael appeared puzzled. "Business relationship?"

"The packages—"

"How?"

Koa smiled inwardly. If a witness thought you knew more than you did, they became wary of getting caught in a lie. "Never mind how I know. Just tell me about the arrangement."

"Dates back more than a dozen years. She knew I got rare earth shipments from China and wanted to piggyback. You know, use the shipments for certain packages. She offered me five hundred bucks a pop for each delivery." He paused, trying to explain himself. "You know how many hours I have to sweat in front of that furnace to make that kind of money?"

"Go on."

"She said she had money coming from her family in China. They couldn't send it the normal way 'cause of Chinese government exchange controls. I made her promise she wasn't shipping drugs. I didn't want to get involved in that. She promised no contraband, so I agreed. The boxes came every month, wrapped up with the rest of the packing material, and I gave them to her. Pretty simple, really."

"What was in the packages?"

Michael hesitated. "I don't know."

"I'm betting you do. Like I said, we can do this the formal way if you're not going to cooperate fully."

Michael looked down at the table, as though the answer might be printed there. "I wasn't supposed to look."

"But you did look, didn't you?" Koa pushed.

"Yeah, once. Just once. It was a lot of freaking money— hundred-dollar bills in bands, five bundles, fifty K, can you believe it?"

The amount surprised Koa. Fifty thousand a month? That was $600,000 a year.

"Who was paying her?"

"She said it was her family."

"And you believed that?"

"Hell. I was getting half a grand a month for doin' nothing. I didn't really care."

That had a ring of truth. A former Special Forces guy like Olina was smart enough to understand that too much knowledge could boomerang. Koa shifted gears. "Where'd you first meet her?"

"What do you mean?"

"She didn't just walk into your shop and ask you to be her delivery boy. How'd she know you?"

Again, Michael paused. "We met overseas while I was on active duty after my reserve unit got called up."

"Where overseas?"

Again, Michael hesitated, and Koa sensed he might not answer. Finally, he said, "Kosovo."

"What was she doing in Kosovo?"

Michael shook his head.

According to Kahaʻi, Michael had been Special Forces. "You were military?"

"SEALS. I was a Navy SEAL and then stayed in the reserves."

"And she was?" Koa pressed.

"It's classified."

Koa knew he was going out on a limb, but he nevertheless tried. "Not anymore it's not, not in my murder investigation."

Yet he'd come up against the witness's red line. "I'm not going to jail for your murder investigation."

Koa swore. He'd been on a roll. Pixels had come alive giving him the barest glimmer of a picture before Olina's hard stop. All investigations had moments like that, but he hated the frustration and wanted to ring Olina's neck.

CHAPTER FIFTEEN

KOA PARKED HIS car near Wailoa Park, on the Hilo waterfront, where the Nihoa rally would be held in two days. Chief Lannua had instructed all his officers, even detectives and administrative personnel, to increase their presence on the streets, keeping an eye on the potentially volatile situation in advance of the Nihoa rally and reporting trouble.

Over a hundred public school teachers were marching with anti-Nihoa placards: "Save Public Schools," "Respect Our Teachers," and "Reject Racial Politics." Across the park, more than five hundred Nihoa supporters paraded. Their placards read: "Quality Education First," "Justice for Native Hawaiians," and, most powerfully of all, "Reduce Government Waste . . . Cut Taxes."

Koa shook his head at the deceptive simplicity of the messages as he recalled Wailoa Park's violent history. Just a few feet above sea level, it had been home to Shinmachi, Hilo's Japanese community. Tsunamis had destroyed Shinmachi twice, once in 1946 when 159 people died and again in 1960 when a wall of water thirty-five feet high flooded most of downtown Hilo, killing sixty-one residents. After the second disaster, the city had turned the area into a park. Koa never walked its paths without thinking of the people who had died there. Suddenly, he had a bad feeling about the political rally.

He wandered through tree-lined paths and across its grassy fields, listening to various factions rally their supporters. His concern grew rapidly. In the shade of an old banyan tree, a crowd of public employees opposed to cuts in government surrounded a speaker, screaming over a megaphone. Three or four other groups scattered around the park held their own rallies. Each had its own agenda, with compromise invisible.

Eventually, Koa noticed a heavyset, red-haired man on a soapbox. The man's crudely hand-lettered "Kill the Sovereignty Movement" placard caught Koa's eye. The word "KILL" was ten times larger than the other words. A crowd of a couple dozen around the speaker was mostly *hoales*. Several were shabbily dressed and unshaven, and Koa guessed most came from poorer communities.

The speaker, also a *haole*, was big, like Sergeant Basa, but fair-skinned beneath a freckled face reddened by the sun and his palpable anger. He wore a Hawaiian shirt and jeans, but his desert combat boots made Koa think he might be a veteran. Koa, trained to take in details that others missed, noticed the man's hands. They were covered with pale-colored blisters or boils, almost as though the man had contracted leprosy.

The man pumped his sign up and down as he screamed through a megaphone: "Nāinoa will turn back the clock. Native Hawaiians will take our homes. He must be stopped." His mouth took on a boar-like snarl that reminded Koa of other political demagogues. "Kill the sovereignty movement! KILL the sovereignty movement!" the man chanted. "Nāinoa must be stopped!" The man seemed to draw energy from the spectators, who pumped fists in the air and yelled, "Right on, brah."

* * *

Koa looked up when a small, wiry stranger walked into his office unannounced and closed the door. Cranky at the chief's treatment of Smithy and annoyed at the unexpected interruption, Koa snarled, "Who are you and what do you want?"

"James Alderson, CIA." The black-haired man, dressed in uber-preppy business casual clothes, opened a leather wallet and placed it on the center of Koa's desk. Alderson looked more like a big-city accountant than a CIA spook. The government identity card featured Alderson's thin face and gray eyes. The credentials appeared to be genuine.

Although he knew the Honolulu PD's counterterrorism unit sometimes worked with the CIA, Koa was unaware of any CIA presence on the Big Island. Alderson must have flown in for this meeting. What, Koa wondered, did the CIA want? He'd worked with agency people in his Special Forces assignments. His experiences hadn't been good. He didn't trust CIA types.

"Okay, Mr. Alderson, what brings the Central Intelligence Agency to the Big Island?"

"Please call me James. I'm here because of the fingerprints you sent to the FBI. We need to know what you found in the Campbell house."

Typical of the arrogant CIA boys, Koa thought. "That's not the way it's going to work, Mr. Alderson. You don't get any information until I understand what's going on."

"They told me you were a straight arrow and tough," Alderson allowed.

"Right on both counts." Koa kept his face impassive. "Who briefed you?"

"Admiral Cunningham and some of your friends in the Honolulu FBI."

The mention of Admiral Cunningham got Koa's full attention. He'd worked with the Coast Guard admiral on civil defense issues, disaster recovery, and criminal cases. He had enormous respect for the officer.

"You can check out my creds with the admiral. He's waiting by the phone, if you want to call now."

Koa called the admiral, whose assistant put the flag officer on the line in record time. The admiral vouched for Alderson. Koa turned to the agent. The man plainly had clout to have the admiral standing by for a confirmation call.

"So, what do you want, Mr. Alderson?"

"Before I get to the guts of it," Alderson began, "I need to warn you I've been authorized to make certain disclosures to secure your cooperation. What I am about to say is classified top secret with several additional levels of security. Indeed, it's among the nation's most closely guarded secrets. If you disclose this information to anyone, and that includes your chief, you will be prosecuted under the National Defense Secrets Act. Do you understand?"

Koa, keenly aware that CIA involvement elevated the significance of his murder case, avoided giving any tell. His taciturn expression hid his surprise the CIA didn't trust Chief Lannua. Was it because the chief talked too freely to the mayor, or might there be some more sinister reason? Koa knew Chief Lannua had once worked in Washington in the Defense Department, but he'd never heard of his involvement with any of the national security agencies. "Yeah. I understand."

"The prints you inputted into the FBI IAFIS created a firestorm at Langley," Alderson said.

"Arthur Campbell's prints?"

"No, the woman you know as Gwendolyn Campbell."

Koa had already guessed that Gwendolyn Campbell was an alias, but he hadn't expected the CIA to have an interest in her. "Is that so? What's the CIA's interest in a local artist?"

"Your local artist was born in the southern Chinese province of Guangxi as Lan Zwang. She worked as a CIA field agent." Koa remained impassive and continued to listen. He now knew why Michael Olina had refused to answer his questions about Gwendolyn's work in Kosovo. Federal criminal statutes imposed stiff penalties for disclosing the identity of a CIA field agent. Lewis "Scooter" Libby had gone to jail for obstruction for trying to cover up the unauthorized disclosure of Valerie Plame Wilson's covert CIA identity.

"Lan Zwang disappeared from a field assignment in May 1999 with highly classified documents, documents of the highest possible sensitivity to the United States. The CIA and the FBI launched a manhunt but failed to find the slightest trace of her. No one in Washington knew her whereabouts until you asked for a routine check on her fingerprints."

Koa waited to ensure that Alderson had finished, giving himself time to digest this news. A poor farm girl from rural China, sold by her father to a rich man, had somehow become a CIA agent and then stolen highly classified documents. She'd disappeared in May 1999 and six months later turned up in Hawai'i with Elian Cervara, alias Arthur Campbell, a former Delta Force operative, who'd purchased the two parcels from South Mauna Loa Farms through offshore trusts. She'd received $50,000 a month through a front company in Hong Kong. Gwendolyn Campbell, aka Lan Zwang, must have stumbled onto some blisteringly hot documents to justify that level of blackmail.

"And you want to know whether we found any classified documents when we searched her house."

"Exactly."

Koa had no doubt the CIA already knew the answer. "The crime-scene boys searched the house from top to bottom, and I have personally been through the papers. We haven't found your secret documents."

"Any leads?" Alderson asked. Koa presumed the CIA hadn't learned of the separate 240-acre parcel behind the Campbell dwelling. Koa considered telling the agent but decided to keep his own counsel until he had better knowledge of this unfamiliar turf.

"None."

"But you'll let me know if you find anything?" The agent slid a card across Koa's desk. "You cannot imagine how vital this information is and how much damage will be done if it falls into the wrong hands."

"I don't suppose you're going to tell me what I'm looking for?"

"Physically, it's a sheaf of papers, a medium-sized file, but I'm not authorized to disclose the contents."

"What language?" Koa pressed.

Alderson looked decidedly uncomfortable. "Some of the documents are in Chinese."

"What about Arthur Campbell? There's definitely something fishy about him, too," Koa said.

"I . . . I can't talk about Arthur."

Aldersen's response meant that Arthur, too, had secrets, secrets distinct from Gwendolyn's and perhaps even more dangerous. "There's more going on here than you're letting on." Koa stated it as a fact.

"That shouldn't surprise you, should it?"

"I'm trying to solve a murder, two murders, to be more precise. I'd appreciate any help you can offer."

"I'll keep that in mind."

Koa wasn't sure why Alderson hadn't simply denied knowledge of Arthur Campbell and repeated his earlier question with a kicker. "While you're keeping my investigatory needs in mind, tell me how Lan Zwang came to have documents in Chinese when she disappeared from her agency assignment in Kosovo."

Even experienced professionals are sometimes unable to suppress their reactions to unexpected challenges, and Alderson's eyebrows flicked up, registering surprise for a fraction of a second. "Who said anything about Kosovo?"

"Your Lan Zwang worked for the CIA in Kosovo before she walked out with your Chinese documents." Although only an educated guess, Koa pretended to be positive. As a Fifth Special Forces Group officer, Koa had worked with the CIA in Afghanistan and Somalia. He knew firsthand the agency piled deception upon deception, and frequently got its hands covered in slime. He wondered whether the CIA sought to protect a highly placed foreign intelligence source or itself. The agency, he knew, wasn't squeamish about using its secret bank accounts to protect its vilest secrets. He took another shot. "Who's she been blackmailing, the agency or some Chinese official?"

Again, Alderson couldn't control the micro-movements of his facial muscles. "What are you talking about?"

"A motive for murder."

"This is serious. You need to tell me what evidence supports your assertions about Kosovo and blackmail."

"If it's so serious, Mr. Alderson, tell me about Arthur Campbell, and I'll tell you how I got my information."

The CIA man glared at Koa for a long moment. "No can do."

"Well." Koa summoned up his best smile. "Come back, Mr. Alderson, when you're prepared to trade."

Long after Alderson left his office, Koa sat staring at his birthday present, Escher's *Concave and Convex*. He tried to imagine the pathways leading from Guangxi, China, to a CIA assignment in Kosovo, to a hiding place in the rain forest on the eastern slopes of Mauna Loa, to a Honda Civic crushed under the front end of a Hawai'i County dump truck. Whose secrets had Gwendolyn Campbell learned along the way? And who the hell was Arthur?

CHAPTER SIXTEEN

KOA DIDN'T KNOW much about Kosovo. He called a friend on the faculty of the University of Hawai'i and ultimately connected with James Kalo, a professor of European history. Koa met Kalo in his office on the UH–Hilo campus. He found the academic dressed Hawai'i style in an *aloha* shirt, shorts, and sandals. Long experience had taught Koa not to pretend to know things for fear of looking stupid, so he let his ignorance show with his first question. "I don't mean to sound dumb, but exactly where is Kosovo?"

"Not a dumb question," Kalo responded with a smile. Moving to a wall-sized map of Europe, he pointed to a small diamond-shaped country somewhat north of Greece. "Kosovo shares borders with Macedonia, Albania, Montenegro, and Serbia. Part of the Roman and Ottoman Empires, Serbia, and Yugoslavia before declaring its independence. That didn't last long, and in 1999, it came under United Nations protection."

"I'm interested," Koa explained, "in events in early 1999."

"Okay, but a little context first," the bespectacled Kalo offered in clipped English. "President Tito kept the lid on Yugoslavia's cauldron of ethnic tensions, but the country went to hell after his death in 1980. Enter Slobodan Milošević, who became president on a platform of repressing the Albanian nationalists in Kosovo. You've heard of Milošević?"

"Vaguely. Wasn't he an international war criminal?"

"Kosovo has had no shortage of criminals on both sides." Kalo paused, gathering his thoughts.

"Milošević forces engaged in brutal repression. NATO sent peacekeepers in to curb ethnic violence, and Serbian Yugoslavia mobilized for war." Kalo adjusted his thick eyeglasses before continuing. "NATO then started a bombing campaign, code-named Operation Allied Force, against Yugoslavia. It ran from March to mid-June, 1999 and involved hundreds of NATO aircraft and Tomahawk cruise missiles."

"Okay." Koa nodded. "I remember something about the air war." Mindful of Arthur Campbell's Delta Force membership and Gwendolyn's CIA employment, Koa asked, "Tell me what U.S. clandestine forces did during Operation Allied Force?"

"Just what you'd think. The CIA was up to its eyeballs in arming the Kosovo Liberation Army, gathering intel, coming up with targeting data for the bombing campaign, and running kill ops against leading Serbian fighters and politicians."

Drawing on his own Special Forces experience, Koa went straight to the essence. "And I suppose the Delta guys worked with the CIA?"

"Sure," Kalo said, "with the Serbs, the Russians, the Chinese, WikiLeaks, and God knows who else watching, the Delta Force role in 'snatch and kill' ops quickly became common knowledge. Hell, you can buy photographs of U.S. Delta Force soldiers in Kosovo Liberation Army camps."

So, Koa thought, both Gwendolyn and Arthur could easily have been stationed in Kosovo. Now he needed to figure out what roles they played. Knowing from Ryan Chang that Gwendolyn spoke Chinese and from Alderson that she disappeared with Chinese documents, Koa asked, "You mentioned the Chinese. How were they involved?"

"Heavens." The professor spread his arms. "We could spend hours talking about the Chinese role."

"Then let's go with the dime-store version."

"Okay. The Chinese and the Russians sided with Yugoslavia and tracked the NATO bombardment to learn everything they could about NATO war plans, equipment, tactics, and capabilities.

"There's also the stealth incident. The U.S. lost an F-117 Nighthawk stealth aircraft over Yugoslavia in March 1999, and the Yugoslavs found the wreckage. At that time, the Chinese military didn't have stealth technology, and the Chinese made a deal with Milošević to supply communications facilities in exchange for access to the downed aircraft.

"The most complicated part of the story involves the Chinese embassy in Belgrade, the capital of Serbia. On May 7–8, 1999, U.S. B-2 stealth bombers dropped five JDAM GPS-guided precision bombs on the Chinese embassy in Belgrade. The incident caused an international uproar. The Americans claimed it was an accident, but the Chinese never bought that line, and lots of subsequent press reports cast doubt on the official American version."

Koa listened intently as the professor continued, "Of the thousands of air operations over Yugoslavia, the CIA directed only one, the embassy bombing. The CIA blamed the error on an erroneous map, but the National Mapping Agency insisted its maps were accurate. Besides, the embassy was on the no-target list. CIA controllers couldn't have missed it.

"Foreign press reports called the bombing deliberate. Theories abound about why the U.S. might strike the Chinese embassy. One version has the CIA striking because the Chinese were rebroadcasting military intelligence for a Yugoslav commander. Another says the Chinese were tracking U.S. Tomahawk missile strikes." Finally, the professor added, "There's also a theory that elements of the U.S. military intelligence community were trying to make President Clinton look bad. And God only knows what other reasons the CIA might have cooked up for a deliberate attack on the embassy."

Koa was skeptical; would the U.S. deliberately bomb a foreign embassy? It seemed far-fetched, yet he'd seen the CIA do crazy things, so he focused on the possible connections. A Chinese-born CIA agent would be invaluable in an operation involving a Chinese embassy. It was also just the thing for a Delta Force operative. Arthur Campbell could have easily met, and worked with, Gwendolyn in Kosovo. Something must have gone wrong; maybe the bombing itself. Whatever happened, they'd fled to a remote farm in Hawai'i. That something would have to be mighty important for a CIA operative to come visiting. With every step Koa took in this case, he seemed to be sinking deeper and deeper into an international morass.

CHAPTER SEVENTEEN

KOA'S DAY BEGAN with a call from a police officer assigned to check on the Campbell property. Someone had broken into the old house and ransacked it. They'd reportedly done a thorough job, dumping every drawer and searching even the tiniest spaces. The extent of the damage suggested that the searchers had not found what they sought, but Koa sent the crime-scene team back to determine what, if anything, was missing.

Everything about the Campbell murders gnawed at Koa, but nothing haunted him more than the mystery of identity. Elian Cervara had become Arthur Campbell. But Elian Cervara had been unwilling, or more likely unable, to discuss his family with Raul Oshoa. Elian Cervara had purported to come from a Catalan family living in Cuba but spoke Caribbean Spanish. And he'd spoken Russian or some Slavic language to Gwendolyn during their car ride with Howie. Koa wanted to know this mysterious man. What he'd done. What secrets he'd harbored and what he'd fled when he'd come to live as a recluse in Volcano Village.

Piki had entered the couple's fingerprints into the FBI's IAFIS system. The CIA spook Alderson had come storming into Koa's office about Gwendolyn's fingerprints, but Koa had heard nothing about Arthur's prints. He called Piki, who reported no known record on either of them.

Given Gwendolyn's CIA background, Koa wasn't surprised that her prints weren't in an accessible database, but that didn't explain the absence of a report on Arthur. The military fingerprinted everybody, including Special Forces soldiers. As a Delta Force guy, the military had undoubtedly classified his fingerprints, but Arthur had been living in Volcano, and therefore out of Delta Force, for well over a decade. Koa couldn't understand why his fingerprints would still be protected.

He felt sure the chameleon behind the Elian and Arthur aliases had harbored secrets, mysteries anchored in his life before his land purchases from Raul Oshoa. Those secrets had to come from his military service—they were most likely Delta Force secrets. The wily lizard had reduced his secrets to some tangible, but cleverly hidden, form. Caught and tortured, this human reptile had kept his secrets to himself. Now someone, most likely his killers, searched for Arthur's hiding place.

He tried to put himself in Arthur's shoes as he thought of the possible hiding places: Liechtenstein, the Cayman Islands, Hawai'i. In Koa's experience, people kept their treasures close. If nearby, but not in the house, maybe the secret lay hidden in the forest. And, if Arthur had arranged the purchase of two adjacent parcels in separate trusts in different offshore countries, the twin purchases must have been intended to conceal Arthur's relationship with the rear acreage.

So if the chameleon were clever, he would have hidden his secrets on the 240-acre parcel, land not legally linked to him or to his home. The house property served as a gateway to the rear property, and the camera system guarded the back acreage, allowing the chameleon to watch for trespassers. Koa guessed that Arthur had buried his stolen treasures somewhere deep in the forest. But 240 acres covered more than ten million square feet. He could spend years searching. Yet somewhere in his head Koa knew there was a clue, a hint that remained tantalizingly out of focus.

His thoughts turned back to the spy who had eyes on him at the Campbell orchid farm. Had the unknown observer been there by coincidence or had the watcher somehow timed his appearance to coincide with Koa's arrival? Had someone known where he would be?

He found Basa and they headed out to the Campbell place with Maru following in a separate car. As they drove, Koa raised an unhappy subject. "Smithy came to see me."

"Yeah, he told me. You gonna be able to do anything for him?"

"I don't know. When I asked the chief about layoffs at the party the other night, he told me to mind my own business. Not in those words; still, that was the bottom line. But I've got a backup plan."

"The grapevine says the chief's in line to become the state director of Homeland Security if Nihoa wins. Did you know he was off campaigning for Nihoa on Kauai yesterday?"

After his conversation with Zeke, Koa wasn't surprised. "Really?"

"Yeah. Got it straight from one of my buddies on the Kauai force."

"*He puhi ka iʻa ʻoni i ka lani* . . . the eel is a fish that moves skyward. No one," Koa muttered, "better stand in the way of his greater glory."

When they neared the turnoff to the Campbell house, Koa stationed Maru near the forest fire lane while he and Basa drove up to the Campbell place. They fired up the generator, and Koa took Basa to the master bedroom, surprising the sergeant by swinging Arthur Campbell's portrait away from the wall to reveal the television monitor. He explained the system—images coming in rotation from cameras around the orchid farm.

"Those two Indonesian goons tortured Campbell to get information or find something he'd hidden. I'm guessing they also tossed this house but didn't find what they were looking for. If Arthur hid something on the orchid farm, he might have set up a camera to keep an eye on it. I want to know where Campbell put those cameras. I'm going to move around out there. I'll be on my cell. Call me when you see me on one of the cameras."

"Got it," Basa responded.

"What's more," Koa said, outlining his plan, "the dude who parked on the fire lane might come back. I'm hoping you'll spot him on one of the cameras. If you see anyone, tell Maru to block the fire lane, and call me. So we're going for a two-for, finding what Arthur hid and catching the spy," Koa concluded with a hint of excitement.

"You got it," Basa responded.

Leaving Basa at the monitor, Koa walked up the trail toward the orchid farm. He moved slowly, taking nearly twenty minutes to reach the orchid-growing tables. For the next hour he poked around the grounds. Whenever he appeared on one of the cameras, Basa called. Koa answered using the voice-activated Bluetooth headset for his iPhone. Basa then directed him where to look: "More to the right" . . . "Higher" . . . until Koa found the camera. Koa then searched the area visible to that camera, looking for anything Arthur might have hidden.

They located three cameras around the periphery of the orchid farm, and then found another camera up the side trail to the water tank and the spring. And another near the compost heap. They also located a camera on the obscure trail leading to the ancient *heiau*. Each time they found a camera, Koa's hopes soared. But the exercise failed to provide a single clue as to what the Campbells might have hidden. At the end of two hours, just when Koa thought he'd been mistaken about an observer, his cell phone vibrated again.

"Koa here," he answered softly using his Bluetooth headset.

"A man just entered one of the forest pictures. I think he's coming from the fire lane. I've alerted Maru."

"Good. Watch and keep me posted on his movements."

Koa drifted back toward the center of the orchid operation, pretending to examine his immediate surroundings while covertly watching for any sign of movement in the forest. Basa continued to report the observer's movement.

"He's moving in behind the shed," Basa's voice warned. "Distances are tough. He's maybe thirty yards back."

Koa moved slowly in that direction, still maintaining the pretense of searching the orchid tables and surrounding area, while occasionally scanning the forest. He caught a flash of movement and recognized a human shape. Drifting slowly to his left, he put the shed between himself and the intruder. When the shed blocked the observer's view, Koa raced around the side of the little building to catch an interloper standing fifty feet away in the forest. The startled man, dressed as a ranch hand, appeared to be Latino. The two men stared at each other for an instant before the invader abruptly turned and ran.

"Police, *stop!*" Koa yelled, but the man kept running. Koa gave chase through the forest, but the man dodged around trees and other obstructions, sprinting like a little axis deer. The intruder was heading for the fire lane. Koa alerted Basa.

"Maru's in position," Basa reported.

"Take my Explorer and back him up," Koa said.

After a quarter mile, Koa lost sight of the man, although he could still hear the occasional crack of branches as the man fled. When Koa finally emerged on the fire lane, he saw a white truck and Maru's brown Chevy with its police bubble—but no sign of the interloper and no Maru. Koa followed the trail out toward the road. He'd nearly reached the intersection when he spotted Maru and Basa bracing a stranger up against the Explorer.

Sergeant Basa handcuffed the man's hands behind his back before checking for a wallet. "Faizon Cimarro," Basa read the name off the man's driver's license, "from Pāhala." Basa handed Koa the billfold.

Koa assessed the watcher. Latino, five foot ten, slim build, but muscled, dressed *paniolo*-style, like a working cowboy. He didn't seem like much of a spy, and his presence puzzled Koa. "Faizon, what were you doing on the Campbell property?" Koa asked.

Silence.

Koa thumbed through the wallet as he waited for an answer. He found little: a driver's license, a few dollars, a picture of a dark-haired woman, and a slip of paper with a phone number. Koa stared at the phone number, and everything clicked into place. The cowboy came from Oshoa's ranch. Someone in the rancher's operation, maybe the big man himself, wanted to know what the police were finding. Koa's suspicions that Oshoa had hidden dealings with Arthur Campbell ratcheted up a notch.

With some punch in his voice, Koa said, "I asked you a question."

Silence.

Other than its registration documents, confirming Koa's suspicions that the vehicle came from Oshoa's ranch, the white truck yielded nothing of interest. They took Faizon back to police headquarters, booking him on criminal trespass charges, failure to obey a lawful police order, and interfering with a police investigation. They let him use the telephone. Like most inmates, he paid no attention to the sign near the telephone warning that jailhouse calls might be monitored.

As Koa had anticipated, Faizon Cimarro made his call to the number on the paper in his wallet. The call went to South Mauna

Loa Farms, the registered owner of the white truck. When the receptionist answered, Faizon asked to be transferred to Jorge Chavez. During the brief call, Faizon explained in Spanish he'd been arrested while checking out the property. Then the jailers led him back to his cell to await arraignment.

* * *

Koa's cell phone buzzed. He picked up to hear Sam Ikeda's voice. "Koa, we've found the cause of the explosion. You're not gonna believe it. No way you're gonna believe it."

The normally placid arson investigator sounded over-the-top excited, but Sam wouldn't talk over the phone, instead inviting Koa to drive to the fire station. As Koa entered, Sam got up from a computer and introduced MK Dexter. "MK's from the fire analysis unit of AFEI Corp. in Honolulu. We use their laboratory and engineering services for difficult arson cases like this dump truck thing."

Koa shook hands with MK before turning to Sam. "By the way, I saw Mike Tolman in the hospital. He's gonna recover okay. In fact, I caught him studying for his arson exam."

"That's great. He's damn lucky. Geez, if he'd been a little closer, he'd have been dead. And he's got a wife and two kids. Is he still in the hospital?"

"Yeah, at Hilo Medical. He'll be there for another day or two. So what did you guys find?" Koa's curiosity hit overdrive given Sam's call and the presence of a professional arson specialist.

"Wait till you see this." Sam led Koa to his laptop computer and ran a program. "MK built this re-creation. It uses wire-frame graphics, but you'll get the idea." The outline of a Honda Civic drove down the road toward the viewer. As it reached the intersection with the dirt lane, the outline of a dump truck hurtled into view from the right side of the picture, smashing head-on into the side of the Honda. The steel front bumper of the truck hit the little car at the level of the driver's window, rolling the car onto its side. The truck continued forward, crushing the smaller vehicle under its front end.

As the truck crushed the car, the Honda's wire-frame gas tank burst open. Yellow coloring showed the fuel running down the underside of the Honda before bursting into a roaring fire, shown in orange.

Koa watched in fascination as the orange tracked the growing gasoline-fed fire while the counter on the bottom of the screen showed the passage of time . . . a minute, two, five, ten, almost fifteen minutes . . . before a massive explosion of red erupted from the hood of the dump truck, blasting the heavy vehicle up and backward while simultaneously shredding the Honda into a thousand pieces.

"I get the gasoline fire," Koa said, "but I still don't understand the explosion afterward. What happened?"

Sam activated another file. This one depicted the front end of the dump truck, exposing its internal components. Koa could see the engine block, the radiator, and the other mechanical parts. But he didn't understand the light pink blob overlaid on the internal structure of the engine compartment, filling all the space around the engine and extending beneath the radiator. "What's that pink thing?"

"A bag made from reinforced polyurethane. We found shreds of the material scattered in the wreckage."

"A bag?" Koa still didn't understand. "Filled with what?"

"Acetylene. It was an acetylene bomb," Sam explained.

"Like the gas used in machine shops for welding and metal cutting?"

"Exactly," Sam said. "You remember, out at the scene, I couldn't understand why the fire got so damned hot. Well, acetylene burns at over three thousand degrees Celsius. That's plenty hot enough to melt steel."

"An acetylene bomb! I've never even heard of one. Have you guys?"

"Unfortunately, we've seen them before," MK responded. "Believe it or not, there's a YouTube video showing kids how to make small ones."

Koa was dumbfounded. "That's insane!"

"Fuckin' YouTube's not just for funny videos. It's a graduate school for terrorists," MK said.

"Why the delay?" Koa asked. "I mean, in your reconstruction there's a fifteen-or-so-minute gap between the gas tank ignition and detonation of this acetylene bomb."

"We're not sure," Sam responded. "We haven't found the triggering mechanism. It probably evaporated in the fireball. So we don't know what the perps intended. Maybe the crash disrupted the trigger mechanism or maybe the perps were targeting first responders."

"Jesus, that's sick."

"Yeah, but it happens more often than you'd think." MK shook his head. "I can also think of other possibilities."

"Such as?"

"Obliteration of evidence. I mean, the shock wave, followed by the heat, basically wiped the accident site clean. No body. No license plates. No VIN. These bastards didn't leave you with many leads."

"Sounds right," Koa agreed. "Cap Roberts translated a tape of the two perps talking. There's mention of their boss wanting a clean job with no evidence."

"And," MK added, "it gave the driver time to disappear." Koa thought of Mrs. Furgeson's description of the dusty truck driver running up the road to be picked up by the black SUV. The delayed explosion made perfect sense.

"Anyway," Sam continued, "for whatever reason the bomb didn't detonate until the gasoline fire burned through the reinforced urethane. In fact, we think heat expanded the bladder, creating an even bigger bang."

"Where'd they get the acetylene?" Koa asked.

"It's pretty common in machine shops," Sam answered, "but after MK figured out the bomb, we checked with the county maintenance depot up in Kurtistown where the perps stole the truck. Four tanks of acetylene went missing about the same time as the truck. That's the most likely source of the gas."

"As you probably know," MK said, "the use of explosives to kill is a reportable terrorist event. We've notified the FBI and the bomb experts at Justice. Agents from the joint task force have already started looking at the wreckage. They're trying to trace the materials, especially the polyurethane."

"Good. Any more surprises for me?" Koa asked.

"A couple." Sam led Koa across the room to a workbench where a blackened, partially shattered hunk of metal—what had once been a handgun—lay in the illumination of a work light.

"We found it in the wreckage from the Honda. A Walther P99 pistol, used by law enforcement officers, but widely available from gun shops. Most likely with a full clip before the ammo cooked off in the explosion. Blew the damned thing apart."

"That," Koa said emphatically, "explains Mike Tolman's memory. He thought he heard gunshots just before the explosion blew his lights out. It must have been Gwendolyn's gun. Ryan Chang said she always carried. You said you had a couple of things. What else?"

Sam and MK exchanged looks, and Koa sensed bad news coming. MK cleared his throat. "We figure the truck bomb used roughly two tanks of acetylene. That means the bad guys probably have at least two more. Enough to make another bomb."

"Christ," Koa swore. "We'd better find these bastards before they blow somebody else to pieces."

CHAPTER EIGHTEEN

Bambang Gunawan, driver of the Hertz getaway SUV, had worked briefly as a chauffeur for the U.S. embassy in Jakarta, which explained why the FBI had his fingerprints in its IAFIS. The thumbprint put Bambang at the Arthur Campbell murder site. And Bambang matched Mrs. Furgeson's description of the older man in the black SUV, the one giving the orders to stage Gwendolyn Campbell's accident.

Immigration and Customs Enforcement in Homeland Security reported Bambang entering the United States at Honolulu airport a month earlier on a temporary work permit. A review of his application led Koa deeper into the conspiracy: South Mauna Loa Farms sponsored Bambang's L1-B visa. A further check of the ICE database revealed that South Mauna Loa Farms had sponsored a second Indonesian, Sudomo Sanjaya, who had entered the United States at Honolulu one day after Bambang.

The evidence pointed to Bambang, and probably Sudomo, as the killers of both Arthur and Gwendolyn Campbell. But Koa knew of no connection between the Campbells and the two Indonesians, and doubted they'd killed the Campbells on their own, especially since they'd referred to a "*kepala*" or chief who wanted a clean hit. It seemed doubly improbable that, acting on their own, they could have used South Mauna Loa Farms as cover. The two Indonesians had to be contract killers. Someone at South Mauna Loa Farms had hired them or at least assisted in arranging their entry into the United States.

Digging deeper, Koa found Customs application forms for both Bambang and Sudomo. According to the documents, they'd worked for the Indonesian subsidiary of South Mauna Loa Farms. In applying for their work permits, South Mauna Loa Farms claimed they were needed in Hawai'i for their coffee-processing expertise. But the Big Island, Koa knew, produced more than two million pounds a year of some of the best coffee in the world. No Hawaiian coffee producer needed to import expertise from Indonesia. Everything about the work permits smelled fishy.

The Customs application forms bore the signature of Jorge Pasqual Chavez, the South Mauna Loa Farms operations manager. Koa smiled. At last, he had a solid link to connect South Mauna Loa Farms to the Campbell murders. He could hardly wait to get his hands on Chavez—the arrogant asshole who'd tried to block Koa's inquiries on his first visit to the ranch.

Koa took the evidence to Zeke Brown, and the county prosecutor readily agreed that Bambang's fingerprint tinged with Arthur Campbell's blood on the doorframe of the torture room at what old Mo had called the "Chinese house" more than supported an arrest warrant. Sudomo presented a tougher case, but Koa had done his homework. Mrs. Furgeson described the dump truck driver as "age about thirty, black hair, heavy face, Asian eyes, thick lips, with a scar or blemish under his left eye and a small round gold earring in his right ear." Except for the earring, her description matched Sudomo's visa photo almost perfectly, right down to the scar under his left eye. And her tape recording of him speaking Indonesian provided a further connection.

Zeke prepared the affidavits and warrants, and they walked across the street to the county courthouse, where Judge Herbert K. Hitachi signed the arrest warrants.

As they walked back to Zeke's office, Koa outlined his meeting with Smithy. He explained the background of his injury in a bungled police raid on a crystal meth lab and his subsequent jobs under four different police chiefs.

"What do you want me to do?" Zeke asked.

Koa offered two alternatives. "I'd like to find a way to save Smithy's police department job, but otherwise we need to get an equivalent job in the prosecutor's office or some other Hawai'i County agency. He's a good guy, Zeke, and he's getting a raw deal," Koa reiterated. "I'd like to see the county do the right thing by him. Think you can help?"

It was a rhetorical question. Of course, Zeke could help. Koa had seen him pull off miracles that made taking care of Smithy a layup.

* * *

Koa worried that Bambang and Sudomo would put up a fight, so he took Sergeant Basa and four patrol officers in three separate cars. When the convoy arrived, Koa stationed two policemen on the road to prevent the Indonesians from fleeing the ranch, while he, Basa, and the other officers headed directly to Chavez's office. Koa led the officers to the headquarters building and up the stairs. The appearance of three police officers stunned the Cuban ranch foreman, who rocked back in his chair and jumped to his feet.

Koa took the initiative. "We've got arrest warrants for Bambang Gunawan and Sudomo Sanjaya. Where are they?"

"Who?" Chavez's brow wrinkled, and he appeared not to understand.

"Bambang Gunawan and Sudomo Sanjaya, the two Indonesians you sponsored for temporary work permits."

Confusion spread across Chavez's face. "Temporary work permits? I don't understand."

Koa was in no mood to put up with the manager's playacting. "Don't act dumb. You signed two temporary work permit applications, vouching for Bambang and Sudomo." Koa let frustration show in his voice.

Chavez stiffened. "You're mistaken. I signed no work permit applications. We have no temporary workers at South Mauna Loa Farms."

"Goddamn it, Chavez. Don't fuck with me," Koa roared. He pulled out the Immigration and Customs Enforcement Form I-129 he'd copied from the Customs database, slapped it down on the desk, and pointed to the signature. Chavez picked it up and read the words "Jorge Pasqual Chavez."

Chavez put the form back on the table. He looked straight back at Koa, his eyes now bright. "That's not my signature." Chavez reached into his pocket for a thin, well-worn billfold and pulled out his Hawai'i driver's license. He slid the document across to Koa. The name read "Jorge Pascual Chavez"; to Koa's surprise, the script looked nothing like the signature on the Customs form.

Some of the heat now gone from his voice, Koa asked, "You're saying your signature was forged?"

"The handwriting is not mine, and Pascual, my middle name, has been in my family for many generations. We have always spelled it with a 'c' and never with a 'q.'"

Koa felt deflated. He'd come to make an arrest, but the prospect had slipped away. "What do you know about Bambang and Sudomo?"

"I've never heard of them."

"Do these men, Bambang and Sudomo, work for the company in Indonesia?"

"I don't know. I'm not familiar with the employees there."

"Well." Koa's anger resurfaced. "Bambang and Sudomo are wanted for murder. If they're working for South Mauna Loa Farms anyplace in the world, you damn well better tell us where they are."

Chavez spread his hands in a gesture of helplessness.

Koa wasn't quite through. There was still the matter of Faizon Cimarro, the ranch hand he'd caught spying at the Campbell farm. "We have your man Faizon Cimarro in custody. Tell me about him."

"You shouldn't have arrested him. He was just checking out the property."

"Why? It's no longer part of South Mauna Loa Farms."

"Fire hazards. Given the drought, we can't be too careful about fire."

The asshole, Koa thought, was a rotten liar. There might be fire risks on parts of Oshoa's ranch, but not in a rain forest.

"Is that why he ran when he saw a police officer?"

"He didn't know you were a police officer."

"Bullshit. I identified myself as police."

"Maybe he didn't hear you."

"Yeah, right."

Koa paused to think. The temporary work permit applications could only have been cooked up by someone with insider knowledge of South Mauna Loa Farms operations. Chavez might have forged his own name or maybe Rachael Ortega had done the deed. Or maybe somebody else. But he couldn't storm around Raul Oshoa's headquarters, interrogating people at random. Oshoa would complain to the mayor or maybe even the governor. Still, Rachael Ortega was Oshoa's principal assistant, and she might know if Bambang or his sidekick worked for the company.

He led his officers down the hall to Rachael Ortega's office. She looked up, surprised when he stepped through the door. The pockmarks on her face seemed more prominent than he'd remembered, and she looked haggard, as though she hadn't slept in several days. He put on his nice face. "Just a quick question, Ms. Ortega." He placed the Customs form in front of her. "You know anything about this form?"

She studied the form for an inordinately long time. He couldn't tell whether she was trying to decipher the bureaucratic language or deciding what to say. Finally, she looked up. "I've never seen it. Have you asked Jorge?"

Koa decided he needed to regroup. On the way back to Hilo, he updated the prosecutor by cell phone. When Zeke finished swearing, Koa asked him to declare Bambang and Sudomo fugitives and notify the FBI, Customs and Immigration, and Interpol.

Something weird, Koa figured, was going on at Oshoa's ranch. The political kingpin set up a sweetheart land deal for Elian Cervara, aka Arthur Campbell, a former Delta Force guy, who moved in with his ex-CIA girlfriend. Arthur grew exotic orchids that wound up all over the ranch's offices. Then years later he's tortured and she's murdered by two Indonesians thugs, who get into the U.S. on phony temporary work permits sponsored by Oshoa's ranch.

Koa guessed the deaths grew out of the Campbells' blackmail scheme. Gwendolyn had stolen CIA files and had been using them to blackmail somebody. Koa saw no other way to explain $600,000 a year tucked inside deliveries from the Dowlong outfit in Hong Kong. Arthur must have been in on the extortion scheme. That would explain why he'd been tortured. And the tough SOB had not revealed a thing. Otherwise, why would anyone toss the Campbell house? And why would Chavez send his ranch hand to spy on police activity around the Campbell property?

Yet, the Campbell blackmail gambit had been rolling along like a luxury car for more than a decade before something happened to make the transmission fall out. Koa couldn't fathom what had changed, but somehow the Campbells had pissed off the wrong person, and the *kepala*—the headman—had sent his goons in to neutralize them and their secrets. Mrs. Furgeson's tape told that part of the story.

Koa saw three avenues to pursue—identify the *kepala*, discover the secret, or figure out what motivated the players to veer off course after a decade in equilibrium. The path to the mastermind led to or through one of three people at the ranch—Oshoa, Ortega, or Chavez. Although logic pointed to Oshoa, Koa doubted that the savvy billionaire would allow his name and ranch to be tied so openly to a murder plot. Koa couldn't see Oshoa using killers so easily traced back to his ranch. That left Ortega and Chavez. The *paniolo* had clearly lied, but was he so stupid he'd forge his own name when importing killers? Maybe, but cowboys didn't run big operations for men like Oshoa by being stupid. The left Ortega, but she hadn't even been an Oshoa employee when Campbell bought the property. Could someone else at Oshoa's ranch be the *kepala* or the *kepala's* agent?

The secret had to be a Delta Force or CIA secret and it most likely came from Kosovo, the place where the strange Campbell pair had last been stationed before disappearing. Alderson, the CIA man, had all but confirmed as much. And Koa was prepared to bet his Escher lithographs that the secret was buried someplace on the Campbell property.

The thing that had changed and triggered the murders was the most puzzling part of all. Why had the blackmail scheme come unraveled? Had the Campbells upped the price? It didn't seem likely. Six hundred grand was a fortune in rural Hawai'i and, except for the orchid farm, the Campbells had lived on the edge of poverty. Koa couldn't see them demanding increased payments after collecting more than six million over the preceding decade. Nor would they have been likely to risk their one-percenter income by threatening to expose whomever they'd been blackmailing. Still, something—something big—had changed, prompting a nasty double murder.

CHAPTER NINETEEN

THE CORONER DEFAULTED on his promise to check for torture marks on Arthur Campbell's body. Nor did he return Koa's telephone calls. Years earlier, after many disasters with Shizuo, Koa had begun a dossier on the coroner's many screw-ups. Suppressing his anger, he pulled out the file and added the obstetrician's latest default to the list. Someday the county would swap Shizuo for a real coroner, hopefully before Koa himself gave up his shield.

For what seemed like the thousandth time since he'd joined the police, Koa trooped over to Hilo Medical to find the arrogant doctor. Not surprisingly, he waited twenty minutes for Shizuo to finish delivering a baby.

He confronted Shizuo in his delivery room scrubs before he'd even removed his mask. "Shizuo, you promised me a report on Arthur Campbell's injuries."

The baby doctor looked genuinely surprised. "It's over."

"So, you finished the autopsy work?"

"No, no. The file is over, done, closed, gone away."

Koa wanted to scream. "What do you mean, it's closed?"

"The national security men, they came last night. Two of them, they had national security credentials."

"Were they Asian?" Koa asked, thinking the two Indonesians might have snookered Shizuo.

Shizuo became agitated. "No, no . . . Americans from the Defense Department. They had badges and Defense Department identity cards with a government seal."

"What did they tell you, Dr. Hiro?" Koa knew from experience that using Shizuo's formal medical title calmed the man.

"The file is secret, a national security secret. I'm ordered to stop all autopsy work."

"Describe them."

"One tall, maybe six feet. The other shorter, maybe five seven. Both American from the mainland. No distinguishing marks I could see."

Koa marveled, not for the first time, how anyone, let alone a medical officer, could give such a useless description. "What about the autopsy? Did you find torture marks on Arthur Campbell's body?"

"Yes, but I cannot show you."

"What do you mean, 'you can't show me'?" Despite his efforts at restraint, impatience again crept into Koa's voice.

"They took my photographs, my X-rays, my files . . . everything. And the body, too. They took Arthur Campbell's body,"

"Why didn't you call me?"

"They told me not to tell anyone."

As he walked out of the hospital, stunned over the unexpected development, Koa's cell sounded. The screen showed an unfamiliar number with a Hawai'i Volcanoes National Park prefix, and Koa wondered if Nālani was calling from a landline. He swallowed his disappointment as a gruff voice said, "Detective Kāne." It was the park superintendent.

"Something just happened you should know. Two men showed up at the park headquarters, asking about the body out near Royal Gardens. Claimed to be federal agents. Demanded to interview Mano, one of the Volcano Observatory guys who found the body.

Said it was some kind of national security investigation. You know anything about this?"

"No." Koa stopped to think. They had to be the same two guys who'd taken Shizuo's files. "Did they interview Mano?"

"Yeah. Acted like a couple of assholes. Scared him pretty bad, and he's plenty tough."

"Are these two dudes still at the park?"

"No, they left about five minutes ago."

"Thanks for the heads-up."

"No problem." The line went dead.

* * *

Driving back to police headquarters, Koa tried to make sense of the situation. The two federal agents—if that's who they really were—hadn't checked in with the police. Instead, they'd gone after Shizuo, the medical records, and the body. Then they'd interviewed the Volcano Observatory tech who'd discovered the body. Weird. Seizing evidence and obstructing his murder investigation. He'd often seen the feds act like arrogant pricks, but nothing in his experience prepared him for this kind of nonsense.

He called Zeke and shared the details of his conversations with Shizuo and the park superintendent, provoking a swearing fit from the prosecutor. "They did what? Who are those bozos? How dare the fuckin' feds interfere with a state murder investigation! Arrest the bastards. I'll indict their goddamn asses."

When Zeke finally ran out of steam, Koa asked if federal agents really could usurp his state murder investigation.

"Hell, no," Zeke responded. "The Tenth Amendment to the Constitution preserves the traditional power of the states to prosecute their own criminal cases. And the federal courts rarely curtail any state criminal investigation."

Hanging up, Koa asked himself what the supposed agents would do next. Their next logical step would be the Campbell house. Perhaps he could surprise them.

He took Sergeant Basa with two patrolmen and directed the officers to shut down their emergency sirens and lights when they turned off the Belt Highway onto the lane where the accident had occurred. Four miles later, they wound their way up the dirt track through the forest to the Campbell house, where Koa spotted a gray Chevy Caprice. He'd guessed right. The federal agents were ransacking the Campbell house.

Koa and his team stopped fifty yards from the house, blocking the access track. They crept though the woods to the front of the house. Koa left Sergeant Basa and the patrolmen outside before tiptoeing up the steps. The entry door, where the yellow crime-scene tape had been torn away, stood open. Koa caught sight of a tall man sorting through a pile of drawings and other papers in the artist's studio.

"What do you think you're doing here?" Koa demanded, stepping through the door.

The man, caught unaware, whirled around. For an instant, Koa thought the man might pull a gun, but his hands dropped to his sides. "Federal agent Christopher, and the question is, what are *you* doing here?"

"I'm Chief Detective Koa Kāne, Hawai'i County Police. This is my crime scene, and I'd like to see your identification."

"Bill Christopher." The agent stuck out a hand. "We're here on a matter of national security."

Koa avoided the agent's outstretched hand. "Your credentials, please, Mr. Christopher." With arrogant slowness the agent withdrew his hand, reached into his jacket, flipped open a leather wallet, and flashed a gold badge along with an identification card. The agent started to close the wallet when Koa took it from him.

"Agent William Christopher, Defense Intelligence Agency," Koa read from the identification card. "You have a search warrant for these premises?"

"We don't need a warrant under the Patriot Act. You need to clear out and let us do our work."

"I don't think so." Koa spoke slowly, emphasizing each word.

"You're interfering with a national security investigation. That's a federal crime."

"And you're interfering with a state murder investigation. That's a state crime, Agent Christopher."

"You've already solved your murder case. Too bad you let those two Indonesians, Bambang and Sudomo, outsmart you. Now you've got to rely on the FBI and Interpol. Good luck."

Christopher's statement caught Koa off guard. How did the man know about the Indonesians?

"Those two were contract killers. I want the mastermind who hired them."

The agent turned away from Koa. "George," he yelled, "you need to come down here. We've got a small-time cop trying to interfere."

Koa heard footsteps, and the shorter agent came down the stairs, taking a position to the right of his partner. Their aggressive stance aimed to intimidate, but Koa had faced worse.

"Introduce yourself, George," Christopher directed.

"George Nixon, Defense Intelligence Agency."

Agent Christopher continued. "Like I told you, we're federal agents dealing with a national security matter of vital importance. Now either you let us work, or we'll arrest you."

"Arrest me?" Koa said. "Not a chance. Now, why don't you two *agents* tell me why you're running around behind my back screwing up my murder investigation?"

"We warned you," Christopher said, and the two agents moved forward.

Koa whistled and stepped to the side, allowing Sergeant Basa and the two patrolmen to rush past him and confront the two interlopers. Koa savored the look of shock on the agents' faces. "Now, would you like to tell me what this is all about?" Koa said evenly.

Silence.

Koa reflected on their possible mission. These DIA agents had to be on Arthur Campbell's trail. "You're here because of the Delta Force guy's prints I sent to the Bureau." Koa detected raised eyebrows and a flash of surprise in Christopher's eyes, but the agent said nothing.

Koa smiled. "You cooperate, I might be able to help you find what your man took when he disappeared from Kosovo in 1999."

George Nixon took a step forward, and Christopher tensed. "I don't know what you're talking about," Christopher said.

Koa heard the words and understood exactly the opposite. They weren't going to answer his questions, but Christopher was as easy to read as a stop sign. His reactions gave away what he sought to hide. "Don't bullshit me," Koa said, watching Christopher's eyes. "Your missing Delta Force operative and his Chinese girlfriend stole the family jewels during the Kosovo war."

Christopher had steeled himself, but his facial muscles still tensed. He took the bait. "What do you know about Kosovo?"

Koa smiled. "You help me, I help you. Otherwise, get the hell outta my crime scene."

"Damn it. You're fucking with a national security matter. You fucking well better tell us what you know."

There was something fake about the two purposed agents. Their approach, rooting around like wild boars, exceeded anything Koa had ever experienced in dealing with even the most obnoxious federal officers. He also found it odd that these supposed DIA agents weren't coordinating with the CIA. Alderson, he knew because of Admiral Cunningham, had backing at the highest levels, but that only made these overbearing characters seem less authentic. He decided he'd had enough. "Sergeant Basa, will you please escort these gentlemen out of the house?"

"You're making a big mistake," Agent Christopher protested, "a career-ending mistake."

"Get 'em out, Sergeant Basa," Koa ordered as he walked down the steps. The patrolmen herded the DIA agents into the yard, where Koa again confronted them. "This house is a crime scene. You gentlemen will stay out until you have a warrant issued by a judge in this jurisdiction. And there'll be a police guard posted to ensure that you don't come back without proper authorization. Understand?" Koa headed back toward his Explorer.

"You're making a mistake," Christopher repeated.

Koa stopped, turned slowly toward the agents. "You threaten me on my turf, I'll put you behind bars."

CHAPTER TWENTY

"WHY THE HELL didn't you keep me in the loop?" Chief Lannua's words hung like a quivering arrow in the air. Koa faced his immaculately uniformed chief across the chief's wide desk. "Why the hell did you act on your own? That's what I want to know." Koa generally enjoyed a decent rapport with Chief Lannua, but deep anger now flared in the chief's eyes.

"Those two guys disrupted a crime scene. I acted in accordance with police regulations." Koa struggled to keep his voice respectful.

"They identified themselves as federal agents, didn't they?" The chief's voice had a hard edge.

"Yes, but they had no right to break into a posted crime scene."

"You could have called me from the Campbell house," the chief said, raising his voice. "You could have asked for instructions." The chief almost never involved himself in the details of cases unless they became political. So, Koa thought, there had to be a political angle to the two DIA boys.

"They acted weird, refusing to explain, and began threatening—"

"They're federal agents, for God's sake!"

The normally soft-spoken chief's anger puzzled Koa. He couldn't figure out why the chief cared so much. What was it about these two so-called federal agents? "Chief," he said, trying to calm his boss down, "they didn't act like federal agents. They didn't coordinate with us, and they went around taking evidence and threatening witnesses. The FBI always—"

"They're not FBI. They're Defense Intelligence officers. You saw their credentials."

"Yes, but—"

"But what?"

"They didn't have a warrant."

"Law enforcement officers don't always need a warrant, especially under the Patriot Act."

"I talked with Zeke Brown and he confirmed—"

Koa realized his mistake before the chief began screaming.

"You briefed the fuckin' prosecutor, but you didn't think to tell your boss! Who do you think you work for?"

Koa coordinated with Zeke all the time on warrants, investigations, and criminal trials. He didn't brief the chief every time he talked to Zeke. "I wanted to check them out. There's something off, unreal—"

"They're real." The chief slammed his fist down on his desk. "Too damn real. Their boss called the mayor and burned his ass."

So that was it. Christopher had warned him, but Koa hadn't been impressed. Apparently, the asshole had clout. Stranger and stranger. "Their boss?"

"The deputy director of the Defense Intelligence Agency. He threatened to send military police in here."

That revelation stunned Koa. "Threatened military action?"

"They warned you. They told you they were dealing with a sensitive national security matter." The chief lowered his voice, but it still had an icy edge.

Koa wasn't backing down. "And we're dealing with two murders, one where the killers tortured the victim and another involving the theft of a county vehicle and a bomb that nearly killed a county firefighter."

"Give it up. They're taking over the Arthur Campbell case."

"What's their jurisdiction?" Koa asked.

"They're federal officers. Hawai'i is part of the United States. National defense is a federal matter with nationwide jurisdiction."

"But we have jurisdiction over killings committed in the county," Koa argued.

"Well, we're not going to exercise it."

What the hell? "Chief, we're talking about murders. Two murders, here in Hawai'i. In our jurisdiction. With all due respect, I think you're making a mistake."

"Well, I don't, and it's my decision to make."

"And so, nobody stands up for these two victims?"

"You've identified the killers, these two Indonesians."

"They're just contract killers—"

"You don't know that."

"I've got a tape of them talking about their *kepala*, their boss, the guy who ordered the killings."

"If that's true," the chief responded, "the DIA agents will get him."

"So I'm supposed to give up the investigation, give up any effort to prove the Indonesians were working for someone?"

"That's exactly what you're going to do, and you're going to give them everything you have on the Arthur Campbell case. Everything. That's an order."

Koa felt his heart rate spike and his face get red. He bore the scars of the exploding car and had been face-to-face with Arthur's tortured body. He owned the case, and the chief was wrong to shut him down. Pissed as hell, Koa got up to leave the office, but the chief stopped him. "I'm not done yet." Koa kept his face stern, though his anger wanted to burst through his skin. "Don't let me catch you meddling in departmental personnel affairs again."

Koa felt his brow furrow. "What are you talking about?"

"A delegation of patrolmen came to see me about reinstating Smithy down in dispatch."

"What's that have to do with me?" Koa asked.

"Don't play games. I know about your meeting with Smithy. You and your chum Basa better stop agitating for him."

"I haven't done a thing, Chief, except meet with him when he came to see me," Koa said, regaining his calm. As least with Smithy he knew the lay of the land. The chief was playing politics, and with the upcoming election, Lannua's lickspittle behavior was out of control. He was sacrificing the department for his own political gain. Koa couldn't resist even in the face of the chief's anger. "You could boost morale and make points with the troops, by reinstating Smithy."

"Butt out. Don't tell me how to run this department," Lannua said without a hint of compassion. "And one other thing. I told you Raul Oshoa had big-time political connections. You were supposed to handle him with a light hand."

"That's what I did, and he cooperated."

"That's not what Chavez, his ranch manager, said when he complained to the mayor."

* * *

Word of Koa's confrontation with the chief went viral through the department. Sergeant Basa appeared in Koa's office minutes later, closing the door behind him. "I'm sorry, boss. I heard the chief shit all over you."

Koa grimaced. "Yeah, he did. Worst I've seen from him."

"That bad?"

"Yeah. Some jerk in the Pentagon—the Pentagon, for chrissakes—called the mayor and crapped all over him. Shit flows downhill, so the chief got burned, and I got dumped straight into the toilet."

"You gonna be okay? I mean, he didn't ask for your badge or anything, did he?"

"No. He just ordered me to give up the Arthur Campbell case."

"Jesus!"

Basa looked concerned. They'd worked together for years. He'd been with Koa on politically sensitive cases, going toe to toe with the mayor and the chief. And he knew how tenaciously Koa pursued criminals. Koa wasn't surprised when Basa asked, "You're not giving up, are you?"

"No. I'm not giving up the Campbell murders, not to those two DIA assholes. I talked to them out at the Campbell place. They're amateurs—obnoxious, heavy-handed amateurs. And they're not here to solve murders; they're here for something else, something I don't understand."

"Be careful," Basa advised. "The chief is already climbing the walls."

"Hey, I'm good at my job. I can get another one by making a few phone calls."

"Christ, you can't be serious."

"Dead serious. My gut says there's something smelly about these DIA spooks. A man gets tortured and a woman burned to death. Whether they were good people or bad, no one deserves to die that way. But these DIA goons don't give a rat's ass. They aren't looking for justice. I don't know what they're doing, but it has nothing to do with finding the truth. Someone needs to find justice for Arthur and Gwendolyn, whoever they were."

Basa, loyal as ever, offered, "I'll cover your back anytime you need me."

"Thanks." When Koa thought about it, every officer on the force knew what was right and wrong in this case. "You can do one thing."

"Name it."

"When Christopher and his sidekick show up, cooperate but stick to the hard facts. No speculation, no guesses, no volunteering. Let them figure out the Oshoa connection and the orchid farm all by themselves."

The sergeant grinned. "It'll be a friggin' pleasure."

"Thanks, Basa." Koa patted him on the shoulder. "Oh, and be careful. The chief thinks the two of us are agitating for Smithy. He warned me off."

Basa wasn't cowed. "He can go fuck himself."

They were interrupted by a door-rattling knock. Koa rubbed his eyes and took a deep breath, summoning reserves of energy and adrenaline. After a moment, he opened the door to see Agent Christopher with his partner standing in the hallway. Koa wanted to punch the son of a bitch in the jaw but restrained his rage. He'd play nice until he found an opportunity to shaft the assholes.

"Got a minute?"

"Sure, we were just finishing up."

Basa left and Koa dropped into the chair behind his desk. The two agents took the chairs opposite. Koa expected Agent Christopher to be overbearing, but the man took a softer tone.

"We got off on the wrong foot. Can we let bygones go and do this professionally?"

"Sure," Koa said, but he didn't trust these dudes and wasn't conned by their "soft-shoe" routine. He had no intention to forgive and every intention to even the score.

"I assume your chief has put you in the picture?"

So that's why they were being nice. Well, he'd cooperate while pursuing his own agenda. Koa, aware the federal criminal code made it a crime to lie to a government agent acting in an official capacity, made only truthful statements, albeit limited ones. He outlined the call from the rangers, the location of the body, and the forensic evidence at the crime scene. He described the fieldwork leading to the Campbell house, and the identification of Arthur Campbell based on the bedroom portrait and DNA matching the samples found in the house. Because they had already confiscated Shizuo's files, Koa left out the discovery of Mo's "Chinese house." They had the body. Let them figure out the cigarette burns and the missing left hand.

Koa gave them as little as possible beyond what they already knew. They didn't ask, and he didn't volunteer information about the ownership of the Campbell house, the existence or ownership of the adjoining 240-acre orchid farm, or his conversations with the South Mauna Loa Farms people. Most important, he never mentioned the staged accident that killed Gwendolyn Campbell, Mrs. Furgeson's descriptions of the Indonesians, her recording, or the visit from Alderson, the CIA agent.

In the end, Koa gained more information than he gave. The two national security agents asked no questions designed to identify Arthur Campbell's killer. Every question focused on a single topic—the search of Arthur Campbell's property. Had police thoroughly searched the house? Inside and out? Including the crawl space? The attic? The shed? What had they found? Did Arthur Campbell have a safe deposit box? Where did he work? Who were his friends?

Koa had never been so happy to be behind on paperwork. The bare-bones file he turned over to Agent Christopher lacked almost a full week of updates. It contained none of the information Koa had withheld. He'd just make a new file—for his own use.

When the agents left, frustrated, Koa smiled. Plainly, they thought their boss's call to the mayor had relegated Koa to the sidelines, leaving the DIA agents an open field. More to the point, their questions confirmed what he suspected. Arthur Campbell, aka Elian Cervara or whoever hid beneath that alias, had secreted something the DIA agents wanted desperately to recover.

* * *

After the DIA agents left, Koa went to see Zeke. He found the prosecutor with his feet up on his desk and a law book in his lap.

"I've been expecting you." Zeke sported a half grin that told Koa the prosecutor already knew about the blowup with the chief.

"You heard already?" It was like Zeke had eavesdropping devices in every county office, but Koa still marveled at the speed with which news reached the prosecutor's ears.

Zeke nodded. "Tell me the gory details."

"First, we're gonna have to go to plan B on Smithy."

"Oh, why?"

"The chief accused Basa and me of agitating to get Smithy's pink slip withdrawn, and when I suggested he could improve morale by reinstating him, he told me to butt out."

Zeke's grimace conveyed his opinion of that staffing decision. "Some people are their own worst enemies."

Koa outlined his confrontation with the two DIA agents at the Campbell house and Chief Lannua's angry reaction. "I'm not giving up the Arthur Campbell investigation," he ended. "Those two Indonesian goons are contract killers. They have to be, and I'm going to nail whoever hired them. The chief can fire me if he doesn't like it, but I am not caving to political pressure, not from some bureaucratic asshole in Washington."

"There's something weird going down," Zeke said.

Koa felt a surge of relief. "Then you agree with me?"

"Yeah, I agree, but we can't have you exposed. Lannua's let politics scramble his brains, but he still runs the police department."

"So you think I should drop it?"

"Hell, no." Zeke stood, dumping the law book onto the desk. "But we need to give you some cover."

"Like what?" Koa asked.

Zeke gave Koa a conspiratorial smile. "The county charter gives me the power to investigate any crime coming to my attention and the power to appoint such deputies as may be necessary. I'm appointing you a deputy to investigate the murders of both Arthur and Gwendolyn Campbell." Zeke picked up a sheet of paper from his desk and handed it to Koa. "It's official."

Koa studied the paper. "The chief will go ballistic," he warned.

"I'll handle the chief when the time comes. In the meantime, he doesn't need to know about this. That way he won't report it back to the DIA spooks."

CHAPTER TWENTY-ONE

KOA MADE ANOTHER sweep of Wailoa Park, hoping political tempers had cooled, but the marches, speech-making, and vitriol had only increased as the date of the Nihoa rally approached. The event was going to be a nightmare. What, he wondered, had happened to negotiation and compromise, the indispensable ingredients for governing a diverse society. Yet, he appeared to be alone in that belief.

He had just completed a circuit of the park when Basa called. Koa knew something was up from the excitement in the sergeant's voice. "We've got a line on those two Indonesian goons."

"Where?" Koa demanded.

"Ka'ū district, off Ka'alāiki Road north of Na'ālehu and south of Pāhala. After we put out the ABP, patrol officers down in the Ka'ū district started hittin' gas stations. One of the operators spotted the rental SUV, and our boys followed up. Looks like those dudes are holed up in a farmhouse."

An image of Arthur's tortured body flashed through Koa's mind. The Indonesians were deadly. "The Ka'ū cops haven't tried to make an arrest, have they?"

"No. I told 'em to stay back but keep a tight watch."

"Good," Koa said, calculating strategy. The chief notwithstanding, he had all the authority he needed. Zeke had seen to that.

Besides, the chief was on his way to Honolulu, probably for another campaign appearance with Nihoa. Koa focused on tactics, thinking about the location and the brutality of the two murders. "They'll be armed. We're gonna need firepower. Call out a tactical group and have 'em meet us down there."

"What about the bomb guys?" Basa asked.

Koa hesitated, thinking through the probabilities. Sure, the Indonesians still had more acetylene, but they'd have no idea the police knew their location. Once the police showed up, they'd have no time to rig a complicated bomb. "I don't think we'll need them, but let's put 'em on standby just in case."

"You got it," Basa said and left.

Koa kept the Explorer at seventy for nearly the whole sixty-five-mile stretch down south past Pāhala. At the Punaluʻu Bake Shop in Naʻālehu, where Kaʻalāiki Road turned off the Belt Road, Koa met up with Basa, tactical team leader Sergeant Awani, and three other officers from the SWAT team. Awani, formerly a police official in Egypt, had fled his native country after a falling-out with the Islamic government then in power. A wiry man with Middle Eastern coloring, jet-black hair, matching eyes, and a neatly trimmed mustache, he had a wickedly irreverent sense of humor. Koa guessed his blasphemy had contributed to his difficulties.

Koa led the group of police vehicles north on Kaʻalāiki Road for several miles and then toward the ocean on an unmarked dirt road until they spotted a patrol car off the verge in the shade of several ʻōhiʻa trees. Everyone got out and Basa led the group up the side of a small hill. The two Kaʻū patrol officers had staked out a position in the cover of several boulders atop the rise overlooking the farmhouse in the distance.

They were southwest of the Kaʻū desert, downwind from the Kīlauea volcanic vents in a semi-desert area. Sulfurous gases mixed with a hint of smoke from faraway lava fires, creating a noxious smell and irritating the eyes. The omnipresent gases turned the infrequent rains acidic, leaving the ʻōhiʻa shrubs stunted and twisted into demonic shapes. Along with occasional ʻamaʻumaʻu ferns, they provided the only splashes of grayish-green on the otherwise barren landscape.

From his vantage point atop the rise, Koa surveyed the scene through binoculars. Across a wide field of jagged ʻaʻā lava broken only by a handful of ʻamaʻumaʻu ferns, a ramshackle farm building sat at the back of a small bowl-shaped valley. A long, rutted dirt track wound through the rough open field from the dirt trail off Kaʻalāiki Road to a patch of bare ground in front of the building, where a black, late model Chevy Traverse was parked. A stand of grotesquely twisted ʻōhiʻa trees guarded the backside of the dwelling. A curl of smoke rose from the farmhouse chimney, but otherwise Koa saw no movement. The place was so remote Koa doubted the Indonesians could've found it on their own. Someone with an intimate knowledge of the local area must have helped them.

He turned to one of the Kaʻū police officers. "That the Hertz rental?"

"Yes, sir."

"Any activity?"

"Not since we've been here"—the officer checked his watch—"about two hours now."

"What's behind the trees?"

"An old fire road, but not much else."

Koa didn't like the tactical situation. The Indonesians had an ideal defensive position. The open field in front of the farmhouse prevented any concealed approach from that direction. Anyone in the building would see a vehicle or even a person coming within five hundred yards, and a gunman could easily target any police officer in the open. The only sensible approach would be from the rear, and a twenty-yard gap between the edge of the misshapen trees and the back of the house made even that approach risky.

Koa conferred with Sergeant Awani, whose tactical skills Koa respected. They agreed to approach the farmhouse from the rear. Koa and the tactical team would drive up the fire road and sneak through the ʻōhiʻa forest. The stunted trees wouldn't provide much cover, but they would have to suffice. The two Kaʻū policemen would stand by in a concealed position on the dirt trail, ready to block the drive in the event the Indonesians sought to escape in the Chevy. Koa assigned Basa to maintain a watch on the dwelling from their current position. Sergeant Awani distributed voice-activated radio packs, and they agreed on a simple communications protocol.

"Be careful," Koa warned. "These hombres have wasted two people and hospitalized a county firefighter."

Everyone except Basa moved out. Koa and the tactical team, screened by the ʻōhiʻa forest, drove up the rough fire road and parked two hundred yards behind the farmhouse. Koa pulled a ballistic vest from the back of his Explorer. The tactical team suited up, carrying Colt LE6940 advanced law enforcement carbines with twenty-round magazines, Luepold M6 tactical scopes, and M6X laser illuminators. With practiced skill they crept silently through the sparse forest. As they approached the rear of the old farmhouse, Sergeant Awani sent one two-man team to the left while he and his colleague took the right side. They slipped quietly into semi-protected positions along the tree line behind the building.

Koa scanned the back of the wooden farmhouse, searching the four rear windows. No light came from the building, and nothing moved in the windows. The rear door was shut. No one seemed to be watching. The stench of sulfur filled the blisteringly hot air. An eerie silence hung over the place. Not even a bird chirped.

Koa used the radio to call Basa. "B, this is K, any movement?"

"Nothing, except the smoke is dying."

Koa checked the chimney himself, confirming the fire inside had burned down.

"A, this is K, ready to recon?" Koa asked the SWAT team leader.

"Affirmative," Awani responded. While two of the four tactical team members covered their colleagues from the tree line, Awani and one of his guys broke cover, and crouching low, sprinted for opposite corners at the rear of the building. Nothing moved in the house as the two men reached the shadow of the building and hugged the wall. Awani moved slowly across the back, checking windows while the other man disappeared around a corner to examine the side and front windows.

Their reports came back to Koa: dark inside, nothing moving, can't see anything, nothing, nothing, no sound inside, nothing. Koa held his breath until the second man completed his circuit of the house and returned to the back.

"Team two, move up," Awani ordered, and the two additional members of the tactical team sprinted to the house and flattened themselves against the wall. "Team two, front door. Team one, rear door. Coordinated entry assault. Signal when ready." The members of the second team disappeared around opposite corners of the building, while Awani and his backup took up positions on either side of the rear door.

They'd reached the point of forced entry, the most dangerous point in any hostile takedown. Koa felt a prickle of unease. What was going on? They'd been on-site nearly ninety minutes with no activity. The local cops had been present even longer. He tried to imagine what the Indonesians might be doing inside. Koa looked at his watch—one thirty in the afternoon. Unlikely the Indonesians would be asleep. Perhaps they were lying in wait, ready to blast the officers as they entered.

His unease blossomed into anxiety. Things were much too quiet. It occurred to him the Indonesians might have fled sometime earlier, leaving a fire burning in the fireplace. No activity for more than three hours. Almost no smoke came from the chimney. But the SUV, the Chevy Traverse, still sat out front.

What if the Indonesians had another vehicle? That would mean they'd left hours ago. God only knew what they'd left inside the farmhouse. Maybe two tanks of acetylene? With a detonator? Pictures flashed through Koa's mind: a brown car under a yellow county truck, the horrific scream, a flash, a pink balloon in a wire frame drawing, a massive explosion under the front of the dump truck, Mike Tolman flat on the ground.

"Ready," team two reported from the front door.

Awani exchanged nods with his team member at the rear door. Awani keyed his communicator. "On my command—"

Nālani's words roared in Koa's ears: Be careful and think about us when you're out there.

"Abort! Abort! Abort!" Koa yelled both aloud and into the radio net.

Awani, who was about to kick the rear door open, turned, looking at Koa. "What the fuck?" he mouthed.

Koa waved him back away from the house. "It's too quiet. It's booby trapped!" Koa yelled. "Get your people back. Take up covering positions."

Koa called the bomb squad. During the long wait for the experts to arrive, Koa retreated through the trees to the fire road. He checked for tracks, starting from the parked police vehicles and heading gradually deeper into the forest. He had gone less than three hundred yards when he found an area of crushed grass. Koa guessed the Indonesians had escaped using a second vehicle, probably not long after the police had located the rented SUV on the isolated farm. Someone had tipped off the Indonesians to the impending police raid.

Koa asked Basa to renew the APB for the Indonesians and arrange for his troops back in Hilo to start recanvassing the car rental companies.

Koa had an awful feeling about what the bomb boys would find inside the farmhouse. The squad used optical fibers with tiny video lenses slipped through cracks under the doors to peer inside the building. What they saw scared the bejesus out of every officer present. Both entry doors and each of the windows had been rigged with tripwires connected to what appeared to be a detonator atop a large polyurethane balloon.

"What's in the balloon?" Sergeant Awani asked.

"I'm betting it's acetylene," Koa answered, surprising even the seasoned bomb experts.

"Holy Mother of God," Awani swore, "that shit would have taken out my whole team. How'd you know?"

"It's the same MO they used to kill Gwendolyn Campbell," Koa explained. "And it shows the bastards were targeting first responders."

Awani's men, guided by bomb experts and dressed in massive protective suits, used a chain saw to cut an entry hole through the side of the building. Then one of the bomb specialists suited up and waddled into the house to disarm the detonator. The process took hours, and night had fallen before the crime-scene techs finally entered the house. Perhaps because the Indonesians hadn't expected the building to survive, the police found a ton of evidence. Two bodies had left their impressions on bunk beds. Puddles of water in an old cast-iron bathtub evidenced recent use. They found fingerprints galore. One of the crime-scene techs even discovered a dog-eared land plan, showing both the Campbell house property and the rear parcel.

A little after midnight, as Koa and Basa made their way back toward Hilo, Basa asked, "Aren't you worried about the chief? I mean, with all the people involved in this clusterfuck, he must've heard something. I'm surprised he hasn't chewed your ass again and maybe mine, too."

"The chief's in Honolulu, cozying up to Nihoa like they're about to get married." Given Zeke's warning, Koa didn't explain that as a duly appointed deputy prosecutor he could flaunt the chief's order to give up the Campbell investigation.

"Still," Basa protested, "he must be in touch with the headquarters staff."

"Probably, but I'm guessing he's too busy kissing political ass. There's something weird going down with the chief. Politics is one thing but blocking a murder investigation is off the chart." Koa paused. "But, there's something else that's been bugging me all afternoon. Those two goons bolted out of the farmhouse this morning. Even if they'd prepped the acetylene in advance, they must've had at least an hour's warning. How the hell did they know?"

CHAPTER TWENTY-TWO

WHEN KOA, BLEARY-EYED and dragging from the tension of the raid, parked in front of his Volcano cottage two hours past midnight, light streamed from the windows. His heart rate spiked. Nālani must still be up, and tired as he was, he rejoiced at the prospect of seeing her. He'd been high on activity for the past twenty-four hours, but even in the maelstrom of the double murder investigation, her words—*be careful and think of us*—had saved his colleagues and maybe even his own life. The intensity of feeling surprised him, and he hurried toward the door.

He opened the door to find her curled up on the couch watching *Casablanca* on cable TV. Light from the TV reflected in her black eyes, and her shoulder-length black hair seemed longer than he remembered. She wore one of his old tee-shirts, pulled down over her knees, and the outline of her nipples telegraphed the absence of a bra. He wondered if she had anything at all under the tee-shirt and felt an unexpected surge of love for her.

With a tiny crooked smile, she said, "I've been waiting for you." She rose from the couch. He stepped forward, and their bodies met in a hungry embrace.

* * *

The death trap at the farmhouse bugged Koa. The police had located the Indonesians at their hideout only the previous morning. They'd initiated the raid immediately. Someone had tipped off the Indonesians—probably just as Koa had ordered up the tactical team. The bad guys had slipped out the back, moved through the woods, and escaped in another car, most likely while the Kaʻū cops focused on the front of the house.

The timing left only four possibilities. A cop could have alerted the Indonesians. Koa rejected that possibility. None of the cops had any motive to help the Indonesians, and all the cops who'd known about the raid had been present. No cop would tip off killers only to risk death in the ensuing trap. The Kaʻū cops could've blown the surveillance, but based on their reports and seeing them in action, he doubted the Indonesians had spotted the local cops. Someone could be tailing him, but Koa would have caught some whiff of any tail. Or, the bad guys might have some form of electronic surveillance.

He thought again about Faizon, spying on him at the orchid farm. Most likely, he, too, had been tipped to Koa's presence only after he had arrived at the Campbell house. Only Basa and Maru had known his location, and Koa doubted they'd been tailed. Putting the two episodes together, he felt sure someone had him under electronic surveillance.

Who, he puzzled, would bug the cops? They'd traced Faizon back to Oshoa's farm. Chavez's explanation had been dodgy. Koa dismissed Chavez's story that Faizon had been checking the property for fire hazards. Faizon had fled even after Koa identified himself as a police officer.

Oshoa and his people had the wherewithal to set up bugging equipment. So, too, did the odd pair of DIA spooks. Although he'd been surprised the DIA agents had known about the Indonesians, he couldn't fathom why the DIA boys would aid the killers. Koa also supposed it could be the CIA, although that seemed doubtful.

Given the chief's orders, he didn't want to use police department resources to check for listening devices. Besides, given departmental budget limitations, Koa doubted Cap Roberts's crime-scene guys had the necessary know-how, especially if he was dealing with something sophisticated, as the DIA or the CIA would use.

Koa knew whom to call. In his time on the force, he'd collected a lot of chits, including one from a former CIA electronics guru, Joe Po, who now ran a spy shop in Honolulu. Joe had breached trespass and eavesdropping laws in his overzealous pursuit of a Ponzi scheme gone awry. Koa had overlooked the violations because Joe had rooted out a fraud, and Joe was now in Koa's debt. Pretty deep in Koa's debt. Besides, the former spook got his kicks playing cops and robbers. When working with Koa, Joe typically waved his usual fees, and Koa covered his out-of-pocket expenses from a police discretionary fund used mostly to pay informers.

Koa made the call, and Joe agreed to fly to Hilo. "You remember me, I'll be the short fat dude getting off the aircraft," Joe promised in his thick Louisiana drawl. Koa smiled. How could he forget the three-hundred-pound former spook? Joe barely topped five feet while sporting a forty-six-inch belt.

"Hate those fuckin' airplane squats," served as Po's only greeting as they shook hands at the airport. Joe retrieved his goody bag from baggage claim, and they walked out toward Koa's Explorer.

Joe stopped him about ten feet from the vehicle. "Let's check this jalopy before we go tooling around."

"You really don't think—"

"Thinkin' don't find no bugs," Joe interrupted. He opened his bag, extracted a pair of headphones, assembled a wand-like device, and slid it under the vehicle. He moved the wand around the undercarriage, adjusted a dial on the wand, and repeated the maneuver. After

Koa opened the door, he used the wand to scan the interior of the vehicle. Satisfied that the car wasn't bugged, Joe repacked his gear.

"There are two places we need to check," Koa explained, "my home and my office. You want to start with my home?"

"Lead the way, Luke Skywalker." Koa smiled, knowing from their previous work together that Joe was a Star Wars fanatic.

At Koa's home, Joe unpacked his stuff while Koa retrieved two cold Black Sand Porters. To his surprise, Joe declined. "Never drink on the job. Makes me fat."

For an obese man, Joe moved like Spider-Man, checking telephone lines, hauling himself in and out of the crawl space under the small post-and-beam cottage, and finally hoisting himself into the attic. After nearly a half hour, Joe emerged. He held a finger to his lips, pointed to the front door, and led Koa outside and some distance from the cottage before speaking.

"Y'all are dealin' with some sophisticated fuckers," Joe drawled.

"You found something?"

"Fuckin' A, I found the latest, the greatest, most expensive electronic shit in the whole fuckin' solar system."

"Government stuff?" Koa asked, thinking of the official agents tramping through his life.

"Could be, but not necessarily. Y'all can buy this shit on the market if y'all got the dough. Could be shops on the mainland, but this electronic wizardry, it's all over the fuckin' web. There're thousands of fat cats spying on their wives an' girlfriends an' the broad next door."

"What's it do?"

"It listens. It records. It transmits, not just the fuckin' telephone, but every goddamn sound in the house. That gizmo widget thing-amabob can hear a friggin' mouse pee."

Koa felt his face get hot as realization dawned. Someone had hacked into his most intimate conversations with Nālani and listened like a Peeping Tom to their lovemaking. Then embarrassment turned to outrage with the realization that the Indonesian killers, or someone working with them, had thrust their criminal conspiracy into his home.

He was furious, ready to kill the motherfuckers who'd burglarized his house to plant their electronic shit. They'd endangered Nālani. He was going to have to tell her, and she, too, would have to deal with an invasion of their privacy . . . her most intimate privacy. And he now had to worry about her safety outside the house. The bug in the house meant the killers knew her whereabouts and her schedule.

He speed-dialed her, and she answered on the second ring. He was relieved to hear her voice but didn't want to discuss the illegal bugging with her over the phone. He said he'd be in the area, and they agreed to meet for lunch.

Koa turned back to Joe. "You disable the damned thing?"

"No. I can, but I didn't know if maybe y'all might wanta leave it in place. I mean, y'all could feed the fuckers on the other end some serious shit."

Koa thought about the options. He saw a number of problems, not the least of which was getting Nālani to go along, but Joe's idea had merit. "You're pretty sophisticated yourself, Joe."

"And there's another thing. I need to check your wheels again. I wasn't looking for this kind of electronic shit. I mean, I haven't seen technology like this since I left the company."

Half an hour later, Joe hauled Koa back across the street. He'd found a tracking device attached to the underside of the Explorer. "The fuckin' thing has a burst transmitter. It only broadcasts for six seconds every five minutes." In the end, Joe showed Koa how to disable the devices, but they left both gadgets in place, at least temporarily.

Koa thought about his office. People who'd violate Hawai'i law by bugging the home of a police officer had the balls to plant listening devices in the police headquarters. He had to figure out where to look. "Can you do the police headquarters now?"

"The whole friggin' building?" Joe asked.

Koa pondered Joe's question. Whoever planted the devices had targeted him, and they'd expect anything important to be funneled through him. "No, just my office and phone lines." He hesitated. "Maybe Basa's, too."

"Y'all got access to the telephone closet?"

"I know how to get access."

"Then I can do it."

They found bugs in Koa's office and on his telephone line. After establishing the devices couldn't overhear activities in other parts of the department, they left the bugs in place. Koa wondered just how the culprits had secured access to police headquarters. A phony janitor could have entered his office, but the telephone closet had been locked and the keys kept in a safe. Had it been an inside job? Had someone bribed their way into the restricted space? Was some police officer on the take?

* * *

Koa and Nālani only rarely met for lunch, and he cherished those moments. Not so this time. He approached their meeting with concern bordering on dread because he'd have to tell her that his job had gotten their life hacked by a pair of brutal killers. He'd rather fight with the chief than deliver such news to Nālani.

He got meals to go—a plate lunch for himself and a fish taco, with extra salsa, for Nālani. They met at the picnic area off the Mauna Loa strip road in the national park. Full of old *koa* trees and all variety of native birds, it was one of their favorite spots. But it might not remain so after this lunch. She'd already settled at a table when he arrived. His stomach churned as he parked the car and joined her.

He couldn't find the right moment to raise the awful subject until Nālani finally said, "Something's bothering you. Out with it."

He told her everything, and then added, "I'm so sorry my job has invaded our life together."

She was quiet for a time, and he watched her experience the same reactions he'd felt when Joe first revealed the existence of the bug. Her silence drove him close to despair as he feared the worst. Then, she looked straight into his eyes. "You've got to stop these bastards."

He'd expected her to be angry at him and fearful for her own privacy and safety, but he was wrong. "You're not angry with me?"

"No, of course not. I'm angry at the people who did this, and I want them to pay."

A huge wave of relief washed over him, giving him the fortitude to forge ahead. "Could you live with the bugging device for a few more days?"

Confusion clouded Nālani's face until it registered. "So we can beat these bastards at their own game?"

CHAPTER TWENTY-THREE

KOA WALKED OUT of the police station around noon to find a paper folded under the windshield wiper of his Explorer. He read: "I need to speak to you in private about AC and GC. Today, 3 pm, Martha's dress shop. Come alone." The note was signed "A."

A hoax? Not likely. A trap set by the DIA spooks? Koa studied the note. No, the spooks would be more sophisticated. And he couldn't see Christopher, the obnoxious federal agent, setting up a rendezvous in a dress shop.

In times past, he might have gone alone, but Nālani's words and the near miss at the bobby-trapped farmhouse made him more cautious. Besides, he couldn't take his Explorer with the tracker still attached. He decided to take Piki and have him wait nearby. They took Piki's wheels and drove around Hilo, making sure they weren't followed before heading to Martha's. It stood at the end of a 1920s shopping arcade with a covered sidewalk. They watched the place, checking both front and back, for an hour before he entered, alone. An old Chinese woman sat by herself behind the counter reading *Vogue China*. He looked around, wondering who'd asked to meet him.

"Detective Kāne?"

He turned to face the old woman. "Yes."

"In the back." The woman's eyes flicked to a curtained doorway before returning to her magazine.

Koa stepped through a beaded curtain to find an attractive, professionally dressed woman in her late thirties or early forties with long lustrous black hair sitting at a small round table. An open law book lay facedown on the table beside a giant black cat with phosphorescent green eyes. He noted a rear exit he'd seen from the outside, but nothing to cause him alarm.

"Thank you for coming," she said in a musical cadence blessed with the tiniest of smiles. "You must think my invite bizarre."

"A bit . . . Ms.?"

"Alexia Sheppard." Her green eyes, matching those of the cat, seemed to twinkle at the prospect of sharing her story. She was pretty—that was his first impression—and her intelligent expression drew him in, intensifying his interest. "You'll find my tale more than a bit strange."

He took the chair across the table from her. "I'm listening."

"I'm a lawyer here in Hilo," she began. That, Koa knew, meant she had a general practice, doing everything from wills to criminal cases. It was the only way to earn a living in the local legal community. "I've been in practice here in Hilo since 1999. When I first hung out my shingle, Arthur Campbell—I'll call him Arthur, but that's not his real name—came to my office. He asked me to do three things—incorporate a flower business, handle certain financial transactions, and maintain custody of an envelope." She gently stroked the black cat as her words poured out in a lyrical, almost hypnotic, cadence.

Her voice captivated Koa. He imagined her charming a jury with those musical tones and huge green eyes.

"I sensed something peculiar about my visitor, but a newbie lawyer needs clients. I wouldn't accept such a client today, but back then I agreed to represent Arthur with some reservations." She tilted her head as if gathering her thoughts.

"I set up his flower business, although I don't think he had many customers. The financial transactions gave me pause. I sought advice from my father."

Her words flipped a switch in Koa's mind. Alexia was Samuel Sheppard's daughter. Everyone in Hilo knew the Sheppard name. Her old man, a lawyer, real estate mogul, and leading local philanthropist, had been a legend in the community. So Sam Sheppard had set his daughter up in a law practice in Hilo.

"Ultimately, I declined to handle his financial transactions, telling him no reputable lawyer would do as he requested." Koa felt an urge to interrupt with questions but restrained himself. Let her tell her story in her own manner. He almost always got more out of a witness by letting them speak freely. He never ceased to be amazed by the things some people let slip. There'd always be time for questions.

"Custody of his envelope presented no ethical issue, but to protect myself against competing claimants, I insisted upon proof of his true identity. He resisted, but, after swearing me to secrecy, ultimately agreed." The black cat rubbed its face against her arm.

"He told me to keep the envelope in a safe deposit box. Initially, I was to give it to his girlfriend, Gwendolyn, in case of his death. Then, about a month ago, he came to my office upset, agitated, and I'd say, fearful. He'd had a premonition of disaster. He said nothing specific, but I think he feared for his life. I urged him to go to the police, but he refused."

Alexia stared off into space, and Koa guessed she was remembering Arthur. "He changed my instructions. He planned to leave a coded message on an answering machine in my office every day. If he failed to call or provided the wrong code, I was to give the envelope to Gwendolyn immediately.

"The coded messages came every day, like the Hilo rains. But then the messages stopped." The music in Alexia's voice faded. "Gwendolyn contacted me. I gave her the envelope."

"Who—"

"I'm not quite finished," she interrupted. "My legal representation has ended. I've done everything according to my agreements with Arthur Campbell. Then I heard about Gwendolyn's accident. I saw the news stories about the burned body. I got nervous." The cat meowed for attention, and then resumed purring as she stroked its fur.

"Under the code of ethics, I'm duty bound to protect client secrets even after death, unless disclosure is necessary to prevent a crime. Arthur and Gwendolyn are dead. Nothing I might disclose could prevent what's already happened, but then there were other crimes—"

"What crimes?"

"Two men vandalized my office searching my files. I guessed they'd been looking for files on Arthur Campbell. I thought they might also search Arthur's flower business. It, too, was ransacked. I'm not sure what's happening, but I believe I'm justified in telling you what I know about Arthur Campbell."

Koa felt a rush. Most investigations had a moment like this. He'd been sorting through possibilities, guessing at what might have happened, but now he was about to get answers. "That is quite a story. You made the right decision."

"Thank you. I hope my father, if he were still alive, would agree."

Koa made a short nod of acknowledgment toward the famous man. "So tell me, who was Arthur Campbell? What was his real name?"

"Ernesto Sapada, a former captain in Army Delta Force with expertise in counterintelligence. I've a copy of his military identification card." She handed him a Xerox copy.

The face in the picture matched Arthur Campbell's.

"Tell me about Sapada."

"A peculiar man, intense with eyes like black diamonds, always darting, searching for danger. Physically powerful, but astonishingly quick, a man who might break your neck with a flick of his hand. I don't much believe in stereotypes, but Sapada was everyman's idea of a soldier of fortune. He was of second- or third-generation Albanian descent. Not a man to be underestimated."

"How do you know he was Albanian?"

"I asked him. I've always been interested in genealogy. I find it useful in dealing with people, given the diversity of ethnicities in the islands."

"What'd you talk about, other than the legal stuff?"

"Nothing, and very little about legal stuff. I've never met a man of fewer words."

"What about his wife?"

Her mouth twisted. "I'm not sure they were married. I met Gwendolyn twice, once at the beginning so I could identify her in case I had to deliver the envelope. He introduced her as his girlfriend. Then I met her again when she came for the letter. Something had frightened her, scared her to the point of panic."

"You have the envelope?" Koa couldn't keep the hope out of his voice.

"No." She gave him a tiny smile. "I gave it to Gwendolyn and never knew its contents."

"Any guesses?"

"I've often wondered. I'd guess Sapada learned a dangerous secret, and—and this is nothing more than speculation—I'd guess he used that secret for extortion or blackmail."

"You think the letter contained the secret?"

"Maybe, but the envelope was quite thin—only a sheet or two of paper. Most likely, it provided the location of the secret, not the material itself. Or maybe the paper documented the codes for a for-eign bank account."

"Anything support your blackmail guess?"

She looked like she'd expected his question. "I told you Sapada wanted me to handle certain financial transactions."

"Yes."

"He wanted me to accept checks payable to my lawyer's trust ac-count and disburse the funds to him in cash."

"But you refused?"

"Yes. There are lawyers who will launder money, but I'm not one of them."

"The name of the flower business?"

"AC Flowers Ltd. The office is on Pōā Street."

"Does it have a bank account?"

"I don't know. I recommended Sam Naupaka at First Hawaiian."

Koa asked a question he'd been holding back. "Not to be rude, Miss Sheppard, but why would Sapada hire a new lawyer, especially one who refused to handle cash for him?"

"A good question I asked myself. I'd guess he cared more about proper handling of the envelope than anything else, and my family is known for its reliability." She favored him with a tiny smile.

Koa reviewed what he'd learned. Arthur Campbell had tried to enlist Alexia in a money laundering scheme. One part of him was disappointed that she hadn't agreed. Then he might have learned where Arthur had stashed his bankroll and maybe even how he got it. Yet another part of Alexia's story left him puzzled. The envelope to be delivered only upon his disappearance or death meant that Arthur had a secret he'd never shared with Gwendolyn. What might he have been hiding even from his ex-CIA girlfriend?

CHAPTER TWENTY-FOUR

PIKI DROVE KOA to Zeke Brown's office, left his car with his boss, and walked back to police headquarters. The county prosecutor helped Koa draw up a grand jury subpoena for AC Flowers's bank records. Zeke greased the way with Sam Naupaka, a senior vice president of First Hawaiian bank. The banker confirmed the existence of an account in the name of AC Flowers Ltd. and agreed to meet Koa.

Driving Piki's car to avoid being tracked in his own vehicle, Koa headed for the main Hilo branch of First Hawaiian. Sam, a bald-headed Hawaiian in a white button-down shirt, led Koa to his private office. Koa handed him the grand jury subpoena, and Sam pointed to a stack of papers on the conference table. "That's a printout of all the transactions since the account first opened in 1999."

Koa scanned the pages. The debit transactions appeared to be payments for orchid-growing equipment—tens of thousands of dollars, stretching back to late 1999. The credit transactions were cash deposits, typically in amounts of $5,000 at a time, but the number of such deposits caught Koa's attention. Arthur Campbell made a lot of deposits, all less than the $10,000 threshold for reporting transactions to the Treasury. Everything about Campbell was cloak and dagger. "Is this the only account?"

"Well, there's a safe deposit box," Sam responded slowly.

"I need access to that box, Sam."

"We'll have to get a mechanic in here to drill through the client lock."

An hour later, a mechanic drilled the client lock on the AC Flowers safe deposit box. Sam inserted the bank key and slid a long box from its place in the vault.

Three small cases held Army medals: a meritorious conduct medal, a Purple Heart, and a Distinguished Service Cross. Koa's own military service told him anyone who could walk eventually qualified for a meritorious conduct medal. Purple Hearts often signified only minor injuries. The Distinguished Service Cross, however, ranked just below the Congressional Medal of Honor.

Ernesto Sapada, aka Arthur Campbell, must have performed an extraordinary act of heroism under hostile fire to earn a DSC. Such medals usually recognized the recipient for risking his or her life to save fellow soldiers. Koa's commanding officer in the Fifth Special Forces Group had worn the Distinguished Service Cross, and Koa had greatly admired his commander as a giant of a man and an inspiring leader. The military medal changed Koa's opinion of Ernesto Sapada.

He thought again of the severed hand in the blacked-out torture room and the horribly burned body in *Pele*'s playground. A military hero had died a horrible death, suffering a tortured end like Koa's buddy Jerry who'd died in his arms outside the Olympic Hotel in Mogadishu. No man—least of all a DSC recipient—should die like that. Anger flared in Koa's gut.

In addition to the decorations, the safe deposit box also contained multiple false identities—passports, government-issued ID cards, credit cards—each in a different name and nationality. All featured pictures of Ernesto Sapada. Koa claimed no expertise in phony documentation, but the papers appeared to be highly professional.

Accompanying the papers, Koa found bundles of hundred-dollar bills held together by rubber bands. The banker put the cash, at least $100,000, aside to be counted before it was turned over to the prosecutor.

Koa also found a Chinese government–issued card with an electronic stripe, depicting Sapada as a Bulgarian national named Biserka Jugoslav, employed by the Chinese embassy in Belgrade. Koa had been skeptical of Professor Kalo's story that the U.S. had deliberately bombed a Chinese embassy. Not anymore. A Delta Force operative with a DSC was a rarity, but one with false identity papers granting access to a Chinese embassy was one of a kind. The U.S. clandestine services had obviously planned to penetrate the embassy.

Finally, Koa removed the last item, a single sheet of paper folded in thirds. Unfolding it, he stared at the TOP SECRET—SPECIAL ACCESS—EYES ONLY—DESTROY AFTER READING designation stamped across the top and bottom of the page. He knew the import of the warning. He'd found classified military orders, dated May 6, 1999, issued by the U.S.-led NATO Operation Allied Force Command. Simple and straightforward, the document ordered Captain Ernesto Sapada, USA, SN 34287621, to proceed forthwith to execute Operation Golden Sting.

The false passports and the money added little to Koa's knowledge of Arthur Campbell. Koa had long pegged him as a chameleon, moving from alias to alias. The safety deposit box contained his escape kit—the identities and money he'd need to disappear once again if he was forced to evade his pursuers. Only he'd never had the chance.

The military orders, on the other hand, put Arthur inside NATO's Operation Allied Force in Yugoslavia, shortly before his arrival in Hawai'i. The words "Special Access" designated tightly controlled, highly sensitive information. Koa knew the designation from his time in Somalia; it usually covered clandestine intelligence gathering or high-value target snatch-and-kill operations. Equally significant, the date on the orders coincided closely with the May 8–9, 1999, U.S. bombing of the Chinese Belgrade embassy.

According to Professor Kalo, the CIA, not regular NATO forward air controllers, had ordered the bombing of the Chinese embassy. According to CIA agent Alderson, Gwendolyn—or Lan Zwang—a CIA agent in Kosovo, had disappeared in 1999 with sensitive documents, written in Chinese. Sapada's Chinese identity card suggested his involvement in a covert mission to penetrate the Chinese embassy. Koa guessed Arthur and Lan Zwang worked together in Operation Golden Sting to raid the Chinese embassy.

If his speculation was correct, NATO Allied Force commanders ordered Sapada to conduct a clandestine incursion into the Belgrade Chinese embassy simultaneously with the CIA-staged "accidental" bombing. If so, Sapada had been sitting on political dynamite—the kind of material that triggered international incidents and ended the careers of military brass, agency heads, cabinet officers, and maybe even a president.

* * *

That night Koa and Nālani engaged in a charade. Nālani put music on their stereo—"Only Wanta Be With You" from Hootie and the Blowfish, popular when she'd been a teenager. They talked for the benefit of the eavesdroppers about the weather, the birds in the national park, and the upcoming Nihoa political rally, while carrying on a more intimate dialogue by texting each other. After dinner they went for a walk. Nālani had developed an avid interest in the investigation, and Koa felt she deserved to know at least some of the details. So he abandoned his usual policy of separating his job from his personal life.

He told her about the raid at the farmhouse, confessing that she had made him more cautious and probably saved Awani's life, along with those of his colleagues. If she was suspicious that he'd called it too dangerously close, she gave no indication.

They continued their playacting and texting until eleven o'clock, when Koa texted, "Time for sex." Nālani texted back, "Not with an audience." He followed with, "Another walk?" She texted, "*Kapu*"—taboo. They went to bed, and he held her close, cherishing their relationship.

CHAPTER TWENTY-FIVE

FOR KOA, POLITICAL fund-raisers held even less appeal than a colonoscopy. He went to the gathering for Nāinoa Nihoa only because Zeke insisted. Local bankers, lawyers, store owners, and ranchers populated the crowd of about forty at the East Hawai'i Cultural Center.

Koa grabbed a beer from the bar and stood in the corner, surveying the crowd, feeling like the outsider he was. Nihoa, dressed in dark blue slacks and an embroidered Hawaiian shirt, topped with a *maile lei*, chatted with supporters. He appeared at ease, comfortable, and exuded warmth, spending time with each supporter, taking an interest in what they said, asking questions, smiling, and even laughing. A politician.

In his mid-fifties, the gubernatorial candidate carried himself with the bearing expected of a former military officer and exuded a friendly command presence. Few men could project Nihoa's aura of leadership without a hint of intimidation. Koa tried to discern the man's formula. He stood straight, shoulders back, and smiled easily. His face was animated, and his bushy eyebrows somehow softened the almost X-ray quality of his blue eyes.

Koa wondered what undercurrents hid beneath Nihoa's veneer. Everyone, including Koa, had secrets. Most were only minor peccadillos, but Koa's time as chief detective had taught him that many people harbored dangerous pasts. He knew only too well that supposedly honorable people stole, assaulted, raped, and killed. The world, like the Escher drawing on his office wall, was full of reptiles. And whether true or not, Koa placed politicians among the most two-faced of human deviants.

"I didn't know you were a Nihoa supporter."

Koa hadn't seen the chief appear at his side. "I'm apolitical, but Zeke thought I should meet him, since he's likely to be our next governor."

"He'll be a great governor."

"You know him well?" Koa asked.

"A lifetime ago we worked together in the Pentagon, and we've kept in touch over the years. He's smart, honest, and effective. Come on, I'll introduce you."

The chief led Koa into the crowd around the candidate. Nihoa shook with a firm, but not crushing, handshake. The candidate said, "I'm a fan. You solved that observatory case last year. Great detective work."

Koa hid his surprise. Not only did the man possess an extraordinary memory, especially since Koa wasn't on the guest list, but Nihoa also knew how to connect with people on their level. Koa had no doubt the pol would be the next governor.

Raul Oshoa joined the group accompanied by Rachael Ortega, his aide-de-camp. Nihoa greeted the rancher enthusiastically. No surprise there. Any politician would welcome a billionaire with a history of writing campaign checks. The two men discussed cattle prices and the crop damage wrought by the coffee berry borer. Koa again noted the politician's knowledge.

Oshoa's aide stood attentively nearby as the men talked. After their meeting at Oshoa's ranch, Koa had sent Piki to the Internet to research the battle-scarred woman. Born in New Hampshire with an Ivy League degree from Dartmouth College, Ortega had occupied various staff positions on Capitol Hill. Never married, she'd finished her career in public service as a congressional assistant to the House Armed Services Committee before becoming Raul Oshoa's aide in 2000.

Rachael's history puzzled Koa. She'd attributed her unfriendliness at the ranch to the death of her brother in a confrontation with police. That might explain why she'd left Washington. But why would a New England girl take a job for a ranching company in Hawai'i? It seemed a reach too far. Maybe she'd tired of the northeastern winters or maybe Oshoa, himself a political animal, had liked her political connections and offered her a fat salary. Still, her move to Hawai'i seemed odd for a political groupie used to playing in the big leagues. He guessed there was more to her story.

She was heavily made up and wore a clingy, silk sheath, revealing ample cleavage, hardly the woman he'd met at Oshoa's ranch. She cleaned up nicely. He wondered whom she sought to impress. Could she and Oshoa be an item? She seemed an unlikely match for the Cuban billionaire.

He struck up a conversation with her. "Quite a turnout, and it's good to see this historic building put to good use."

"Yes. Nāinoa's impressive. He always draws a crowd." She paused. "This is a historic building?"

"Yes, my predecessor many times removed had his office right over there." He pointed toward the right front corner and gave her a brief history of the structure and the successful community efforts to have it placed on the national register. He saw her eyes dart repeatedly toward Nihoa. At first, he thought his history lesson bored her, but then everything made sense. The makeup, sexy dress, her casual use of Nihoa's first name, her attention to his every move, and even the excited glow in her eyes. She had a crush on the gubernatorial candidate.

Koa doubted it was reciprocal. Nihoa, an attractive, popular politician, with a multimillion-dollar bank account, courtesy of his wealthy wife, had a vast array of opportunities to cheat on his wife. Couples often made strange alliances, but Koa couldn't see this pairing. No amount of wardrobe or cosmetics could put Rachael Ortega in Nihoa's league. He found her imagined romance pathetic.

Still, they obviously had a history, and he wondered how they'd first met. He was about to ask, when a woman screamed and a commotion broke out near the door. Koa pushed his way through the crowd to find two people dressed in skeleton costumes and masks, splashing what appeared to be blood over the guests closest to the door. One of them yelled "Fuck Nihoa."

Koa yelled, "Police! Stop!" and sensed, rather than saw, the crowd moving back, escaping the confrontation. He faced two protesters, but no one, not even the chief, came forward to help. He'd have to remember that.

The skeleton nearest to him turned and swung a blood-filled bucket at Koa's head. Koa ducked and charged the protester, driving a shoulder into the assailant at waist height. His attacker was much slimmer and lighter than he'd expected. A female. She flew backward, released her hold on the pail, smashed into the wall, and collapsed to the floor. Blood spilled everywhere.

"Oh, my God. Oh, my God," the second skeleton, also a woman, screamed. She rushed to the side of her fallen comrade. Blood covered Koa's pants from the knees down, and his shoes stuck to the floor. A press photographer covering the fund-raising event began snapping pictures. Shit. Nālani would see photos of him drenched in blood. Why the hell had he let Zeke persuade him to come?

Police sirens sounded outside. Nihoa's guests streamed out the exits. Neither Nihoa nor the chief were anywhere in sight. Only Zeke remained with a grin at Koa's predicament.

CHAPTER TWENTY-SIX

KOA HADN'T HEARD the unnaturally squeaky voice in a while, and it brought back memories. Jimmy Hikorea, an ex-Marine and park service archaeologist, had helped unravel the most difficult case of Koa's career. While investigating a murder, they'd discovered an ancient adze makers' underground workshop in the Army's Pōhakuloa Training Area and ultimately brought a killer and grave robber to justice.

"You find another pile of quarry flakes?" Jimmy asked, referring to their first-ever conversation.

"No, but I've got a Houdini-class puzzle. Game?"

They agreed to meet at the observatory on the rim of the Kīlauea caldera. When Jimmy rolled his wheelchair into the conference room, he wore the same black jacket with the same "Federal Archaeologist" logo as when they'd first met. His hair still fell to his shoulders under the same black baseball cap, sporting the Marine Corps insignia. He shook hands with the same bone-crushing grip.

They got down to business. Koa spread Rachael Ortega's large-scale map of South Mauna Loa Farms on the conference table.

"Let's suppose that an Army officer—"

"The fuckin' Army, again?" Seeing his friend tense, Koa regretted mentioning Sapada's Army connection. Jimmy had lost his legs and his voice in a friendly-fire accident caused by a newbie Army artillery officer.

"The officer in question was tortured to death," Koa said with some bite.

"Sorry. You know how I feel."

"Let's suppose this man wanted to hide the family jewels in this area." Koa drew a circle with his finger around the property owned by South Mauna Loa Farms. "Let's further suppose he chose three potential locations. Here . . . here . . . and here." Koa pointed to the two areas Ortega had marked on the map and then to the parcels owned by Hansel and Gretel. "Finally, let's suppose the first two areas weren't available and the man had to settle for this site." Koa tapped the Hansel and Gretel property.

"What kind of treasure? Small, big, light, or heavy?" Jimmy asked.

Koa ignored the squeak in Jimmy's voice. He'd gotten used to it in their first case together. "I'm not sure, but I think it's small, most likely a file of documents. So maybe these three properties have features in common, something that might give us a clue as to a possible hiding place."

"That's some friggin' puzzle. Not much to go on. Why were the first two unavailable?"

"Both the first two parcels held historic sites the owner had agreed to protect."

Jimmy frowned and stared at the map. An interminable silence followed. Koa would've gotten annoyed, but he'd seen Jimmy work out equally difficult problems. He wheeled his chair around the table. Then the archaeologist looked up. "You might as well take a walk. I need an hour to make some calls."

Koa walked outside to the observation area overlooking the Kīlauea caldera. A cloud of whitish-gray sulfur dioxide–laced

steam rose from Halemaʻumaʻu, the half-mile-wide pit crater within
the larger caldera. According to Hawaiian legend, *Pele* made her
home inside Halemaʻumaʻu, where she fought unending battles with
Kamapuaʻa, a Hawaiian demigod who attacked *Pele* with rainwater.

During daylight, the goddess inside Kīlauea's cauldron of fire appeared to rest, but at night the glow from the boiling lava deep
within turned the steamy, sulfur-laden clouds a bright fluorescent
red-orange, and *Pele's* awesome voice deep within the earth rum-
bled like a dozen jet engines. No wonder the ancients left tributes to
the goddess of volcanic fury on the edge of Halemaʻumaʻu, and more
recent visitors donated bottles of gin for the fire witch.

For Koa, like most true Hawaiians, Kīlauea was magical—the
place where the earth father *Wākea* and the earth mother *Papa*
were still giving birth to the islands. Kīlauea, like the majesty of
the star-spangled night sky, expressed the awesome mystery of nature and reminded Koa of his insignificance in the universe. As a
man, he might live four score or more years, but *Pele* existed for
millennia and created the firmament.

When Koa returned to the conference room, he found Jimmy
hunched over the map. The archaeologist had placed red and blue
dots on the designated parcels. "Water and graves," he announced.

"What?" Koa asked, baffled.

"Each parcel has at least one year-round spring, and at least one
ancient grave."

Koa grasped the import. "That makes sense."

"Why?"

"Our man had a major orchid farm buried in the forest. He
needed a reliable supply of water. And," Koa spoke slowly, "graves
make good hiding places."

"Dead-on. There's a grave here," Jimmy pointed to the red dot
he'd placed on the Gretel property. It appeared to be a hundred

yards uphill from the spring that supplied the Campbell orchid farm.

"How do you know the grave's location?"

"Thousands of ancient graves dot the island. Hawaiians buried the *iwi*, the bones, of their loved ones so only the family would know the location. The *maka'āinana*, the common folk, buried their dead in tiny caves, sometimes just crevices in the rocks. Several groups, like the Hawai'i Island Burial Council, have cataloged known burial sites. The public can't get access to the exact locations—for obvious reasons—but I tapped a friend on the council while you were out gawking at the crater."

"I need to make another trip to the Campbell place," Koa responded. "I need to see if Campbell hid his secrets in this grave."

"I'm going with you."

"I don't see how . . ."

"I'll use my scooter."

Koa pictured the battery-powered, three-wheeled chair Jimmy had used to navigate the long tunnel out at Pōhakuloa. "It'd never make it through the mud on the trail, Jimmy."

"There's got to be a way. I'll hop if necessary. How do you navigate out there?"

"I walk, but . . ." Koa thought of the motorcycle in the shed and the cart Campbell used to get supplies to the orchid farm. "Maybe we can rig up something, but this little adventure could be dangerous. I'm hoping to trap two Indonesians, real nasty dudes. They tortured the Army officer and killed the woman he was living with. If they show up, things could get hot."

Jimmy gave him a thumbs-up.

Koa had anticipated Jimmy's reaction. The ex-Marine was no stranger to danger. "But we're going to wear body armor. These dudes set off one bomb and tried to nail a bunch of cops with a second. I don't want you unnecessarily exposed." *And*, Koa thought, remembering Nālani's words, *I, too, need to be careful.*

* * *

Koa planned meticulously for the outing. He would use his Explorer with the tracker still activated, hoping to draw the bastards who'd bugged his car. Trapping them would be reward enough, even if his foray with Jimmy into the Campbell orchid farm failed to find Sapada's secret. He instructed Sergeant Basa and three of his patrolmen to hide in the forest near the Campbell orchid farm. They were in place before dawn.

Koa, Piki, and Jimmy met at dawn at the Campbell place. They spent almost two hours preparing. Koa gassed up the motorcycle and rode it up to the orchid farm before returning with the cart. Koa pulled three body armor vests from the back of his Explorer. Each vest met or exceeded the NIJ, Level II standard, having been designed to stop a .357 Mag slug. He and Piki suited up, then helped Jimmy into the third vest, and everyone replaced their civilian clothing. Koa and Piki checked their weapons.

They lifted Jimmy into the cart, loaded his wheelchair, and made their way up the path toward the orchid farm. Koa drove. Jimmy gripped the sides of the cart with his massive arms and powerful hands. Piki walked not far behind them. They slowed to a crawl around the rocks and tree branches to ensure Jimmy's safety, but he seemed unconcerned. Koa knew the archaeologist relished the chance to get out into the field.

The little caravan made its way through the forest to the orchid farm and then up the path along the aqueduct to the spring. After that, the path narrowed and became too rocky for the cart. Koa and Piki carried Jimmy to the base of a cliff slicing through the forest like a barricade.

"An earthquake, centuries ago," Jimmy squeaked. "Fault lines run all along this side of Mauna Loa. A big shake left this *pali*." Koa didn't find the thought of an earthquake comforting. "Just the kind of place the ancients used for burials," Jimmy added.

"I don't see graves." Piki voiced Koa's unspoken thought.

"You're not going to see tombstones like in a Western cemetery," Jimmy warned. "We're looking for some kind of cave or maybe just a hole in the rocks, most likely in the cliff face." Jimmy pulled a calculator from his pocket and studied the screen. "We need to move about fifty feet that way." Jimmy pointed away from the spring.

"How do you—" Koa sputtered before realizing his mistake. Jimmy's calculator was a portable GPS receiver. Jimmy had located the graves on the map because he had the geographic coordinates. If he'd just given us coordinates, Koa thought, this could have been so much easier.

They carried Jimmy the additional distance. The man weighed 140 pounds, and Koa's back hurt by the time they lowered Jimmy to his cushion, facing a twenty-foot-high section of the *pali*. He and Piki were sweating heavily inside their protective vests. Koa still didn't see a grave and began to doubt the wisdom of the expedition.

Jimmy studied the cliff face, searching the cracks and crevices in the rock. He pulled his cushion from beneath his body, shoved it forward with the stubs of his legs, and hopped. Hop. Hop. Hop. He moved down the *pali*, stopping to recheck the GPS receiver and examine the cliff face again and again. Check the GPS. Search the *pali*.

After another fifteen minutes, Jimmy focused on a particular place. The archaeologist scrutinized the spot from one angle, hopped to the left, checked again, and then moved back to the right to re-focus. "There." Jimmy pointed. Koa saw nothing unusual about the place Jimmy had chosen. "Look for the edges. See how that slab of rock has been fitted into the cliff?"

Koa still couldn't pick out the slab. Jimmy picked an overripe *ōhelo* berry from a nearby bush, and with a precise throw, splattered it in the middle of the slab. Instantly, Koa understood. Just above head height, an irregular block appeared to have been fitted into the *pali*. The subtle outlines disappeared into the jumble of surrounding cracks and crevices. "There's a cave behind that slab?"

"Dead-on. A cave or maybe just a small crypt."

Koa felt a surge of anticipation. *"Ahuwale ka nane hūnā . . .* the secret is no longer hidden." Sure they were about to discover Arthur's secret, Koa moved toward the cliff and reached up toward the slab.

"Stop!" Jimmy's voice cracked like a rifle shot. He pointed toward the top of the cliff, and Koa saw the problem. A massive stone slab hung ominously over the top edge of the *pali*, ready to tumble down at the slightest provocation. Koa wondered how they were going to remove the slab and get into the crypt without getting crushed.

"You do much work for us," an Asian voice said.

Koa knew the voice from Mrs. Furgeson's tape. It came from behind them. He spun around to see the two Indonesian thugs standing several feet apart, blocking the route back to the orchid farm. Koa took his first look at the two killers. Bambang, the older of the two, was closer. Mrs. Furgeson had described him accurately but failed to capture his aura of menace. He had jet-black hair, a broad face above a narrower chin, and beady black reptilian eyes—cold, calculating, and devoid of any human warmth. The eyes of a cold-blooded terrorist. A man who would find entertainment in torture. Sudomo, although physically larger, lacked the menace of his partner. Both held small-caliber semiautomatic pistols.

"What the hell do you think you're doing?" Jimmy yelled.

At the sound of Jimmy's voice, Bambang spun toward the archaeologist and fired at Jimmy's chest. BLAM! The bullet slammed into the former Marine, knocking him off his cushion.

Piki started forward, but Bambang whirled back toward Piki and fired again. BLAM! The bullet hit Piki in the left side, twisting him around and knocking him off his feet. Bambang steadied his weapon to Koa and screamed, "No move." The Indonesian emphasized his command with a warning shot that barely missed Koa's head.

Koa stiffened. The Indonesians had somehow slipped by Basa, but the gunshots would alert him. Unless the Indonesians had disabled his backup. Not a good thought. Koa couldn't tell how badly Jimmy or Piki were hurt, but for the moment he was alone against the two gunmen. "You're making a mistake," Koa said, like he was in command.

Bambang fired another warning shot, this one careening off the rocks at Koa's feet. "Shut up. Drop gun," Bambang shouted.

Taking his time, Koa backpedaled, moving several steps away from the cliff before unholstering his pistol, and, using only his thumb and forefinger, placing his gun on the ground.

"Back! Back!" Bambang shouted.

Koa backpedaled another dozen paces, moving further from the *pali* and drawing the killers away from Jimmy.

"Who's paying you, Bambang?" Koa deliberately used the killer's name and saw the Indonesian's face register surprise. "That's right, asshole," Koa continued, "we've got your name and your prints. You'll never get off the island."

"I kill you this time. Not like farm," Bambang growled as he advanced. He spoke in Indonesian and pointed at Piki. Sudomo moved forward and bent over Piki, who appeared to be unconscious, taking the young detective's weapon.

Where the hell were Basa and his patrolmen? Koa wondered. While Bambang's shots must have alerted them to trouble, they couldn't come busting through the forest. The noise would alert the Indonesians, endangering all of them. Koa needed to stall.

"How'd you know we'd be here, Bambang?" Koa asked.

"You much stupid," the Indonesian responded. Sudomo moved forward to where Koa had placed his gun on the ground. The Indonesian picked it up and retreated toward Bambang, handing one of the police guns to Bambang and pocketing the other. Again, Bambang spoke in Indonesian and pointed to the slab in the rock wall marked with the red skin of the *ōhelo* berry. Behind the two Indonesians, Koa searched the edge of the forest for Sergeant Basa. Jesus, where was he?

Sudomo reached the base of the cliff and used a pocket knife to pry the edge of the stone slab loose. Millimeter by millimeter he edged it outward. It stuck, and he moved to the opposite side to continue. Neither Indonesian noticed Jimmy slowly pushing himself up off the ground. *Thank God*, Koa thought, *we put him in body armor*. The archaeologist forced himself to a sitting position. He was fifteen feet behind the two Indonesians. Bambang must have assumed his shot had killed Jimmy and had forgotten his presence. Koa watched out of the corner of his eye as Jimmy picked up a round stone the size of a baseball. Koa saw Jimmy's massive arm, honed into solid muscle by years as a substitute for his legs, pulse in readiness.

Koa needed to keep the Indonesians occupied. "Bambang, who hired you to kill Sapada?"

"Fuck you," the Indonesian killer shouted.

Bambang made a show of aiming his pistol toward Koa.

The two thugs never saw the end coming. Focused on Koa and the rock wall, the two killers had completely dismissed the crippled archaeologist. Bambang, coaxed forward by Koa's gradual retreat, had his back to Jimmy. They had no idea of Jimmy's courage or the extraordinary strength of his upper arms. Neither of them saw Jimmy cock his right arm and take careful aim.

With a last vicious twist of his knife, Sudomo dislodged the huge chunk of rock. It started to fall, and he jumped backward. A sound like a thunderclap rang through the forest and echoed off the *pali*. The mass of rocks at the top of the cliff seemed to hang in the air for an instant before crashing into Sudomo, crushing his skull.

Jimmy timed his throw perfectly, launching the rock at the moment the massive rock slide hit Sudomo. It slammed into the back of Bambang's head with a crack. Koa launched himself at the killer but need not have bothered. Piki scrambled to his feet, and Sergeant Basa, joined by three patrolmen, charged out of the forest with guns drawn. Raising his hands in mock surrender, Koa said, "About time, guys."

Only then did Koa climb over the pile of rocks to peer into the grave Sudomo had opened. A yellowed human skull, laid sideways across a pile of bones, glared accusingly back at him. He shivered at the macabre sight. There was nothing else in the crypt. They'd disturbed the dead without finding Arthur's secret.

While Basa, Piki, and the patrolmen took Bambang, woozy but conscious, to the lockup in Hilo, Koa enjoyed an enormous sense of relief. He and the team had eliminated a deadly threat to himself and Nālani. He shuddered when he remembered the killers had been inside his house, planting the listening device. It could just as easily have been a bomb.

* * *

Koa knew the invasion of their home had upset Nālani and called her cell from the Campbell place to share the good news. He checked to make sure she was at work, and not at home where an eavesdropper might overhear, before telling her what happened. Overjoyed, she asked for details. He gave her a truthful description of the trap he'd set and the ensuing fight with the Indonesians. He was struck by just how close to death he'd come and feared Nālani's reaction. When he finished, his concern grew at her pregnant pause. Maybe calling her hadn't been such a good idea.

After a moment, she said, "It's a good thing you were wearing body armor and had the other guys with you." Then she added, "I'm tired of texting, Koa. Can we get rid of the damned bug?"

He thought for a moment. With the *kepala*, the Indonesians' boss, still on the loose, there was some risk in leaving the bug in place, but the capture of the actual killers had drastically reduced the danger. And, he'd kept the listening device in the house only in part to catch the Indonesians. What he really wanted was to smoke out the *kepala* behind the two killers. There was also another problem. If he shut down the bug in his house, the eavesdroppers would likely figure he knew about the one in his office. With some trepidation, he decided to press his luck. "Can you live with it for another few days?"

"Your loss," she responded with a naughty inflection.

CHAPTER TWENTY-SEVEN

THE CHIEF—HIS face red with fury—stood behind his desk with his hands on his hips glaring at Koa. "I ordered you to turn over the Campbell investigation to Agents Christopher and Nelson. You disobeyed that order."

"No, sir," Koa responded. He spoke softly, trying to lower the tension. "You ordered me to turn over the Arthur Campbell investigation, but not the Gwendolyn Campbell investigation,"

"Oh, for chrissakes. It's the same fuckin' investigation."

"No, sir, I don't think so. Remember, a county dump truck hit Gwendolyn, and the driver did a runner. We had to investigate to protect the county from losing a lawsuit. That's why the mayor wanted me out there. At least that's what you told me."

"You're splitting hairs," the chief responded, sounding less antagonistic. Koa hoped he'd found the right response.

"That's not fair, sir. You ordered me to turn over the Arthur Campbell investigation. I briefed Agents Christopher and Nelson. I turned over the file. Pursuing the Gwendolyn Campbell investigation didn't violate your order."

"But it did. At the very least, it violated the spirit of my directive. And you deliberately disobeyed my instructions by continuing the Arthur Campbell investigation."

Koa's stomach churned at the chief's harsh accusation. He'd pushed the envelope by continuing to run with the case, but he wasn't sorry. He'd caught two heinous killers, goons those DIA bozos had no interest in pursuing. He thought about telling the chief about his appointment as an assistant prosecutor, but Zeke had warned him against doing so, and Koa's close communication with the county prosecutor would only reinforce the chief's fury.

"You went behind my back, called out the tactical team, staged a raid on the farmhouse used by those two Indonesians, and nearly got everybody killed."

"I didn't go behind your back. You were out of town. And I tried to arrest them because they stole a county truck, created an acetylene bomb, killed Gwendolyn Campbell, and injured a county firefighter. And nobody got killed because I sensed a trap."

"You're playing games. They're the principal suspects in the torture and murder of Arthur Campbell."

"That may be true, but I was after them for Gwendolyn's murder."

"Bullshit. And you were on Arthur Campbell's orchid farm, searching for his papers."

Koa said nothing.

"Answer me."

"We caught the Indonesians who murdered Arthur and Gwendolyn."

"That's not the point." The chief's face grew redder. He was running out of patience. "I can't have a chief detective disobey my commands."

The chief paced back and forth across the office. He stopped and turned to assess Koa, and then resumed pacing. Koa had worked with Chief Lannua for years and never seen him so upset. "The governor called me this morning. Do you know why?"

"No, sir." Koa had a bad feeling.

"He wants your head. You stepped in shit, deep shit. You ticked off powerful people in Washington. They jumped down the governor's throat, and he blistered my ass."

"I'm sorry, sir."

"A fucking lot of good that will do."

Koa said nothing, maintaining his stance of innocence.

"You are suspended from the police force as of this moment, Mr. Kāne. I'll take your gun and your shield." The chief held out his hand. "And I'll have you terminated from the force by next week."

Slowly, ever so slowly, Koa surrendered his shield and his Glock pistol. He knew he shouldn't, but he couldn't resist. "Give my regards to the future governor."

CHAPTER TWENTY-EIGHT

BACK IN HIS office, Koa ripped off his shoulder holster and hurled it across the room. It bounced off the wall and fell with a useless plop to the floor. He thought about removing his artwork, but instead stormed out of the building without his badge for the first time in a dozen years. Once in his Explorer, he exceeded the speed limit all the way to his home outside Volcano.

Koa had downed two Black Sand Porters before Nālani arrived. She stopped short in the doorway, surprised to find him slumped on the sofa, beer bottle in hand, with empties on the floor. "What happened? What's wrong?"

"The chief fired me. I'm unemployed," he announced more abruptly than he'd intended.

"Oh, my God." Her hand flew to her mouth. She ran to the sofa and put her arm around his shoulders. "I'm so sorry. Tell me what happened?"

"Maybe it's for the best. I couldn't do my job. Fuckin' politics. Goddamn fuckin' politics." He downed the rest of his beer. "Did you know Arthur Campbell had a Distinguished Service Cross? That's almost like a Congressional Medal of Honor. His country honored him as an exceptional hero, and nobody cares he got tortured to death. Nobody gives a flying fuck. Not the police chief, not the goddamn fuckin' politicians."

Koa gazed blearily at the bottle in his hand. He had a mind to drink himself into oblivion, but Nālani's arrival had changed the tenor of his party. At any other time, he had zero use for self-pity.

Nālani stepped back outside the house with her cell phone, while he continued to reel from his blowup with the chief. A long string of images flashed through his mind: sitting at his grandfather's feet, listening to stories of his Kāne ancestors . . . that awful day when they'd pulled him out of school to tell him his father had been crushed to death . . . the death scene in the Kohala cabin where he'd killed Hazzard . . . Jerry's bright face talking about becoming a cop in Seattle.

He'd kept true to his promises to himself and Jerry and reached a place in life far beyond anything his father or grandfather could've imagined. And now everything he'd worked for had vanished. Doing the right thing had cost him his job. All because of fucking politics and goddamned politicians. He opened his wallet and stared at the dog-eared picture of the Hāmākua Sugar Mill where his father had died, for him the symbol of failure. Koa had escaped the fate of his father. Until now.

The guilt he'd long ago buried returned like a flash flood. He'd gotten away with killing Hazzard, and created his own penance, but it wasn't enough. This must be his punishment for the Hazzard killing. He descended into a black mood.

Then, like a seesaw, his cop instincts came back. Why had the chief blocked the investigation? The question kept nagging at him. Just because he'd been stripped of his badge didn't mean he'd stop asking questions. Lannua had blamed telephone calls from the mayor and the governor. True, the chief was a political animal, but he held one of the top law enforcement jobs on the island. Even the chief wouldn't let a killing go by for political reasons. That mystery

led to another. Who had given the wiretappers access to the secure telephone cabinet in the police station? Suddenly, Koa felt
bad about the chief. Except now he lacked the power to do anything about it.

He went to the fridge, opened another beer, and called for her.
"Nālani . . . Nālani."

"Here." She came back into the house.

He looked at her, his beautiful, lighthearted Nālani. He'd lost his
job. Now, he was afraid he'd lose her, too. The image of a former girlfriend filled his mind—a beautiful woman whom he'd loved and
whom he'd lost. Lost because of his job, because he hadn't appreci-
ated the magic they'd shared, because he'd let trivial annoyances infect their relationship. They quarreled about stupid things. She'd
met another man and left him. He'd been in shock for weeks. And
he'd vowed if he were ever lucky enough to find another wonderful
woman, he'd never let her go.

In a rush of emotion, he understood how vital Nālani was to him.
In his self-pity, he'd ignored something that mattered greatly to her.
She had her dream job at Hawai'i Volcanoes National Park, and any
uncertainty in his job situation would make her nervous, afraid his
unraveling would be her own undoing. "I'm sorry, my *ipo*." He spoke
softly, using their Hawaiian term of endearment. "I've screwed it up.
I've screwed up our lives."

"Don't be sorry." She cupped his chin, lifted his face to hers, and
kissed him. "You did what you thought right, what is right, so don't
be sorry, my *ipo*."

"I'll find another job on the island."

"Of course you will. After today, no one will ever have any respect for Chief Lannua."

* * *

Hook Hao came through the door carrying a plastic bag from the Suisan fish market and two six-packs of Paniolo Pale Ale. "I brought *aʻu*. We're gonna be rid of this trouble." Hook made a play on words. *Aʻu*, Hawaiian for swordfish, also meant trouble because a jumping swordfish could maim any fisherman who got speared. Hook lit the grill and loaded *kiawe* wood, Hawaiian mesquite, on top of the charcoal. He bustled around the kitchen, slicing a dozen swordfish filets, firing up the rice cooker, and preparing a giant skillet full of *hōʻiʻo*, an edible native Hawaiian fern like a thin asparagus.

Basa and Piki soon arrived. Chef Hook drank Paniolo Pale Ale and regaled the group with fishing stories. Hook's energy, storytelling, and friendship slowly lifted Koa out of his dour mood. The charcoal grill burned hot with the rich smell of *kiawe*. Combined with Hook's marinade of ginger and wasabi, it perfumed the air.

"You okay, Koa?" Sergeant Basa asked.

Koa nodded, and then felt a pang as he realized he and Basa would no longer be working together. "It's tough, really tough, after twelve years, but I'll find something. I've been through worse."

"Jesus, Koa, all we've heard is scuttlebutt around the station. Can you give us the blow-by-blow?"

Koa outlined the meeting, replaying the chief's anger and his own efforts to defend himself. Nālani served the grilled *aʻu*, and the five of them sat down to eat.

Sergeant Basa finished first and pushed his plate away. "*Mahalo*, Nālani, for getting us over here tonight." He addressed the group. "It means a lot to hear how this thing went down straight from Koa."

Although he'd been too wrapped up in himself to ask why all his closest friends had appeared at his doorstep, Koa knew she'd called them. He looked at Nālani. "Thank you, my *ipo*."

"I invited Zeke, too." Nālani didn't hide the bitterness dripping from her voice. "He was supposed to have your back on this investigation, and he didn't even bother to show up."

Why, Koa wondered, hadn't Zeke come? Was it possible he'd somehow lost Zeke's support? The county prosecutor did, after all, hold a political office. He wondered if Zeke had withdrawn his appointment as an assistant to investigate the Campbell murders. Koa's mood darkened again.

"The chief is gonna regret this, big-time," Basa warned.

Koa gave Basa a wan smile. "How? How's the mayor's lapdog gonna regret this?"

"The chief is gonna have my resignation on his desk before he wakes up in the morning. I'm really pissed about Smithy, and for me this is the end. And from what I heard, mine won't be the only fuck-you on the chief's desk."

"Damn straight," Piki added. "I'm out of there. If we can't investigate crimes without political interference, there's no honor in being a policeman."

Koa sat up straight, realizing the ramifications. "Hold on. Hold on. You guys can't put your careers at risk because of me. You've got to think—"

Koa's cell phone sounded the opening bars of "The Star-Spangled Banner," the ringtone reserved for the chief. Koa dug his phone out of his pocket. "It's the chief." Koa gave a sneering half laugh and, ignoring the call, flung the phone across the room. "He can go fuck himself." He looked first at Basa, then at Piki. "And you guys can't resign on my account. You've got careers and families to think of."

"Oh, yes, we can," Basa responded hotly. "Like the wonder boy Piki said, if you can't look yourself in the mirror and know you're doing the right thing, then what's it all about? It's time to bail. This fucking job ain't about prestige, and it sure as hell ain't about the money. It's about doing the right thing."

Nālani's cell phone buzzed, and she answered. After listening for a minute, she walked into the bedroom to speak in private. She returned to the room a little later. "That was the chief. He wants to see you in his office tonight."

"I'm not going," Koa retorted.

"Yes, Koa Kāne"—she emphasized his full name, and now spoke with a distinct firmness—"you are going. Zeke has apparently explained some facts of life to the chief. I don't know what he wants to say, but it's not to chew you out. And you owe it to your buddies to hear what the chief has to say."

Koa understood. The chief wouldn't have called unless he'd been forced to do it. "I've had too many beers. I can't even drive."

"No," Nālani said, "you're the one who's always bragging about an iron stomach. I'll make some strong coffee." She went to the kitchen and returned a few minutes later with a cup. "Drink up, iron man."

Hook drove him to police headquarters with Basa and Piki in tow. Koa promised they'd be the first to hear the outcome. When he walked into Chief Lannua's office, Zeke Brown was perched at the chief's conference table, and the chief sat slumped behind his desk. He looked beaten down. Koa's badge and Glock pistol sat in plain view on the desktop.

"Sit down." The chief indicated a chair across the table from Zeke. Koa took his seat and waited.

"Zeke explained some things to me." The chief spoke so softly Koa had to lean forward to catch the words. "I'm damned unhappy about your lack of communication, but I was too hasty in suspending you. I'm going to withdraw your suspension and schedule another meeting about all this later in the week after we get past this Nihoa political rally and I have some time to sort everything out."

Koa knew to accept the peace offering. "Thank you, sir," he began slowly. He felt a wave of relief, but he knew now more than ever he couldn't sacrifice his promises to Jerry and to himself. "I appreciate your candor. But you must understand, sir, if I am to be chief detective, I must be able to investigate crimes, *all* crimes."

The chief appeared to bristle. His face turned bright red, and his eyes bulged. "You're pushing your luck."

Koa thought the chief would explode and saw his chances of reinstatement fade. The chief plainly wanted to block the Campbell investigation. Koa would have to give up the investigation or his job. So be it. He continued to stare at the chief, not yielding an iota.

"Chief Lannua." Zeke's loud voice cut through the air. "Remember what I said."

The chief didn't take orders from anybody, but Zeke was resolute. The two men glared at each other before the chief broke eye contact. The tension drained from his body, and he slumped back in his chair. What, Koa wondered, had Zeke said to the chief before he arrived? The county prosecutor plainly had some powerful hold over the chief. The room became quiet, and the silence stretched.

Chief Lannua finally spoke. "I understand your position, but you must realize that I can't run this department without adequate communication from my team."

"I understand, Chief." Greater communication was a concession Koa could make. And it gave the chief a way to save face.

Again, the chief paused. "For tonight, I am withdrawing your suspension and returning you to good standing, subject to a discussion later in the week."

"And I intend to participate in that discussion," Zeke announced. "So, gentlemen, we have an understanding." Both men nodded. The chief stood with Koa's badge and pistol in hand, and slowly carried them across the room to him.

CHAPTER TWENTY-NINE

Police officials hoped for rain on Nihoa rally day but had no such luck. Nature brought warm, sunny weather, with just a whisper of trade winds, so the day grew unusually hot. Traffic poured into Hilo creating a massive jam. By eleven a.m., an hour before the scheduled address, people lined the roads from the airport to the rally site in Wailoa Park where twenty-five thousand voters had assembled. Vendors circulated through the crowd selling plate lunches, hot dogs, *malasadas*, drinks, and souvenirs. Musicians, joined by *hula* dancers, entertained the masses.

Workmen added the finishing touches to the stage, decked out in patriotic bunting and a giant banner proclaiming: "Limit Government for Freedom's Sake." Smaller posters, supporting "Nāinoa Nihoa for Governor," dotted the scene. Hundreds of red, white, and blue balloons tethered to the stage provided a backdrop behind the podium, and matched the colors of *Ka Hae Hawai'i*, the official Hawai'i state flags, flying high above.

Police officers, augmented by dozens of law enforcement personnel borrowed from federal agencies and several hundred county employees with green armbands, protected public order and manned support facilities. Bomb-sniffing dogs checked the stage for explosives, and local police cordoned off access, except through the official entrance from the rear. Police helicopters roamed back and forth over the crowds, providing intelligence to the police officials on the ground. Koa, his detectives, and two dozen undercover FBI, DEA, and TSA employees circulated through the gathering looking for potential troublemakers.

The early crowds frolicked in the sunshine, exhibiting the Hawaiian "*aloha* spirit." Families spread picnic blankets on the grass and children played *pā'ume'ume*, tug-of-war, and *'io*, a form of tag. The mayor and council members circulated, shaking hands and slapping backs.

But as the clock ticked toward noon, more and more provocative political placards appeared throughout the crowd and tensions rose. The majority of participants were Nihoa supporters, but clusters of his political opponents made their presence known. Competing slogans screamed at each other. "Save the Public School Teachers" vied with "End Teacher Bargaining Rights." "It's America, Stupid" challenged "Sovereignty 1883."

The *aloha* spirit wore thin with the rapidly growing crowds, the rising sea of slogans, and heightened anticipation of the main event. People jockeyed for position. The police radio net began to register shouting contests, minor acts of vandalism, and even a few fights. While police officers aggressively stepped in to reassert control wherever necessary, temperatures rose and nerves frayed. To Koa, the rally looked increasingly like a tinderbox searching for a match. And Nāinoa Nihoa had yet to arrive on the Big Island.

Koa's earpiece crackled with the news: the big man's campaign plane had entered its Hilo airport landing pattern. The crowd grew more tense. The police command center confirmed Nihoa's plane had landed. A Piper Cub circled overhead, trailing a banner, "Vote Lower Taxes—Vote Nihoa." Koa got word from senior police officials at the airport that Nihoa had entered his motorcade.

Koa and his people were in position, his detectives split into two groups. He and several others stood toward the front of the crowd, not far from the edge of the stage. A second row of detectives circulated farther back. All wore casual clothes and mingled with the rally participants, alert for suspicious activities.

Koa heard crowds along the street cheering as the motorcade approached. VIPs began to take their positions on the platform with Republican council members prominently positioned, and lesser county officials and major political donors at the edges. Koa spotted Raul Oshoa and Rachael Ortega, among them.

Police observers on the nearby roofs reported that Nihoa had exited the motorcade. Nihoa's campaign aides walked onto the stage, and the crowd roared as the mayor appeared with the aspiring candidate, his wife, and nineteen-year-old son. The two men stood together, arms extended, giving the *shaka* hand signal with thumb and pinky extended—Hawai'i's sign of *aloha*, friendship, compassion, and solidarity. The crowd screamed, "Nihoa, Nihoa ... we want Nihoa."

Koa scanned the crowd, checking faces, as he circulated around his assigned area. No one escaped his scrutiny, but he paid particular attention to protesters, those wearing anti-Nihoa buttons, and people carrying anti-Nihoa placards. He dismissed the happy, laughing faces and focused on the less effervescent people who appeared nervous, yelled harsh words, or stared malevolently at the candidate.

He paid little attention to the mayor's words describing Nihoa's military career, Pentagon service, and political successes in glowing terms. When the candidate stepped up to the microphones with his wife on one side and son on the other, the crowd again began chanting: "Nihoa ... Nihoa ... Nihoa ... we want Nihoa." Then the chant changed to "Lower taxes. We want lower taxes." People threw their arms in the air, waved placards, and shouted slogans. In the midst of everything, Koa found it hard to concentrate on watching for suspicious behavior.

Nihoa began speaking, his voice booming over loudspeakers. "It's time to reject the failed policies of the Democratic governor and his legislative cronies. We must reduce our bloated state government. We must free our citizens from the onerous state tax burdens. We must not be held hostage to public employee unions." Many in the crowd cheered, but others began to raise their voices in protest.

Koa's earpiece erupted with excited voices. A fight had broken out on the outskirts of the crowd. The police moved to restore order, but more disruptions sprang up. The crowd seemed to pulse with pushing and shoving. Nihoa's amplified voice, the cacophony of the crowd, the flow of police reports, and the distracting sea of placards created an increasingly tense atmosphere.

"In my administration, we will slash the public-school budget. We will open more charter schools. We will return control of education to families." Nihoa's words drew cheers and hisses from the assembled masses. A man carrying an "Elect Nihoa" poster on a stick brushed past Koa. He'd seen the man before but couldn't place him. Koa turned as a noise behind him erupted. Two men looked to square off. Koa started toward them, and then it registered—the man with the poster had red hair. In that instant Koa knew where he'd seen him. He was the same red-haired man Koa had pegged as a troublemaker on his pre-rally foray into the park. Last time the red-haired man had been shouting, "Kill the sovereignty movement."

Koa pushed his way through the crowd. Red hair flashed amid a group of people closer to the stage. Koa shouldered a man out of the way and nearly knocked over a small woman holding a child. But still he plunged forward. The red-haired man marched resolutely toward the platform, weaving around others as he went. Koa bolted after him. "Code Red . . . Zone C," Koa yelled into his microphone, broadcasting the emergency signal for a potentially catastrophic situation. He raced forward. Twenty feet . . . fifteen feet . . . ten feet.

The scene unfolded in nanoseconds, but Koa lived it step by step, like the individual pictures of a comic book seen one by one. The red-haired man stopped. His placard fell to the ground. He pulled something from beneath his baggy brown shirt. Koa saw a long-barreled pistol emerge. The man's gun hand, covered with pale-colored boils, rose. The black barrel glinted in the sun. Eight feet away. The barrel swung to the right, aiming up toward the platform. Six feet away. The gun settled on its target. Koa was too far away. He wasn't going to make it. The red-haired assailant was going to shoot Nāinoa Nihoa.

Koa dove forward. He felt the impact of his head against the assailant's legs just as a blast of gunfire shattered the air. The man fell forward. The gun discharged again, and a shock wave of sound ripped at Koa's ears. On the ground, Koa scrambled to get on top. The gun rotated toward him. He tried, but failed, to knock it away. He saw the dark round hole in the muzzle bearing down on him.

Nālani's face flashed through his mind. Then he felt a massive jolt. Fire burned his forehead, and a thunderclap pummeled his ears.

CHAPTER THIRTY

KOA OPENED HIS eyes amid a tangle of bodies. Tears blurred his vision, bells rang in his ears, and the side of his face felt like raw meat. The body sprawled atop him shifted as Piki slowly stood and helped Koa to a sitting position. Koa touched the side of his head; pain radiated down the side of his face. Piki said, "You've got some blisters and a hell of a bruise, but it's not bleeding much."

The red-haired man kicked and screamed "Kill the mother-fucker ... kill the motherfucker" as two patrolmen pinned him to the ground. The long-barreled pistol lay at his feet. A bystander slumped nearby, holding his shoulder, blood seeping through his shirt. A crush of bodies encircled them. Electronic flashes popped. Someone yelled questions.

Policemen and federal agents appeared from every direction, pushing the crowd back and reestablishing control. The deputy chief pushed through the spectators, followed by emergency medical personnel. Police led the red-haired man, still shouting obscenities, away in handcuffs. EMTs treated the wounded bystander and helped him to an ambulance. Within minutes, law enforcement officers had restored calm.

The chief, Zeke Brown, and an FBI agent debriefed Koa, establishing the timeline, placing the events in sequence. The pieces snapped into a coherent picture. Koa had foiled an assassination attempt on Nāinoa Nihoa. Piki, responding to Koa's emergency broadcast, had jumped the assailant just as he turned his gun on Koa, saving his life. Amid the discussions, Zeke stepped out of the debriefing to call Nālani, letting her know what had happened and telling her Koa was all right.

Television bulletins screamed "Hawai'i Cop Stops Assassination Attempt." Commentators talked over successive pictures of Koa tackling the assailant, the resulting tangle of bodies, and police officers restraining the struggling red-haired man. The police did not immediately release the man's name, but the media reported that he was Kevin Narcotti, a former Army grunt, court-marshaled and dishonorably discharged for brutality against Afghan civilians. He'd been living alone off the grid in a shack in the Puna district of the Big Island for the past several years, but even the investigative journalists couldn't decipher his motive.

Chief Lannua, always eager to present the department in a favorable light, called a late afternoon press conference. Koa became the star attraction. When he took the microphone, he credited his fellow officers for their professional handling of the rally and singled out Piki for saving his life. Diplomatically, Koa explained how Chief Lannua's superb planning and thorough preparations for the rally enabled Koa to spot the abnormalities in the red-haired man's behavior, and thus position himself to act when the gun materialized.

Nāinoa Nihoa's campaign headquarters issued a press release lauding Koa for saving the candidate's life and inviting Koa to Honolulu so Nihoa could thank the brave police officer in person. The evening news broadcasts reported the rally but focused on the assassination attempt and Koa's bravery. The following morning, the local newspapers carried headlines like: "Officer Foils Assassination

Attempt" and "Hero Cop Saves Nihoa." National newspapers carried shorter versions.

Koa reflected on making it through one hell of an afternoon and
saw an obvious personal benefit. The politically sensitive chief would
never suspend a police detective who'd just saved the life of a major
political figure. For now, he'd secured his position as chief detective
and, as hero of the day, increased his leverage with state and local
politicians. There were, in fact, some advantages to coming so close
to death.

CHAPTER THIRTY-ONE

KOA FLEW TO Honolulu to meet Nāinoa Nihoa at his campaign headquarters. The gubernatorial candidate's staff arranged a news conference. Koa stood beside Nihoa with the Hawai'i state flag in the background. Cameras flashed. "In my own service as a senior military officer," Nihoa began, "I've seen many brave men, but few cross that invisible line separating bravery from true heroism. Brave men fight well and hard, but heroes put themselves in mortal danger to save the lives of their comrades. There stands beside me here today a true hero, Chief Detective Koa Kāne."

Nihoa proceeded to describe how Koa had singlehandedly tackled an assassin, disrupting his aim. "In saving my life, he put his own life in grave danger." The candidate railed against the forces of lawlessness in society and recited his own plans for improved public safety. While Koa sensed Nihoa's genuine appreciation for his heroism, he also understood it advanced Nihoa's campaign to be seen praising a police hero, and Koa felt used.

When Koa took his turn at the microphone, he repeated what he'd said at the first press conference. He considered exploiting the opportunity to highlight the deleterious effects of slashing budgets on the police department's ability to protect the public but thought better of it.

Afterward, Nihoa invited Koa into his private office, a spacious retreat with windows overlooking the Honolulu harbor and its famous Aloha Tower, now in a state of disrepair. The opulence of the richly appointed office created a contrast with Nihoa's cost-cutting public persona. Still, the man had a super-rich wife, and Koa recognized the difference between spending your own and the public's money. The gubernatorial candidate shed the obligatory *lei* he'd worn for the press conference, seemed visibly to relax, and sprawled behind his desk as they chatted.

"You know, Detective, we come from similar backgrounds, your father in a sugar mill and mine on a pineapple plantation. Growing up, my family lived the plight of farm laborers, working terrible hours for pennies."

Koa, having read Nihoa's newspaper bio, asked, "You grew up on Lānaʻi?"

"Yeah, with three brothers in a tiny two-room shack in Lānaʻi City. It's a miracle I ever got out. I can thank the demise of the pineapple plantations for my escape. With no jobs on the island, I joined the Army."

Koa nodded. "My dad had friends on Lānaʻi who lost their jobs when cheaper Philippine labor depressed pineapple production in Hawaiʻi. The same thing happened to the sugar workers on Maui and the Big Island. A lot of them never recovered."

"You got that right. My dad was one of those lost souls. Wound up drinking himself to death. But enough of that. How about you? Why'd you become a cop?"

Koa, seeing a new, more down-home side of the politician, explained how Jerry's death had motivated him to come back to Hawaiʻi to join the police. He omitted his guilt over Hazzard's death and wondered whether Nihoa also harbored such secrets.

Surely, Koa thought, the press would have sniffed out any scandal like the one hidden in his own history.

Koa expressed his support for public school reform and restrictions on the bargaining rights of the teachers' unions. When Nihoa asked about his experiences as a police officer, Koa seized the initiative. "If I can be candid with you, sir, I am worried about what across-the-board cuts will do to our ability to ensure public safety."

"I'd love to hear your views."

Koa laid out his concerns. He warned against the effects of manpower shortages, inadequate police training, and subpar crime lab facilities. He detailed the lack of funds for police cars and helicopter support.

"Police departments across the country are stepping up their commitment to sophisticated technology in fighting crime. I'm not talking about firearms and protective equipment. I'm talking about high-tech communications equipment, surveillance equipment, emergency radios, CATV cameras, facial recognition software, and computer systems that identify drivers and vehicles, inform officers of warrants, and alert officers to repeat offenders.

"We're falling further and further behind the curve, and our people here in the islands will ultimately pay a heavy price in increased crime, less security, and maybe even terrorist attacks. I mean, do you know, sir, we don't even have a coroner? Yes, that's right. We're forced to rely on a seventy-six-year-old Japanese obstetrician with no forensic training."

To Koa's surprise, Nihoa became engaged and asked questions, probing for details until he seemed to understand fully the problems. "So, you're saying my proposal for an across-the-board cut in government expenditures will endanger public safety, if not immediately, then in the longer term."

"Exactly. That's what I believe."

"Well, you might be surprised to hear me say this, but I think you've made a strong case. I thank you for your courage in speaking up. You have no idea how many people are afraid to tell me what they really think."

"Thank you, sir."

"And," Nihoa said as he ended the conversation, "if I am elected, you'll have a real coroner. Just you wait and see."

CHAPTER THIRTY-TWO

KOA, ZEKE, AND Hook Hao met for dinner at the Kīlauea Lodge just outside Hawai'i Volcanoes National Park. After they were seated and ordered beers, Hook said, "So the detective who hates politicians got co-opted at the hero conference with the gubernatorial candidate in Honolulu."

"I guess," Koa responded, sheepish at his old friend's tease. "I mean, it did feel strange when he started in on his public safety plans, but afterward, I laid it on the line about inadequate police resources, and he listened. In the end, I think he agreed with me. He said he'd consider changing some of his positions."

Zeke snorted. "Seeing's believing."

"On a lighter note, guys, Nihoa made me a promise," Koa responded. "I told him about Shizuo, and he promised to get us a real coroner if he's elected."

"I'll drink to that." Zeke raised his glass, and they toasted Shizuo's demise.

After dinner, Zeke asked about Koa's next steps in the Campbell investigation. Koa described Jimmy Hikorea's identification of graves on the three parcels Arthur had selected. "I was sure we'd find something in that grave, but we didn't. So now, I'm going to tackle the *heiau* in the forest behind the orchid farm."

Hook nodded. "It's just like old times when the religious *kahuna* hid their *mea hūnā*, their secrets, in the forest. I tell you, the more things change, the more they stay the same. History twists and turns, but at the end of the day, it just repeats itself."

"True," Zeke agreed. "We prosecute the same crimes—murder, rape, robbery, burglary, and assault—that my grandfather prosecuted."

On that note, they split the bill and rose to exit. A large canvas on the opposite wall caught Koa's attention. It depicted a *heiau* in a forest clearing surrounded by all manner of creatures—birds in the trees, insects on the flowers, and a gecko perched on a plant in the foreground. Koa recalled Betty Galant's words. "Anatomically correct birds are . . . like medical school texts. It's the Chinese education system, very rigid and formulaic." In the lower right-hand corner, Koa found Gwendolyn Campbell's signature.

Koa realized he'd seen the *heiau*, deep in the forest on the 240-acre parcel behind the Campbell house. He studied the stone platform in the painting, taking in the difference between the picture and his memory of the actual place. He used his cell phone to snap a photo of Gwendolyn's painting.

Driving home, Koa's thoughts returned to Nālani. After he'd intentionally minimized the danger he'd faced when Gwendolyn's car exploded, she'd demanded honesty. He could honor her need going forward, but she knew nothing of his secret history. And he couldn't tell her. He could never tell anyone. Would that, he wondered, ultimately infect their relationship?

He was still mulling that question when he opened the door to his cottage. Nālani stood in the soft glow of candlelight. Her short nightie obscured nothing, and her coy smile excited him even more than the curves of her body. He'd never seen her more alluring. He took her in his arms, and they kissed, a long, probing union. All thoughts of his secret criminal past succumbed to her magic.

Then he remembered the listening device and thought about crawling up in the attic to kill it. Nālani was more practical. She inserted a Springsteen CD in their stereo and turned up the volume. "Born in the U.S.A." thundered from the speakers, filling their little cottage with sound, while a grinning Nālani led Koa to the bedroom. The Boss entertained the eavesdroppers as the lovers entertained each other.

Afterward, Koa lay in bed pondering their relationship. They were like magnets. Turned one way, a powerful attraction brought them together. But his secret crime could spin them apart with nearly equal force. The positive magnets seemed to be getting stronger, pulling them together, but he wondered how long they could go on before the ultimate secret in his life began pushing them apart.

Koa slept fitfully. Dreams clouded his sleep. Men in *malo*, loincloths, paraded up the stone steps onto the platform of a *heiau* where ancient priests in strange masks performed rituals. At one point in the darkness, he sat bolt upright. He'd just awakened from a dream about Gwendolyn's *heiau* deep in the forest. The dream was so vivid he might've been standing on the stone platform. He tried to go back to sleep, but his mind cycled through all the bizarre events of the preceding days, and sleep eluded him. Finally, he got up and tiptoed down to the kitchen for coffee.

Why, he wondered, had his dream about the *heiau* been so compelling? Something he'd seen in the *heiau* in Gwendolyn's painting tugged at the corner of his mind. Gwendolyn's picture showed two holes in the surface and piles of stones on the old *heiau*, yet the platform he'd visited had no holes or piles. The precision with which Gwendolyn rendered living things led him to conclude she wouldn't have painted piles of stones if they hadn't been there. The existing *heiau* had a more pastoral quality. Gwendolyn, he thought, wouldn't have deliberately added ugly rock piles. She'd have copied reality, as she'd done when Howie took her around to make drawings of various *heiau*.

With a jolt like an electric shock, Koa understood. The old *heiau* had been ravaged, and then *restored*! The pieces snapped together like a Rubik's Cube solved. He knew where to look for Sapada's *mea hūnā*, his secret, but not *exactly* where. The platform, he knew from his previous visit, stretched a hundred feet in each direction. Ten thousand square feet altogether. Maybe fifty thousand stones, depending on the number of layers. He'd need an army to take it apart. There had to be a quicker way.

He thought of X-rays—the way to see inside objects—then switched to radar and finally to astronomers. In a previous case, he'd discovered that the astronomers atop Mauna Kea had ground penetration radar. The astronomers used a portable unit to locate and avoid ancient burial sites when doing construction on the mountain. It had been stolen and used to locate ancient artifacts. If a GPR machine could find ancient treasures hidden in lava caves, it should be able to see inside a stone platform. In the earlier case, he'd recovered the machine for the Alice Telescope Project, and now he needed to borrow it, along with someone who could operate it. Later that morning, ten minutes on the phone to Allen Maples, the director of the Alice Telescope Project, got him what he needed.

Koa met Gracie Roberts, a young technician from the Alice Telescope Project, at police headquarters. He asked Sergeant Basa to come along with a patrolman, and they took Basa's vehicle because Koa's Explorer still had the tracker. On the way, Koa explained what they were about to do. Once at the Campbell property, the three men struggled for over an hour getting the GPR machine up the rough trail to the *heiau*. It was the size of an electric lawn mower, but much heavier.

Gracie's eyes went wide at the sight of the large square platform, covered with dark brown stones, fitted together like a cobblestone street. "I've never seen one intact," she gushed. "It's big, really big. It's gonna take forever to scan that whole thing."

She attached the computer console to the machine's handlebars and activated the electronics, taking several minutes to adjust the controls, run self-diagnostic tests, and calibrate the device. When she had it operating to her satisfaction, the police officers placed it on the platform, and Gracie began to scan at one corner. Moving a few inches at a time, she guided the gadget down one side of the stone square. At the far end, she turned the machine and inched back. The process took an hour, and Koa offered to give her a break by running the machine himself. She showed him how to read the wave pattern on the LED screen, and he took over for another hour.

By midafternoon, they had covered less than a fifth of the stone platform and found nothing. Koa realized they'd never finish by sunset, but they kept going, inch by inch. An hour later, they hit an anomaly. Koa retrieved his cell phone and checked Gwendolyn's painting from the Kīlauea Lodge—a picture depicting the same *heiau* with two holes and two piles of stone. The spot with the anomaly bore no relationship to either of the piles of stone. "You keep going," he suggested to Gracie, "while we take up these stones."

The men went to work, prying the stones loose and lifting the heavy slabs. After almost an hour of work, they found nothing except a small, empty depression beneath the stones. At least, Koa thought, the GPR machine could find hollow spots, even small hollow spots. He studied the platform, checking Gracie's progress. As he'd guessed, they weren't going to finish before dark. He wondered if there was a faster way.

Koa sat on the stump near where he stood on his previous visit. He studied the *heiau*, then the photograph of Gwendolyn's painting. The hole they'd dug up didn't match either hole in the painting. The painting placed the pile of stones on the opposite side. It didn't make sense.

Koa walked around the *heiau*, viewing it from every angle. He tried to imagine how Gwendolyn had constructed her composition. He found the same vantage point she'd used and visualized her sitting with her sketch pad. Suddenly, he remembered the apparatus in Gwendolyn's studio, the overhead projector she'd used to project her sketches onto canvas. Had she used the overhead projector to transfer her sketch of this *heiau* to her canvas?

He recalled the photo apps that Nālani had given him for his smartphone. One of them included tools to manipulate photographs. He loaded Gwendolyn's *heiau* picture into the app and with a few clicks succeeded in transforming the photo of Gwendolyn's painting into an image that resembled the real *heiau*. He looked at the transformed photograph and again at the landscape in front of him. The location they'd already dug up now matched one of the piles of stones in the photograph of Gwendolyn's painting.

He walked back onto the platform. "Gracie, mark your current position, so you can return to the pattern. Bring the machine over here."

He walked to the place on the *heiau* where the second stone pile in Gwendolyn's painting would have been if she hadn't reversed her sketch when projecting it onto her canvas. He stepped aside, letting Gracie roll the ground penetration radar machine over the spot.

"Hey! We've got something," Gracie said excitedly. Although Koa felt strongly they'd found the hiding place, he sent Gracie back to the original pattern while he and the other men began tearing up the stones. Koa said a prayer of thanks when they first uncovered the corner of a metal plate. Forty minutes, and gallons of sweat, later, they'd removed the stones from a four-foot-square area, around a rusty two-foot-square steel plate.

Sergeant Basa reached for the edge of the steel plate. "Don't," Koa shouted, and Basa withdrew his fingers like they'd been singed.

Light dawned in Basa's eyes. "You think it's booby trapped."

"I'd bet a composite canoe paddle on it," Koa responded.

Basa allowed a small smile at the reference. "You want to get the bomb experts out here?"

Koa checked the sky. They had less than an hour before dark. "Let's rig something ourselves." They mounded a pile of rocks into a small parapet beside the square hole, then Koa, using Basa's small but sharp pocketknife, cut a long, straight sapling from the forest.

He positioned Basa, the patrolman, and Gracie more than fifty yards back in the woods, then fitted one end of the sapling under the edge of the steel plate and laid the other end over the stone wall they'd created. He stretched out flat behind the parapet. Reaching up with one hand, he pulled the end of the sapling down, levering the steel plate upward. He felt the plate shift. He pulled harder. The plate began to lift.

A pop rent the air. The heavy steel plate shot upward, followed by an explosion. The whine of shrapnel filled the forest. Chunks of steel clanged off the little rock wall in front of Koa, ricocheted off the stone platform, and shredded several nearby trees. The thick steel plate sailed across the *heiau* like a Frisbee. One corner hit and buried itself in the closest *koa* tree; the sheet of steel hung there like a shelf.

Koa slowly stood as the sound died away and the smoke drifted off in a light breeze. Basa came running. "Are you okay?" They gathered on the platform, ears still ringing, but otherwise unhurt. Koa walked over to the tree impaled by the steel plate. Bolted to its underside, Koa found the remnants of Claymore antipersonnel mines. He hadn't seen this kind of weapon since his combat days.

Gracie picked up one of the irregularly shaped steel scraps scattered over the *heiau*. "That was awesome." Excitement bubbled in her voice.

"Only because no one got hurt," Koa said. They were really lucky. He hadn't expected anything like that level of violence.

He moved to the large square hole in the platform. A gray steel file box lay nestled at the bottom of the depression. Koa poked it with the remnants of the sapling, checking for further booby traps, before stooping to pick it up. He wanted to open it but wasn't about to take the risk before running it through an X-ray scanner.

CHAPTER THIRTY-THREE

ZEKE STOOD BESIDE him in the county prosecutor's conference room when Koa finally pried open the steel box. He and Basa had transported it to a safe site, where it had been pronounced clean before Koa brought it to the prosecutor's office. He drew out a series of red folders, three of which were labeled TOP SECRET.

The first folder contained a lengthy CIA Ops Plan. According to the executive summary at the beginning of the document, a secret CIA asset, named De Xiaoping, the First Deputy Ambassador in the Chinese Belgrade embassy, had disclosed the existence and location of plans, technical drawings, orders, invoices, delivery schedules, and other materials detailing the Iranian nuclear program. With De Xiaoping's assistance, the CIA planned to penetrate the embassy, steal the documents, and cover up the raid by bombing the embassy. Koa passed the folder to Zeke. After reading through the description, he scribbled De Xiaoping's name on a scrap of paper and left the room.

The second folder held technical drawings and other papers in Arabic and Chinese. Koa couldn't decipher them, but they appeared to be Iranian nuclear documents, most likely the target of the CIA's plan. In Koa's mind they confirmed that the CIA had, in fact, raided the embassy and bombed the place to cover up the theft.

Zeke returned and handed Koa a one-page printout. The headline of the Reuters news story, datelined Beijing, China, October 24, 2005, read: "Guangdong Party Chief Elected to Seven-Member Politburo Committee." The story outlined the election of De Xiaoping, formerly of the Chinese Foreign Diplomatic Corps, to the highest governing body in China.

Koa was dumbstruck. "Holy shit. No wonder the CIA is desperate to get this file back. They've got a spy at the top of the Chinese government."

The third folder contained handwritten notes in Chinese and a number of eight-by-ten photographs of an Army officer in uniform—a lieutenant colonel, Intelligence Corps. Koa peered at the first photograph before the shock registered and disbelief followed. He knew this man. Nāinoa Nihoa looked younger in the photo, but Koa had no doubt. He turned the photograph over to examine the next one and noticed Chinese characters covering the back.

The next photograph showed the same officer in civilian clothes with a young Caucasian woman of extraordinary beauty. They were standing on a street but appeared to be unaware of the photographer. The picture looked like a high-quality surveillance photo. More pictures followed. In one, the couple sat close together in a nightclub, his hand on her thigh. In another they were dancing, her head on his shoulder, his hands on her ass. None of the shots had been posed—the couple was oblivious of the camera. More surveillance photos. Then the pictures turned pornographic. The man undressing the woman. The woman naked on her knees before the man, he, too, unclothed. Then the couple in bed, he on top, she on top, more positions. The bedroom pictures had been taken with professional cameras from different angles, and each bore Chinese markings on the back.

The pictures nauseated Koa. Not the pornography; cops saw plenty. The man, the uniform, and the markings on the back spelled treason. A senior American military officer had been caught in an affair or more likely a sting. Not just any officer, but the future governor of Hawai'i.

Koa passed the pictures to Zeke. "Holy shit," Zeke said. "You know who this is?"

"Yeah." Koa guessed the look on his own face matched Zeke's stunned expression. "Our future governor. And look at the Chinese on the back."

Zeke turned the first photograph over. "God help us."

Koa had a good idea what he'd find in the next folder. He wasn't mistaken. It contained cables from NATO headquarters to senior military officers, including generals and members of the Joint Chiefs of Staff. Koa read cables from U.S. military planners to the operations directorate of the Central Intelligence Agency and the Bureau of European and Eurasian Affairs in the State Department's Office of South Central European Affairs. They detailed personnel rosters, strategies, capabilities, target lists, and operational plans from the Allied Force bombing campaign in Yugoslavia. All the documents bore SECRET or TOP SECRET labels.

A fifth folder contained an audiocassette; its label was dated May 24, 1999, two and a half weeks after the Belgrade Chinese embassy bombing and about nine weeks before Oshoa had sold the Campbell property to the two offshore trusts. Zeke asked a secretary to find a machine to play the old-fashioned audiocassette.

Koa understood the importance of the materials and exactly what the package as a whole represented. The woman, a Chinese spy, had led Nihoa to her supposed *pied-à-terre*, already rigged by her Chinese spymasters with multiple cameras. That's the only way the Chinese could have captured the bedroom shots from various different angles. They'd caught the colonel in a classic honey trap. With the pornographic pictures in hand, the Chinese must have pressured the colonel, and with his career, his marriage, and his family on the line, Nihoa had caved. He'd stolen the classified documents, with his name listed among the recipients, and turned them over to his Chinese masters. The Chinese had turned the American officer into a Chinese agent and blackmailed him into stealing U.S. military secrets. He'd engaged in espionage and betrayed his country.

The CIA had sent Ernesto Sapada into the Chinese embassy. Gwendolyn had assisted in the operation by enlisting the aid of De Xiaoping, a highly placed spy. Sapada had risked his life, as well as the life of a vitally important CIA asset, and found these materials. They must've been stored near the Iranian nuclear documents—the raid's objective.

Koa felt his rage blossom. He's been on the front lines. Soldiers had died in his arms. For him, treason was worse than murder. The colonel had risked his country's honor and soldiers' lives to hide his illicit affair. The secrets he'd delivered to the Chinese had put soldiers and aircrews at risk, and Koa felt sure some died because of the colonel's perfidy.

Koa tried to put himself in Sapada's position. The man goes into a foreign embassy on an important mission for his country, only to discover pornographic pictures of a senior American officer, together with a stash of classified NATO documents, addressed to the same officer. It wouldn't have taken Sapada long to reach the same inescapable conclusion Koa had reached. Sapada must have been dumbfounded, shocked, revolted.

The secretary delivered a tape player, and Zeke put the cassette in the machine, punched the play button, and adjusted the volume. The voices sounded scratchy but plainly audible.

"*Good afternoon, Colonel.*"

"*Thank God you're okay. Where are you, Sapada?*"

"*Where your fuckin' friends can't find me, Colonel.*"

"*What the hell are you talking about?*"

"*I have the pictures, Colonel.*"

"*What pictures?*"

"*Cut the crap, Colonel. I know about your little tryst with the Yugoslav whore. Was she worth the fuck?*"

"*I don't know what you're talking about.*"

"*When did you find out she was working for the Chinese, Colonel?*"

The colonel's voice had lost its stridency. "*What do you want, Sapada?*"

"*Did the Chinese let you screw her even after you started passing secret documents?*"

"*Secret documents, what are you talking about?*"

"*I have the documents, Colonel. Secret and top-secret battle orders, target lists, operational plans. Copies addressed to you. You gave the Chinese everything they ever wanted. You're a traitor. A goddamn fucking traitor.*"

The man's voice was now abject. "*I didn't have a choice, Sapada. That Yugoslav whore came on to me and set me up. Chinese agents confronted me in her apartment with the pictures. They were going to ruin my life. They made me get the documents for them.*"

Sapada laughed harshly. "*Made you, Colonel? You couldn't keep it in your pants, you got caught, and you weren't man enough to take the heat.*"

"*Please, Sapada, you've got to understand.*"

"*Yeah, I understand. You sent me into that embassy to save your goddamn skin. You knew where to look. That's why you told me to do the second safe and to make sure I got everything. Did you think I wouldn't look? And you had the CIA bomb the god-damn Chinese embassy just to save your own rotten fucking ass."*

"The Chinese were helping Milošević. We had to bomb the goddamn embassy. We had to."

"Is that the line you fed the CIA hawks at Langley?" Sapada paused. "Tell me, Colonel, did you tell the Chinese about De Xiaoping? Did you sink that low?"

"Jesus, Sapada. Just tell me what you want. I've got money."

"You did, didn't you, you scumbag? You told the fucking Chinese De Xiaoping was working for us. I can't believe you compromised him. The Chinese will kill him or turn him into a double agent. You fuckin' traitor."

"What do you want?"

"I should cut your balls off and send 'em to the FBI."

"You don't want to do that. I can set you up for life. Just give me those pictures."

Sapada laughed again. "Trust you, Colonel? Not fucking likely, not ever again."

"Please, Sapada . . ."

"Shut up, asshole. I'm going to milk your sorry ass for the rest of your life. Twenty thousand dollars a month, every month . . . every fucking month until they bury your rotten corpse. You'll get the instructions in the mail. You miss a single payment, and you'll be sitting in Leavenworth unless your CIA buddies put a bullet in your head.

"One last thing, Colonel, traitor, sir. If anything happens to me or to Lan Zwang, the FBI will automatically get the pictures of you with your prick in the Yugoslav woman, along with the top-secret documents you handed to your Chinese spymasters. Understand?"

The colonel's voice only confirmed what Koa already knew. Nāinoa Nihoa, candidate for governor of Hawai'i, was a traitor and almost certainly the *kepala* behind Sapada's murder. Koa had no doubt, none whatsoever. Still, he found it hard to believe Nihoa had orchestrated the torture and killing of an American military hero.

His treachery was worse than Koa had imagined. Sapada hadn't discovered the pictures by accident. The colonel had ordered the raid and sent Sapada to get the pictures. Koa couldn't guess how the intelligence officer had planned for Sapada to steal the compromising materials without looking at them. Maybe they'd been in a lockbox. But Sapada had looked and discovered the intelligence officer's espionage. Koa understood why Sapada had disappeared from Kosovo.

Koa felt he had to tell Zeke about Alderson's visit. "Earlier this week, I had a visit from a James Alderson, a CIA agent. Admiral Cunningham vouched for him, so I know he's the real deal. Alderson told me Gwendolyn, a former CIA agent named Lan Zwang, went missing from Kosovo in May 1999 with highly classified information. She and Sapada must have worked together."

"Explains why someone"—for once Zeke spoke in a low tone of voice, almost a whisper—"and I'll bet it was the fucking CIA, was willing to pay Gwendolyn six hundred grand a year to keep her mouth shut. It puts those agency pricks at the top of the suspect list."

Koa shook his head. "I'm not so sure."

"What do you mean?" Zeke demanded, his voice regaining volume.

"Alderson told me that the CIA and the FBI had been looking for Gwendolyn since she disappeared. He might be lying, but I don't think so. And while I don't doubt the agency would kill Gwendolyn without remorse, they wouldn't pull the trigger without first getting their hands on these papers." Koa pointed at the documents spread on the table. "Better the devil you know than one you don't."

"Good point," Zeke conceded.

"Besides, the rest of the facts don't fit."

"Which ones?"

"That traffic accident. That doesn't have the hallmarks of an agency hit, and don't forget Arthur. Despite all the press stories about waterboarding, the CIA doesn't burn people with cigarette butts, break fingers, and cut off hands, at least not on American soil."

"If not the CIA, then who?"

"Nāinoa Nihoa."

"Holy fuckin' shit," Zeke said. "That tape's a nuclear bomb."

"Yeah, with multiple warheads. It proves the CIA was behind the embassy bombing, and it shows that the CIA's spy at the top of the Chinese government is likely a double agent. It's also going to end the career of our governor-in-waiting."

Zeke grew pensive. "We have to alert the CIA."

"Agreed, but we play our cards one at a time."

"What's that mean?"

"It means I want that bastard, Nihoa. I want him and all the conspirators who helped the motherfucker. I want them on murder charges. And I'm going to end the fucking CIA cover-up that's been going on for almost two decades."

Zeke looked skeptical. "We don't have proof that Nihoa's behind the killings, and we haven't identified the conspirators."

"Not yet," Koa said, "but I'm going to flush them out."

"How?"

"Give me an hour," Koa said. "I'm going for a walk. I want to think this out." Koa walked through the park where he'd saved

Nihoa's life. All the while his mind raced, building a plan, rejecting it, and starting over on a new one. Finally, the fragments came together. They could do it. They could expose the bastard and get a confession.

Back in Zeke's office, Koa laid out his plan.

CHAPTER THIRTY-FOUR

THEY INVITED JAMES Alderson to Zeke's office. The CIA agent flew in from Honolulu and showed up, looking like he'd just stepped out of a Brooks Brothers ad. After introducing the county prosecutor, Koa began to question the CIA agent about Arthur Campbell.

"I thought I made it clear when we met before. That's off limits," Alderson responded.

"I thought maybe you might want to trade for the CIA operations plan you worked out with De Xiaoping's help." Koa made no mention of Sapada's tape or the other documents they discovered under the *heiau*.

Koa might as well have used a Taser on the CIA agent. It took him several seconds to respond. "Jesus Christ, you found the file, and to know that name, you must have opened the file. That's a crime." He looked around the room as though searching for the file. "You'd better hand it over."

Koa remained cool. "In exchange for some information."

"Don't fuck with me. I'll get the FBI in here. They'll take you away in handcuffs."

"I'm conducting a murder investigation, Mr. Alderson. I want answers."

"I'm warning you. Hand over that goddamn file." Alderson pulled a cell phone from his pocket and began to select a prepro-grammed telephone number.

"Put that phone away, asshole!" Zeke's voice boomed across the conference room. Alderson spun around toward the prosecutor and slowly lowered his cell phone.

"You think we're a couple of jerks?" Zeke let his words sink in before continuing. "If you want to get the U.S. attorney over here, we can have a judicial battle royal. Hell, we can have a congressional investigation into the loss of your fucking file and the goddamn agency cover-up. Might be fun to see some of you CIA pricks in the hot seat for a change."

Alderson put his cell phone back in his pocket. The room became silent.

Alderson said, "Okay. What do you want?"

"Complete cooperation," Zeke responded. "First, I want suffi-cient information to satisfy myself that the CIA had nothing to do with the Campbell deaths—"

"Christ, you think the CIA killed them?"

"Don't interrupt me, Mr. Alderson." Zeke might've been talking to a wayward schoolchild. "Second, I want complete co-operation with the county's murder investigation. You shits from Langley might not care who gets murdered in Hawai'i, but Detective Kāne and I do. Koa, you want to explain a little about Arthur Campbell?"

"Sure. Arthur Campbell, aka Elian Cervara, aka Ernesto Sapada, won a Distinguished Service Cross fighting for his country. What-ever else Arthur might have been, he achieved a level of heroism experienced by damn few men. Then he was tortured, burned with cigarettes, had his fingers broken, got his hand cut off before he bled to death, and was dumped in a lava field. And I'm here to tell you,

Mr. Alderson, regardless of whatever else Arthur Campbell may have done in his life, I intend to find the people who ordered his torture and murder."

Alderson, apparently stunned by the depth of Koa's feelings, waited before responding. "What you ask is way beyond my authority. I'll have to get instructions from Langley."

"Fair enough," Zeke responded. "You have until this time tomorrow. After that I'll be on the horn with our senior senator, and your bosses at Langley will be sitting in front of a congressional committee."

* * *

The following morning, Alderson, accompanied by Deputy CIA Director Clancy Blaines, appeared half an hour before Zeke's deadline. Blaines looked tired, no doubt from a hastily arranged flight from Washington on a CIA jet. He took the lead.

"Gentlemen," he said, nodding first to Koa and then to Zeke. "I understand you're prepared to hand over the file if we answer your questions."

"We'll give you the CIA op plan to invade the Chinese Belgrade embassy," Zeke responded, "if you cooperate fully and truthfully with the county's murder investigation and if I'm satisfied that the CIA wasn't involved in the Campbell deaths."

"I understand." Blaines appeared ready to pay almost any price to get the file back. "May I ask one question before we begin?"

"Sure," Zeke said. With the upper hand, he could be magnanimous.

"Who else besides you two knows the name De Xiaoping?"

"No one in county government," Zeke answered.

"Okay. And can I have your assurance neither of you will ever disclose that name?"

Zeke and Koa agreed.

Blaines opened a locked case and removed three sheets of paper. He slid one across the table to Zeke and the other to Koa. "Those are nondisclosure forms under the National Defense Secrets Act. What I'm about to disclose is way above top secret, and I'll need your signatures to proceed."

Zeke read the form through, then took out a pen and added the words, "except as permitted by court order in a criminal proceeding," before sliding the paper back to Blaines. "We'll sign with that caveat." Blaines looked unhappy with the modification but nodded his agreement. Zeke and Koa signed the forms.

Blaines began to read from the third sheet: "Ernesto Sapada, the man you know as Arthur Campbell, was a U.S. Army Delta Force captain assigned to clandestine operations in Kosovo. Lan Zwang, whom you know as Gwendolyn Campbell, was a CIA field agent also assigned to Kosovo. They met, and, we believe, began a personal affair."

Blaines had obviously memorized the script, but he nevertheless referred to the paper. "The U.S.-led NATO command selected Captain Sapada for an operation to penetrate the Chinese embassy in Belgrade. The CIA had previously recruited a Chinese diplomat, De Xiaoping, who was then the first deputy ambassador in the Belgrade embassy. He told us where to find certain documents pertaining to China's sale of nuclear technology to Iran and facilitated Sapada's entry by providing false Chinese documentation."

Blaines looked up. "You two with me?"

Koa and Zeke nodded.

"We knew going in that Sapada would have to use explosives to get into the room where the Chinese kept the targeted information, so the agency arranged for the Air Force to bomb the Chinese embassy to cover up the incursion."

Again, Blaines looked up. "I'm sure you remember the hulla-baloo over the bombing of the Chinese Belgrade embassy on May 7–8, 1999."

Again, Koa and Zeke nodded.

"Sapada pulled off the incursion, and the Air Force bombing raid successfully covered his tracks. We know he got out because he sent the mission-complete signal. But after that, both Sapada and Zwang disappeared, vanished. The CIA and the FBI have been looking for them without success ever since the early morning of May 8, 1999."

Blaines stopped. Zeke and Koa waited patiently. They had arrived at the make-or-break point of the meeting, the point that would determine whether Blaines and the CIA intended to cooperate fully.

"Then we heard from Lan Zwang through an intermediary, or more probably, a series of intermediaries. By late 1999, De Xiaoping had returned to Beijing, where he was a rising star in the Chinese government. Lan Zwang threatened to expose him unless we paid her. We weren't happy about it, but, as you can imagine, the information from De Xiaoping was worth almost any price to the United States government. That's it, gentlemen. That's the whole story."

"The code name for the embassy incursion?" Koa asked.

"Operation Golden Sting."

Koa made a mental check mark. The name matched the code name on Sapada's orders.

"How did you pay Lan Zwang?" Zeke asked.

"Cash. $600,000 a year through a blind drop in Hong Kong."

"Did the agency set up offshore trusts or land transactions for Lan Zwang or Sapada?" Koa asked, watching Blaines's eyes.

"No, nothing like that, just cash."

"What did Sapada take from the Chinese embassy?"

"We know what he went after, but he disappeared before we debriefed him so we don't know what he actually took. Why?"

"Sapada was after just the Chinese nuclear documents . . . nothing else?"

"Correct. Documents dealing with Chinese-Iranian transactions for centrifuges and other industrial equipment related to Iran's nuclear program." He stopped, realizing he was volunteering too much. "What's this have to do with your murder investigation?"

Koa turned to the payments to Sapada. "Has the agency been paying him off, too?"

"No. Why would you ask?"

Blaines appeared annoyed by the cross-examination but curious at the same time.

"Because someone set up offshore land trusts for Arthur Campbell and has been delivering cash to him."

Koa caught a hint of surprise in Blaines's eyes.

"It wasn't us."

Koa turned to Alderson. "When you first came to see me, you didn't want Chief Lannua to know what you disclosed. Why?"

Alderson looked to Blaines for permission to respond, and the deputy director shrugged. "Before he came out here to head your police department, Lannua worked in the Defense Department. While he wasn't officially assigned to Operation Allied Force, he was involved in oversight of certain operations during the Kosovo war. He was one of many officers investigated after Sapada and Zwang went missing. That investigation is still open."

Koa and Zeke exchanged looks. Their suspicions about the chief were dead-on. He could easily have a connection to the Campbells.

"He was suspected in Zwang's disappearance?" Koa asked.

"Yes," Alderson responded, "he, along with several others, but no allegations or charges were ever made."

Koa had a sinking feeling, but this wasn't the time to discuss the chief's possible perfidy. "Okay, Mr. Blaines, you get us two more pieces of information, and Zeke'll return your file."

"And what do you want now?" Blaines asked. He plainly just wanted to take his precious file back to Washington.

"There are two agents from the Defense Intelligence Agency running around interfering with my murder investigation. I want the lowdown on them."

Blaines appeared perplexed. "Who are they, these DIA agents?"

"Bill Christopher and George Nelson."

"I'll check them out for you. What else?"

"I've got an Indonesian hood in custody, Bambang Gunawan. He used to work for our embassy in Jakarta and entered the United States on a temporary work visa a month ago. I can get you a picture and prints if you need them. He's a contract killer, who tortured Arthur and killed Gwendolyn. I want to know what the CIA has, if anything, on him."

"Okay."

"You'll get the information I requested?"

"Yes. You'll have your answers as soon as I get back to Langley."

"And then you'll get your file."

CHAPTER THIRTY-FIVE

KOA WORKED WITH Zeke for two days. They played out one scenario after another trying to anticipate how the target might react to various approaches. They tried to plan for every countermove and every glitch. They'd have only one shot, and they had to make it count. They considered a dozen alternative rendezvous sites. They debated the culpability of the secondary players, disagreeing on their probable identity.

Zeke believed that Raul Oshoa had to be the intermediary between the *kepala* and Sapada. He alone had the connections and the power to orchestrate all the steps. Zeke outlined the land transactions, the entry of the Indonesians into the United States, their housing, transportation, financing, and their use of eavesdropping equipment.

Koa disagreed, arguing that Zeke had boxed himself in with the unstated assumption that a single intermediary had helped Sapada initially and orchestrated his murder. "It could be that Oshoa helped at first and another facilitator helped the mastermind execute the murders. As you said the other day, Zeke, something happened to upset a blackmail train that had been running smoothly for almost two decades."

"So, other than Oshoa, who might have been accomplices?" Zeke asked.

"I see four other possibilities," Koa responded. "Jorge Chavez, Rachael Ortega, the DIA spooks, and you know who."

"The chief?" Zeke asked.

Koa nodded.

Disgust clouded Zeke's face. "That would be awful."

"Yeah, but it would explain a lot of his actions."

"Jesus, let's hope not." Zeke changed the subject. "What's your take on the two DIA turkeys?"

"High on my list, real high. When Blaines told me those numbskulls aren't regular DIA types, but field operatives on an off-the-books gig, I figured somebody in the DIA got wind of Sapada's location and wanted to deep-six some really nasty and politically explosive military history. Just imagine how this story would go down on the front page of the *Washington Post*. The Pentagon would be up to its eyeballs in congressional investigations until the end of time."

"If you're right, about this thing going down in phases, then Rachael Ortega is a real possibility. As Oshoa's aide, she runs his operation, she knows Nihoa, and could easily have forged Jorge Chavez's name to the visa applications."

"She more than knows Nihoa. She's infatuated. You should have watched her at that fund-raiser. Still, what's her motive? What does she get out of helping the Indonesians kill Sapada?"

"Maybe she's in it for money," Zeke suggested.

"She must have done all right as an aide on Capitol Hill." Koa wondered yet again why Ortega, once a Washington somebody, had taken a job on a remote Hawaiian ranch.

"I'm sure," Zeke responded, "she lived well, but I doubt she put away enough to retire."

"Maybe. There's definitely something odd about her."

"That leaves Jorge Chavez, the ranch foreman and operations manager."

"I try not to let my personal feelings cloud my judgment, but it'd make my day to nail Chavez. He tried to cut me off when I first interviewed Oshoa, he lied about sending his guy Faizon to spy on us, and I'd love to prove he forged his own signature on the visa applications. Plus, he tried to interfere with the investigation by complaining to the mayor."

After all the analysis, they settled on a plan. They chose the abandoned bank building on Hilo's main street as a rendezvous site. They wrote the script for their stage play in meticulous detail, with Zeke providing advice on what would cross the line into police misconduct or entrapment. Koa practiced his lines twenty times until they came naturally. Then Zeke played the role of their target, trying every trick he could imagine to throw Koa off.

He and Zeke hammered out two short introductory scripts for the opening scenes, the lures that would set the whole takedown in motion. Again, Koa practiced his lines until he had them memorized.

For these initial stages, they had a huge advantage—the ability to feed the intermediaries misinformation through the listening devices the culprits had planted in Koa's home and office. Koa was glad he'd talked Nālani into living with the damned bug, despite all the inconvenience, and smiled as he remembered the way she'd turned up the music to cover their lovemaking. That had been pure joy.

On the second day, they drafted the affidavits needed to support court-ordered wiretaps. They went back to see Judge Herbert K. Hitachi, asking to meet with the judge alone in his chambers.

Although he'd already heard parts of the evidence in connection with various warrants he'd signed, he listened with attention as they outlined the evidence to provide a solid basis for the court to order wiretaps.

They described the sale by South Mauna Loa Farms of the two parcels to the Hansel and Gretel offshore trusts at the request of Raul Oshoa's unidentified Bay of Pigs collaborator. They showed photographs of the torture room at the ruined Royal Gardens house and the body found partially buried under a toe of lava. Koa added that the crime-scene team had found Bambang's lone thumbprint, tainted with the victim's blood, on the doorframe of the torture room. Zeke told the judge how immigration records purportedly prepared by South Mauna Loa Farms had enabled the two Indonesians, including the one who had left a bloody fingerprint, to enter the United States. Koa reminded the judge about Mrs. Furgeson's description of the truck driver and his companion, and repeated the contents of her tape recording, including the reference to the *kepala*.

They described the contents of Arthur's bank safe deposit box. Koa told the judge about the two DIA agents and the steps they'd taken to thwart his investigation. "The DIA agents took Shizuo's medical records," he said before describing how they'd entered the crime scene at the Campbell house. When he told the judge about the listening devices in his home and office, the judge reacted with indignation.

Finally, they laid the pictures on the judge's desk. Although the judge recognized the man, they nevertheless identified the lieutenant colonel caught in the Chinese sex trap. The judge studied the pictures, turning them over to examine the Chinese writing on the back. "Did they turn him?" Judge Hitachi asked.

"Yes, Your Honor," Koa answered. "They did. We found these with the pictures." He passed over the sheaf of top-secret NATO documents from the box Sapada had secreted under the *heiau*.

The judge scanned the papers. Koa could tell from the judge's grim expression that he was disturbed by the scope of the colonel's treachery.

The judge signed the wiretap orders for the South Mauna Loa Farm lines, including several home and cell numbers, the DIA agents' cell phones, and the target's lines. Neither Koa nor Zeke had ever supervised such an extensive telephone surveillance operation, so they enlisted the aid of the Hawai'i state police. Lieutenant Mokulani from the Honolulu division of the state police helped them make arrangements with Hawaiian Telcom, Verizon, and Mobile One, and provided the equipment necessary to set up a listening post in the basement of Hawaiian Telcom's central office in Hilo. Sergeant Basa assigned officers to man the listening post around the clock and record the calls.

They discussed timing. They needed to give the intermediaries a head start, but not too much of a lead. They settled on twelve hours. They would feed false information into the listening devices in the late afternoon and evening and call the target early the following morning.

That afternoon, Koa and Sergeant Basa staged the first act in Koa's office.

BASA: *Anything new in the Campbell investigation?*
KOA: *Yeah, we found Arthur's hidey-hole, but someone beat us to it.*
BASA: *Where?*
KOA: *Buried in an old* heiau *up the hill on the property behind the Campbell house.*

BASA: *And there was nothing there?*

KOA: *No, unfortunately not. When we got to the* heiau, *all we found was an empty space. Like I said, somebody beat us to it.*

BASA: *Any idea who?*

KOA: *I'll bet those two DIA spooks, Christopher and Nelson, got there first.*

BASA: *Why do you suspect them?*

KOA: *There was some kind of explosion up there, but no bodies. They're smart enough to pull off something like that.*

BASA: *Are you going to bring them in again?*

KOA: *I can't. The chief would lock me up.*

BASA: *So what are you going to do?*

KOA: *I'm not sure.*

That night, Koa and Nālani went for another walk to get away from the listening device. "Are you sure you're okay with what we're about to do?" he asked.

"Yes. We've talked about this, Koa. I know there's risk, but I can live with it."

He squeezed her hand. "While I think it'll improve our odds of catching this creep, it isn't absolutely necessary after what Basa and I did in the office."

"I'm not worried about me, Koa. You forget. Back in California, before we met, I was a park ranger at Yosemite for four years. I went through the Federal Law Enforcement Training Center, so I'm not just an interpretive guide. I can arrest you if you misbehave in the national park." She grinned at him. "So let's go do it."

Back at the cottage, they sat in their living room and performed a second and far more intimate recitation with essentially the same content. When Koa described the scene of the explosion at the *heiau,* Nālani ad-libbed, "Oh, Koa, I'm so glad you were nowhere near that explosion," and when he complained about the chief, she added, "Don't cross him, or he really will fire you." All in all, Koa thought it was a pretty persuasive performance. He hoped that the intermediaries were listening to their pillow talk.

CHAPTER THIRTY-SIX

LATER THAT EVENING, when Koa dropped by the wiretap listening post, he found two patrolmen smiling. "You are not going to believe it."

Koa returned their smiles. "Enlighten me."

"Agent Christopher, that DIA guy, called your target and reported that an unidentified third party found the Sapada papers."

"What else?" Koa asked, thrilled the intermediaries had taken the bait.

"The boss dude blasted them for not getting the papers first. He really chewed on them. Then he wanted assurances you didn't have Sapada's papers. Agent Christopher told him that you didn't have the papers. He said he overheard you admitting somebody else got there first."

"Anything else?"

"Yes, the big man bragged he'd used his Washington contacts to scare the shit out of both the governor and the mayor, and almost gotten you fired."

Koa grinned. He had a lock on an obstruction of justice case. "Any activity at the Oshoa farm?"

"No, not yet."

"Buzz my cell if you get anything more, anything at all."

* * *

The following morning, Koa called Nihoa from Zeke's office on a pre-paid cell phone. As expected, an assistant answered and informed him the man had various engagements and would be unlikely to return his call. If he wished, she said, he could talk to a campaign assistant.

Koa responded coolly, "Tell your principal I'm calling about Operation Golden Sting, and he has thirty minutes to return my call. And, young lady, I promise you your boss will be very angry if you do not get this message to him ASAP." Koa left the prepaid cell number and hung up.

As Koa had hoped, Nihoa called back within fifteen minutes. "With whom am I speaking?" He spoke his strong, cultured voice that he'd used at the start of the 1999 call with Sapada.

Koa ignored the question. "I have some photographs of you as a lieutenant colonel in Kosovo, rather interesting photographs with a young lady . . . a most attractive young lady. I also have some classi-fied documents that passed through your hands."

Nihoa's voice became tense. "Who are you?"

"I want to return the photographs to you, along with the docu-ments. I'd imagine you'd like to have them."

"You can send them to my office marked personal and confiden-tial." Koa thought he heard the man's voice ease a bit.

"That's not the way this is going to work. You must come to me." Koa heard the man take a deep breath.

"I can't do that right now."

"Oh, I think you can. I don't think you want me to send these pictures to you on the Internet."

"No. Of course, don't do that. How much money do you want?"

Koa feigned irritation. "Don't insult me. I want to return these pictures to you in person."

"Where?"

"Right here in Hilo."

"In Hilo?" The voice showed relief.

"Yes, right here in Hilo and soon, before I change my mind." Koa sank the hook deeper. "You wouldn't want me to change my mind, would you?"

"Where would I meet you?"

"Call me at this number tomorrow, and I'll tell you where to meet."

"Why not tell me now?"

"Because we'll meet alone and in the place of my choosing."

Koa had conditioned Nihoa for the next act of the drama he and Zeke had planned. Nihoa might be suspicious, but he'd have to show up. He couldn't afford to let Sapada's papers become public. Koa ended the call. He wanted to go back to the listening post, but he knew the officers would call him if they heard anything. Waiting was agony.

*   *   *

Koa's cell went off at three a.m. and he hurried to the listening post. Nihoa had called Rachael Ortega at home. The two had spoken for forty-five minutes about the Sapada documents, the police investigation, and the Indonesians. They'd speculated about who'd found the documents and his motivation for wanting to return them. The man praised Rachael's loyalty and renewed his promise of a great reward for her in the near future. The call ended with an exchange of intimate endearments.

Koa used many analogies to describe what he did for a living—he peeled away the layers of onions—turned over rocks—peered through a glass darkly—but lifting the veil was one of his favorites.

The intercepted call lifted the veil around Rachael Ortega. Raul Oshoa hadn't enticed her to Hawai'i with a big signing bonus. She wasn't in it for the money. She had somehow met a powerful man and been seduced by the promise of a bright political future. With glowing stars in her eyes, she'd sold her soul.

Koa called Zeke, and they met in the prosecutor's office. Together they replayed the conversation.

"Okay," said Koa, "now for the last act."

CHAPTER THIRTY-SEVEN

THE FOLLOWING AFTERNOON, Koa's prepaid cell phone rang. "Where do we meet?" Nihoa asked.

"Come to the back of the abandoned bank building on the corner of Kalakaua and Kamehameha. The back door will be open. Come alone. Up the back stairs at midnight." Koa hung up.

Zeke had worried that Koa might be recognized. He was well known to Nihoa. They weighed that risk against a greater threat—their inability to predict how Nihoa would react. Koa, who knew the case inside and out, was best prepared to deal with any unexpected actions on Nihoa's part.

To improve their odds, Koa turned to a local theater makeup artist, who padded Koa's shoulders and stomach, streaked his hair with gray, built up his cheeks, and added a false nose, three days' growth of beard, heavy black eyebrows, and owlish wire-rim glasses. When she applied a large black mole near his nose, he protested that she'd gone too far.

"Go with it. The eye always focuses on an obvious blemish and overlooks most everything else."

He knew she was right. When she finished working, he'd dressed in a loud, oversized *aloha* shirt and size 44 jeans. He appeared to have gained sixty pounds. Even Nālani wouldn't have recognized him. Then while he waited for the appointed hour, he practiced altering his voice, dropping it down the register and adding a twang.

Because he'd heard the two DIA spooks, Christopher and Nelson, reporting to Nihoa on one of the wiretap lines, Koa wasn't surprised when they drove Nihoa into downtown Hilo and parked up the street from the rendezvous location. Koa had concealed cops on every corner for two blocks in all directions, and one of them reported Nihoa's arrival.

Nihoa approached the abandoned bank building by himself and looked around to be sure he wasn't under observation. He entered the building and stood in silence for more than a minute before heading toward the wooden staircase.

Four police officers surrounded the parked car where the two DIA spooks sat waiting. Christopher started to yell out a warning before Sergeant Basa rammed the barrel of his pistol into the side of the agent's neck. The warning died on Christopher's lips. The two agents protested, threatening arrest, jail, and disgrace, but their warnings went unheeded as the police handcuffed them, placed them in patrol cars, and bundled them off to the county jail.

The *kepala*, unaware of the arrests taking place a block away, reached the top of the stairs in the old bank. Light pouring through an open door guided him into the room where Koa in disguise sat behind a small desk.

Photographs of the lieutenant colonel in uniform as well as several of the more pornographic pictures lay spread across the desk. A NATO document prominently stamped TOP SECRET partially covered one of the photographs.

"Sit down," Koa instructed. He spoke in a deep voice, pointing to the chair stationed about six feet in front of the desk.

"I don't have much time," Nihoa said.

"Don't patronize me," Koa snapped. "You have as much time as it takes to get these pictures back, and you know it."

Nihoa sat down. "Are we alone?"

They were alone if you didn't count the microphones connected to the concealed recording system, the two policemen in the room next door, and Zeke behind another connecting door. "Do you see anybody else here?" Koa asked. His cold voice echoed in the small room.

"Then we should be able to wrap this up very quickly." Nihoa spoke in an unnaturally loud voice, almost as if firing off commands. Koa grasped the significance of the signal. Nihoa was wearing a transmitter and had just signaled the two agents to come upstairs to help him reclaim the photographs.

"Tell me about the woman." Koa held up the picture of her riding the lieutenant colonel.

The man frowned. "That fuckin' Yugoslav whore, Dejana, suckered me. She worked in a German sex club where I used to go to relax, you know, to get a little on the side when my wife was having our kid." The man paused before adding, "Dejana was hot, and there was nothing, I mean nothing, she wouldn't do." The man's frown morphed into a leer. "After the first few times, we started going to her place, a tiny little squat with this big fuckin' bed. I never guessed the bitch was a damn Chinese spy."

Koa kept his face impassive. "When did you find out she worked for the Chinese?" Koa reversed the picture to display the Chinese lettering.

"Worst day of my life. Dejana was so blisterin' hot takin' me up to her apartment, kissing me, and rubbing my crotch. Then she opens the door, and three chinks grab me. They'd been watchin' me screw her for weeks. Musta had six hidden cameras in that squat.

They were gonna send the pictures to my wife, my boss, the counter-intelligence guys, maybe even my mother. I didn't have a choice."

"That's when you sent Sapada into the embassy?"

The man glanced toward the door before turning back to face Koa. "I wasn't gonna let those chink assholes own me."

"But Sapada doubled-crossed you?"

"Rotten cocksucker."

"How'd Sapada come to be in Hawai'i? You help set him up?"

"Nah. Son of a bitch had it in for me. Told me he'd watch every fuckin' thing I did. Not sure how he pulled it off, except I heard he knew some old-time buddy of Oshoa's."

"Twenty thousand a month. That's a lot of money."

"Yeah, but he wanted more. A month ago, he upped the ante. The greedy prick." Nihoa shifted nervously. He turned to look back at the door.

Koa decided to twist the screws. "Expecting someone?"

"Nah, but it's warm in here. Are you gonna give me the pictures? I'll pay you."

"I don't want your money."

"Okay, okay." Nihoa shifted. Beads of sweat appeared across his forehead.

Koa understood. The man's backup, his insurance, hadn't come through. He was getting frantic. Koa could see it in his body language. The man's right hand slid down to his outside jacket pocket and closed around the butt of a gun.

"Drop the gun," Koa ordered.

As Nihoa turned in response, he found himself staring down the barrel of Koa's Glock. "Nice and easy. Drop the gun to the floor." Nihoa let go of the gun, and it clattered on the boards. "Kick it over here." Nihoa obeyed. Koa laid his own gun on the table within easy reach. "Now we can finish our conversation, and I can give you your pictures. Okay?"

"Okay," the man responded softly.

"Now tell me, a month ago when Sapada asked for more, how much did he want?" Koa was enjoying himself.

"Double . . . he wanted double."

Good, Koa thought. He thinks I'm ultimately going to ask for money and he's haggling. "From 20K a month to 40K?"

"Yeah, and that wasn't gonna be the end of it. He'd want more. He was always gonna want more, more, more. He was gonna suck me dry."

"That's when you decided on extreme measures?"

"Hey, hey, what is this?" Alarm sounded in Nihoa's voice.

"Settle down." Koa kept his deep voice soft and friendly. "I know what happened to Sapada, and I don't want to suffer the same fate."

"Just give me the pictures." The man spoke rapidly, his nervousness getting the better of him. "I'll give you whatever you want, and that'll be the end of it. Sapada was different. He kept upping the ante, the greedy bastard. I had to put an end to it."

"How did you get Rachael to do it?"

The question was asked so casually, his target forgot who he was talking to. "Stupid fuckin' cunt. She made a mess of it with those two assholes from Indonesia. They were supposed to get the pictures from Sapada, not kill him and his girlfriend. But Sapada wouldn't cooperate, and the Indonesians got sloppy and killed him."

"How did you hook Rachael into it?"

"She was a naïve cunt. You give 'em a little sex, a little money, promises of a fancy job. They're yours. It's easy." Koa realized, to his disgust, Nihoa was bragging.

"You met her in Washington, didn't you, when she worked on the hill for the House Armed Services Committee?"

"Yeah, she was a sucker for the uniform."

Koa stood up, making a gesture like a party host. "There's someone I'd like you to meet."

Nihoa began to panic. "Hey, hey. You said we were alone. What's going on?"

One of the side doors opened, and Rachael Ortega entered the room. The woman looked haggard, and her handcuffs rattled as she advanced, glaring at Nihoa. "So your stupid fuckin' cunt made a mess of it," Rachael shrieked, "because she followed your directions! And you would be elected governor."

The man whirled back toward Koa, pointing an accusing finger. Then he jerked around again as Zeke Brown stepped through the other side door, followed by two uniformed policemen. "Nāinoa Nihoa, you're under arrest for conspiracy to murder Ernesto Sapada and Lan Zwang."

Koa felt satisfaction, relief, and sadness as the cops handcuffed Nihoa and led him away. He and Zeke had nailed the bastard, successfully ending another major case. He'd ended the threat to Nālani and saved his job. He grinned at the prospect of telling the chief. But mostly, he found the story painful. Nihoa had embarrassed his country, wrecked Sapada's career, driven the hero into exile, and ultimately killed him. All to cover up his screwing a whore.

CHAPTER THIRTY-EIGHT

"WE ARRESTED NĀINOA Nihoa and Rachael Ortega for conspiracy to commit murder. And we got the two DIA agents for obstruction of justice," Koa announced as he walked into the chief's office at seven a.m. the following morning. The smile on his face hid Koa's still simmering anger at the way the chief had treated him.

"You did *what*?" The color drained from the chief's face.

"Your buddy Nihoa masterminded the Campbell murders. He's in jail as we speak. I hate to tell you, but he isn't running for governor anymore."

Koa would have paid a fortune for a photo of the stunned look on the chief's face. "Jesus Christ, you'd better have an airtight case."

"The evidence will put him away for life, if the feds don't hang him for treason."

"What are you talking about?"

"Calm down, Chief. Let me tell you what we've got." Koa outlined the nature of the complex sting operation and the evidence. The chief sat in cowed silence. When Koa finally finished, summarizing his tape-recorded exchange with Nihoa in the abandoned bank building, the room remained silent for long beats.

Finally, the chief spoke. "How—how did you know?"

Koa almost responded, "Good detective work," but kept the resentment out of his voice. "It all fell into place when I saw the Chinese markings on the back of those photographs. The classified documents and Sapada's tape only reinforced the damage the traitorous son of a bitch did to his country."

The chief was starting to recover. Nihoa might be out of the picture, but the chief was around to stay. "Are you sorry you saved the SOB's life?"

"Hell no, Chief. He'd have died a martyr," Koa pointed out. "This way, every American will see Nihoa for the cockroach he really was."

"And the DIA boys, when did you figure out their game?"

"No disrespect, but I knew they were squirrely from the beginning. After we agreed to return the CIA file, CIA Deputy Director Blaines tipped us that the DIA agents were freelancing for the DIA deputy director, who served in NATO headquarters during the Kosovo war. It didn't take a genius to figure out he was working with Nihoa to cover his own ass."

"And Ortega?" the chief asked.

"We knew Oshoa or one of his people had to be an accomplice, but we weren't sure who till we heard Nihoa and Ortega talking on a wiretap. Once we had the wiretap, we flipped her. It wasn't hard. She started out tough but crumbled like stale bread. She admitted forging Jorge Chavez's name to the temporary work permit applications, monitoring the listening devices in my home and office, and passing information to the DIA agents and the Indonesians. And you should've seen her face after Nihoa called her a stupid cunt. She'd have killed him if she hadn't been handcuffed."

"What was her motive?" the chief asked.

"Nihoa played her. It started back when they were both in D.C. Nihoa sweet-talked her into bed, and she thought they were in love.

Fed him info about personnel decisions, budgets, and military appropriations from the Armed Services Committee while he was in the Pentagon and after he was assigned to Kosovo."

"How'd she get out here?" the chief interjected.

"When Nihoa got out of the service in June '99, and became deputy undersecretary of defense, it was only a two-year deal. He planned to move back to Hawai'i, run for state representative, and parlay that job into a run for governor. Then Sapada started blackmailing him. Nihoa was in D.C. and didn't want to pass the money himself, so he recruited Ortega with promises of marriage, a job in his administration when he became governor, and the glamour of living in Hawai'i. Nihoa knew Oshoa, the anticommunist and Republican moneyman, from his time in D.C., and leaned on Oshoa to give Rachael a job."

The chief shook his head. "She doesn't sound all that bright."

"Love, ambition, and greed warped her judgment. That's for sure."

"She puts Oshoa in the clear?"

"Yeah, Chief. Oshoa was straight with us. One of Oshoa's old anticommunist buddies was Sapada's mentor at the Army War College. The guy put in a good word for Sapada, and Oshoa sold him a life estate on an unused parcel of land. That, his friendship with Nihoa, and undeserved trust in Ortega were Oshoa's only failings."

"Strange."

Koa nodded. He'd seen the look on the chief's face many times before: gratitude that his chief detective was so good at what he did. "I guess I owe you an apology," the chief acknowledged.

Koa wanted to laugh. The chief had fired him. But for Zeke's intervention, he'd have stayed fired, Basa and Piki would have quit, and Nihoa would have been elected governor. The chief's apology felt like a joke.

"You owe the entire department an apology. The whole force knows you laid off people because you were campaigning for Nihoa and angling for the homeland security job in his administration. And the troops are royally pissed about it."

The chief appeared incredulous. "The whole department?"

"Yes, the whole department. The troops have been talking about nothing else for the last week."

"Jesus," he said, and Koa could tell he was scheming for a way out. "I take it you have recommendations for me?"

"You need to make an announcement canceling the layoffs. And a personal apology to Smithy and some of the others you targeted would go a long way toward restoring morale."

"You don't ask for much, do you?"

"I think it's what you have to do, if you want to continue to be an effective leader of the force."

"I guess I don't have a lot of choice, do I?"

"No, not much." Then Koa added, "Oh, and here's the good news. The county prosecutor is holding a news conference at ten o'clock this morning to announce the arrests. He wants you to join him."

EPILOGUE

THE NEWS THAT Hawaiʻi County police had arrested Nāinoa Nihoa and Rachael Ortega for conspiracy to murder Ernesto Sapada and Lan Zwang caused turmoil. Nihoa's supporters marched on the Hilo police station demanding his release. But the political repercussions in Hawaiʻi were nothing compared to the superstorm that struck Washington after Koa played the Sapada tape for CIA Deputy Director Clancy Blaines.

A week later, the U.S. attorney in Washington indicted Nihoa for espionage and treason. In the Senate, the Armed Services, Intelligence, and Judiciary Committees announced hearings into the scandal, to be followed by House of Representatives committees on the Armed Services, Government Operations, and Foreign Relations. The military, the DIA, and the CIA all retreated to their defensive corners. The deputy director of the Defense Intelligence Agency resigned, followed by two Air Force generals and three top CIA officials.

* * *

Stiff trade winds slowed Koa's climb to the 1880s church in Kapaʻau. He wasn't a churchgoer; unable to forgive himself, he felt unworthy.

Bypassing the sanctuary, he entered the adjacent cemetery and picked his way through the headstones. He knew the path to Hazzard's grave; he'd been there before. Hazzard's death was the black hole of his life. He'd escaped, but the gravity of his guilt pulled him back.

Koa had come to this graveyard after the Pōhakuloa case and returned each time he brought a murderer to justice. It was his way of atoning for killing Hazzard, a crime that had driven him into the military and ultimately led him to become a detective. Redemption governed his life.

Standing in front of Hazzard's gray marble monument, he took Sapada's Distinguished Service Cross from its case. The American eagle at its center glinted in the sunlight. The medal represented the honorable side of Sapada's contradictory character, and Koa felt a powerful bond with the former soldier. In arresting Nihoa, he'd thrown Sapada's last dart and completed the Delta's final mission. Sapada would approve, Hazzard might someday forgive, and Jerry, who'd inspired Koa to be a cop, would cheer.

Koa wanted to leave the military decoration atop Hazzard's gravestone, but knew he couldn't. To keep his secret safe, nothing must ever connect him to Hazzard. Still holding Sapada's medal, he retreated from the cemetery, knowing his guilt would bring him back.

* * *

Only late that night, sitting alone with Nālani in front of the fireplace in their Volcano cottage, did Koa ask the question that had bothered him ever since he'd first heard the Sapada tape. "Why would this guy—a genuine military hero—choose blackmail instead of outing his treasonous boss?"

Nālani turned from the fire to face him. "Men do strange things for women. Maybe it was Gwendolyn."

Koa stared into the fire, watching the flames dance. "That's what I thought for a while, but not anymore."

"Why not?"

"The DIA guys had a file on Sapada, which they put together after he disappeared from Kosovo. People described the Sapada-Gwendolyn affair in Kosovo as an on-again, off-again thing. That fits with what I heard from witnesses. She wasn't faithful to Sapada or anyone else. I just can't see him sacrificing his honor for her."

"So what's your best guess?"

Koa took a sip of his wine. "He was afraid."

"Of Nihoa?"

"No. Sapada had the pictures and the tape. Nihoa had money and was content to buy Sapada's silence until he ran for governor. Then Sapada tried to up the ante. That was his big mistake."

"Why would Sapada do that? He didn't need the money."

"Hatred. He hated Nihoa for his treachery, for what he did to Sapada. Sapada spent hours tossing darts at Nihoa's picture."

"That explains why he kept the blackmail up for so long, even after he had his big orchid farm."

Koa looked at Nālani. "I never did figure out where the orchids fit in."

"Who knows?" Nālani said with that impish smile he loved. "You hear about him and you think he's such a tough guy, but maybe all he ever wanted to do in life was tend his orchids."

It was her turn to pause. "So what was this Delta Force soldier afraid of?"

"The CIA. Blaines hinted as much in my last conversation with him. After the Belgrade embassy bombing, our government ran for cover. Officially, the bombing was an accident. Sapada knew he couldn't come forward and say 'see what I found in the Chinese embassy.' The higher-ups—the ones who approved the embassy bombing, maybe all the way up to the White House—couldn't have Sapada talking. The CIA would have had him killed. Then Gwendolyn only made it worse by blackmailing the CIA."

It was Nālani's turn to stare at the crackling logs. "So the government that awarded Sapada the Distinguished Service Cross turned on him."

"Yeah. Governments do things like that."

AUTHOR'S NOTE

As an author, I'm frequently asked about my creative process. In its simplest form, I assemble, reimagine, and fictionalize events from my own experience, weaving them into a new and hopefully engaging tapestry. The story of Ernesto Sapada and Lan Zwang draws from such personal experiences, as you can see from the following sampling.

I have always loved stories of military heroism and been fascinated by international incidents—none more bizarre and intriguing than the "accidental" U.S. bombing of the Chinese embassy in Belgrade in 1999. Although much has been written about the event, I've never read a satisfactory explanation and doubt the truth will ever be told about what really happened in Belgrade on the night of May 8–9, 1999.

I first visited Hawai'i in 1986, and it's been my second home for twenty years. My wife and I were saddened when a small restaurant we frequented in the tiny town of Hawi closed because its owner was arrested as a fugitive from justice. We once bought a painting from an artist who lived off the grid deep in the forest. We've often visited a talented glassblower's studio on the edge of Volcano village, and we love to stand at the edge of the Kīlauea crater, especially at night when the sounds and the glow are magical. Hawai'i's orchid growers supply the world with their unique flowers. Until it finally closed, I often visited the Suisan fish market to watch its giant auctioneer wield his gaff, much like a pirate swinging his hook. You used to be able to arrange an overnight stay in one of the few remaining houses in Royal Gardens before *Pele*'s lava buried the last of that community.

Much of my practice as an attorney involved piecing together what happened from documents and witnesses, like any good detective investigating a crime. And I've always admired the dedicated prosecutors who devote themselves to preserving the fragile line between civilization and anarchy.

You can find these personal threads—and many more—that I've gathered, twisted, and embellished into the characters, scenes, and events of *Off the Grid*. I can only hope you enjoy reading as much as I've relished writing.